CRUCIFIED IN THE DARK

BROOKLYN CROSS

TK
JIMMY
RINGO

SCOOTER
MEL
PEREZ

Trademark Acknowledgements

The author Brooklyn Cross acknowledges the trademarked status and trademark owners of familiar wordmarks, products, actors' names, television shows, books, characters, video games, and films mentioned in this fiction work.

 Created with Vellum

This is a dark novel and is intended for mature audiences ONLY.

This book is for sale to adult ONLY, as defined by the country's laws in which you made your purchase.

This book may contain violence, course language, graphic content that includes alcohol, tobacco, drug use, addiction, mild kink scenarios and PTSD.

For a complete breakdown of the warnings please see Brooklyn Cross's website

WWW.BROOKLYNCROSSBOOKS.COM

SPECIAL DEDICATION
TO ALL THOSE THAT
RISK THEIR LIVES SO WE CAN
LIVE FREE AND TO THE FRIENDS AND
FAMILY THAT SUPPORT THEM.
Thank You

ALSO BY BROOKLYN CROSS

The Righteous Series

(Vigilante/Ex Military Romance - Dark 3-4 Spice 3-4)

Dark Side of the Cloth

Ravaged by the Dark

Sleeping with the Dark

Hiding in the Dark

Redemption in the Dark

Crucified by the Dark

Dark Reunion (Coming 2023)

The Consumed Trilogy

(Suspense/Thriller/Anti-Hero Romance - Dark 4-5 Spice 3-4)

Burn for Me

Burn with Me

Burn me Down (Coming 2023)

The Buchanan Brother's Duet

(Serial Killer/Captive Horror Romance - Dark 4-5 Spice 3-5)

Unhinged Cain by Brooklyn

Twisted Abel by T.L Hodel

The Battered Souls World

(Standalone Books Shared World Romance/Dramatic/Women's Fiction/All The Feels- Dark 2-3 Spice 2-3)

The Girl That Would Be Lost

The Boy That Learned To Swim (Coming Soon)

The Girl That Would Not Break (Coming Soon)

The Brothers of Shadow and Death Series

(Dystopian/Cult/Occult/Poly MMF Romance - Dark 3-4 Spice 3-4)

Anywhere Book 1 of 3

Backfire Book 1 of 3 by T.L. Hodel

Seven Sin Series

(Multi Author/PNR/Angel and Demons/Redemption - Dark 2-5 Spice 3-5)

Greed by Brooklyn Cross

Lust by Drethi Anis

Envy by Dylan Page

Gluttony by Marissa Honeycutt

Wrath by Billie Blue

Sloth by Talli Wyndham

Pride by T.L. Hodel

PLAYLIST

The Only Thing We Know - Bob Moses

Funhouse - PINK

You're My Best Friend - Don Williams

I'm Not The Only One - Sam Smith

Memory - Kane Brown x blackbear

Leave Before You Love Me - Marshmello & Joans Brothers

Cold Heart - Elton John & Dua Lipa

Ex's & Oh's - Elle King

S.O.B. - Nathaniel Rateliff

High Enough - K.Flay

You Oughta Know - Alanis Morissette

Bartender - Lady A

Love Again - Dua Lipa

Old Time Rock & Roll - Bob Seger

Stressed Out - twenty one pilots

Die a Happy Man - Thomas Rhett

Survivor - Nathaniel Rateliff

CHAPTER 1

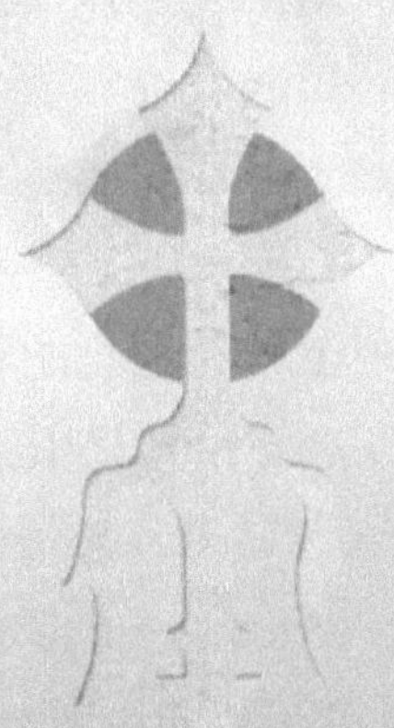

Morry held up her finger as Judd walked into her office without knocking. Typical.

"I told you that I don't care what you think. Kyle is still my son, and until a judge says otherwise, you can't keep him from me, Andrew. I will see my son for the weekend," she said into the phone, happy that she chose not to video call. There was no way she could keep things moderately civil if she had to look at her ex's arrogant face.

"You came back and decided to become a fucking biker. Our nine-year-old son doesn't need that kind of influence in his life. He's already influenced enough by you. Do you know what he told me the other day? Kyle said he wanted a leather jacket for his birthday and that when he grew up, he wanted to join the army just like his mother."

"Nothing wrong with either of those things. My entire family has served this country, and leather is stylish. Not that you would know anything about that. You're lucky if your socks match in the morning."

"Oh, so funny, always the comedian, then you wonder why we divorced. The point is, you're a bad influence. I never wanted you to leave for the army and now look where we are."

Her anger burned white hot, and even though she wanted to keep the peace and knew she shouldn't, she couldn't hold back. "No, I'm pretty sure your cock in my used-to-be best friend got us to this place, Andrew. No one forced you to fuck her while I risked my life for our country. Or do you absolve yourself of any part of the shit that went down between us?"

"Holy fuck, are we on this again? I said I was sorry," his temper flared as it always did whenever she pointed out why they got divorced in the first place. At least this way, they both lost their cool. Andrew had proven that he wasn't above lying or exaggerating the truth to get what he wanted. She almost felt bad for Lindsay...almost. She'd learned through a couple mutual friends that Andrew had been spreading around that she was not only gone for the long stretches of time, but that she was sleeping with the men on base. It was bullshit. She didn't sleep with TK until after Andrew had been outed with his sleeping around.

"I'm pretty sure the fact you brought up the topic of my deployment automatically includes what you did to get us to this point," she growled into the phone as her hand gripped the cell tighter. "There are always two sides, you just seem to like the version where this is all my fault."

"Whatever, Mores. You want to argue in circles, go ahead, but I'm not going to," Andrew said.

She would've reached through the phone and pummeled the shit out of him if she could. Why did they ever get married? How had they gotten to the point that a simple conversation couldn't stay civil?

"It's not a circle, it's called the truth. You really should try it sometime, you might find it refreshing."

"Wow Mores, you've really become a bitch. I'm happy we're divorced and thank god we only have one kid to fight over."

That was cheap shot and hurtful since she'd had to have a full hysterectomy after Kyle was born due to complications. He knew it was still a wound, and one that took a long time to move past. She could feel the limit of her boiling point coming and she was going to completely lose her mind shortly.

Andrew twisted any conversation to the point that everything that came out of her mouth was snide, snippy, or sarcastic. She honestly felt the same way about him, but the difference was he never saw cheating with Lindsay as something he did wrong. He placed that blame at her feet. *She* chose the army over her family. Deployment was too difficult for *him*.

She was done being blamed for his shit. It was time Andrew owned his part in their failed marriage. Meaningless half-hearted apologies didn't count.

"Don't fucking call me Mores. I always hated that nickname

and let you get away with it because I loved you. We can clearly say we are both past that point. I'm coming over Friday night to take Kyle for the weekend, whether you like it or not, and if you try to stop me, we can get the police involved again. I'm sure that will look great in front of the judge. You once more refusing to hand over my son and needing the police to step in and making a scene to get it done."

The cops getting called had become an almost bi-weekly occurrence and she could tell by the looks on their faces when they arrived that they were sick of coming to the calls as much as she was having to make them.

"Fine. What time?" Andrew sighed like she was the annoying one.

"Seven o'clock. And Andrew, he better fucking be there. If you pull the same shit as last time...."

"Are you threatening me?"

Judd leaned up against the door and signaled to hand him the phone. She shook her head no. The one time Judd answered the phone in the office when she was out hadn't gone swimmingly.

"Of course, you'd go there. You always did manage to make yourself the victim. I'm done with this conversation. Seven o'clock, Friday night, don't forget." Morry hung up before she said something that really would get her in trouble with the judge handling their messy divorce. They weren't even supposed to be talking now, but arrangements for Kyle had to be made. "That man may drive me to day drink. Sorry, Judd, what's going on?"

"We've got one of your fancy Humvees approaching. Should be reaching the gate any second."

She couldn't recall a meeting with any Righteous members, but that had to be who it was. Someone mentioned that Dean called, but he was a day's drive from here, so that seemed unlikely.

"You want us to let them in or not?"

"Tell them to let in whoever it is. I'll come out."

Grabbing her gun, she checked the clip and shoved it in the back of her cargo pants. Morry caught sight of her reflection on the way past the small mirror in her office and wiped at the grease mark on her face, but it was useless. That would need a hard scrubbing later. Whoever it was, better not give a fuck what she looked like because she'd seen a dog's asshole look more appealing than what she had going on. That was probably Andrew's plan in the first place. Make her look rundown and crazy so he could look like the golden boy.

She followed Judd outside. His massive six-seven height almost forced him to duck under the door frame. He was her second-in-command. He was a little more than that from time to time, but it wasn't anything serious. She wasn't ready for anything serious, not after all her heart had been through in the last year. Fuck, she wasn't sure she ever wanted anything serious ever again.

It was almost dark, but she could easily see the cloud of dirt that rose in the air behind the black vehicle coming through the gates. The guys outside looked at the Humvee, their eyes wary of the newcomer. Only a handful of them knew about the Righteous, Judd was one of them. She knew every single one of her gang would pull a gun and fire if they thought she was in danger. They were a cutthroat group, the most she'd ever encountered, which said a lot, but they were loyal fuckers. It had taken some time to get them there, but now she'd trust them as much as her boys, Dean, Trev, Arek, Kes and Wolf.

"Did they say who it was?" Judd spoke into the two-way radio.

The radio on Judd crackled. "Guy said his name is Dean."

A smile broke out across her face as she heard who it was a moment before the vehicle came to a stop. She marched for the Hummer and the man behind the wheel. She missed Dean's face. There were few who she missed more than this man. They'd pulled asses out of the fire together and kept one another sane. That was more than most people did in a lifetime, and it bound them together like fucking spirit animals.

"Well, well, well...as I live and breathe, it is you. I thought someone was pranking me when I was told you called."

He smiled widely, something he didn't often do. "Yeah, I didn't expect to be out this way either," he said.

The loud rumbling of a mass of motorcycles starting up vibrated the air. It always gave Morry chills to hear them fire up like that. It was accentuated with them all inside one of the large metal outbuildings. The shed was too large to be called a garage. Anything that could hold five hundred motorcycles was more like a plane hangar. The group drove past, and each rider dipped their head with respect.

"Business is good," Dean asked as he watched the last of the line pass.

"Of course it is." The sun was setting in just the right direction to catch all the sexy angles on Dean's face. "You're still a sexy S.O.B. You finally going to let me ride that gear stick of yours," she asked teasingly.

That was their thing. How they always spoke to one another, but there had never been any sexual tension, which was what made it fun. They loved each other like family and would die for one another, but sex was never on the table.

"You're still the hottest fucking grease monkey I've ever laid my eyes on, but the answer is still no."

"Fuck, you are a tough nut to crack," she said, laughing as he wrapped her up in one of his signature hugs and spun her in a circle.

Giving his arm a playful smack when he put her down, she put her hands on her hips. "So, what brings you to my neck of the woods," she asked, her eyes finally registering that there was a second person.

Dean held his hand toward the young guy, who looked like a terrified mouse. His hair was too long and greasy, hanging over half his face and hiding it from the world. She figured the guy would've hidden his entire face if given a chance. Morry looked the guy over. His jeans were ripped and dirty, and he wore a thin hoodie that he held tight around his narrow frame. He was tall but mostly bones, from what she could see through the material. The one eye she could see was the brightest shade of blue she'd ever seen.

"This is Jeremy, and he needs the works."

She stepped past Dean and gave the guy an even closer inspection. The sheen of sweat on his forehead, dark sunken eyes and hollowed out cheeks were a tell-tale sign that he was an addict and starting to suffer some serious withdrawal symptoms.

"You keeping this one?"

Dean leaned against his Hummer and crossed his arms. "That is yet to be decided." She knew that he'd already made up his mind and intended to take the guy under his wing. The threat was more for Jeremy's sake.

"What's your drug of choice?"

Jeremy crossed his arms, the false bravado evident in the unsure look in his eyes and the way he looked down at his boots. "What does it matter?"

"If you want to fucking stay here, it matters. Now answer the question or get back in the Hummer, and Dean here will bury your body in the desert on his way out."

Jeremy glared at her before his eyes found Dean. "Are you and all your friends this bitchy?"

Wrong first impression. Morry reached out and grabbed him by the front of that threadbare hoodie. She easily picked him up and slammed him down on the front of the Hummer, despite his much taller frame.

"Respect, learn it, and fast, or you're going to get on the unfriendly side of my personality. Trust me. You don't want to go down that road," she said and released him.

Morry laced her fingers behind her back and stuck her chin out for a cheap shot. Would he take it? She wanted to judge what kind of person this guy was in his heart. Sniveling and untrustworthy weasel, or broken man just needing a chance? She'd defied all expectations for women in the military and then some. She earned the respect of the men in her class and unit. She met Dean on her first day, and they quickly became friends, pushing one another to their ultimate limits. She finished second only to him.

"Let's try this again. What is your drug of choice," she asked and loved how Dean never lifted a finger to interfere. He knew she could handle anyone here and had never offered to show her up. It was part of the reason they were friends.

The brief mask of anger was replaced with fear. "I don't have one. I took whatever I could get my hands on, depending on how much money I could pull together. Flakka, Liquid Ecstasy, China Girl, and Serial Killer if I was really desperate."

"Fuck, kid, you're lucky to be alive."

"You sure you want to back this pony?" Morry spoke to Dean but never took her eyes off Jeremy.

"Too much of a challenge for you?" Dean smiled, and her competitive streak bristled to life.

"You always knew how to irritate me more than anyone else," she said and smiled.

"It's my special charm."

"Alright, Jeremy, if Dean here says you are worth the effort, I'll take his word for it. I'll get you checked in and have one of the other enrollees show you around. Dean, you staying the night?" Convinced that Jeremy didn't intend to try anything stupid, she turned to Dean.

"Yeah."

"Well, then, let's go."

She led the way, and it felt like old times having Dean here.

She wished he were closer but understood why he chose to live in the middle of buttfuck nowhere, Kansas. If she had a father like his, she would've stayed hidden as well. She glanced back at Jeremy. There was no telling what she was getting herself into this time; with Dean, it was always an adventure.

CHAPTER 2

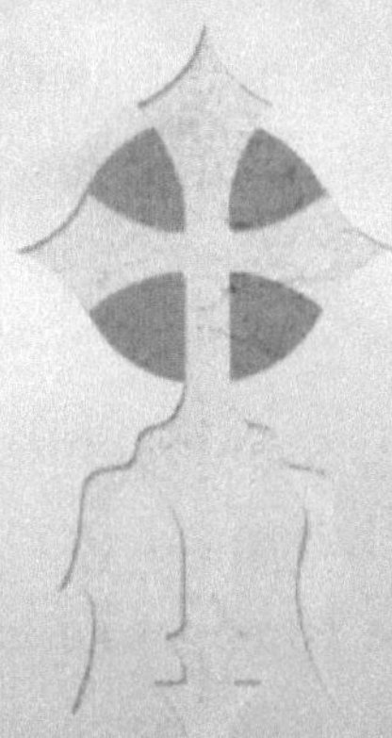

Present Day

"Hey, asshole, you better not die," Morry said as she knelt and looked in the smashed window. Wolf's eyes opened slightly and then closed again. At least he was still breathing. "How the hell did you end up like this?" she mumbled as she crawled inside the Hummer that looked like a crushed soda can.

"Mae..." he whispered, his lips barely moving.

She felt his pulse and flicked a flashlight over his wounds, trying to assess the best way to get him and Duke out of this. She ran her hand over Duke's head. He opened his eyes and then closed them again. Fuck. She couldn't lose any more teammates. The emotion that she normally pushed down lower than her stomach was lodged in her throat as she stared at Wolf's bloody face.

"Here you go," Jeremy said. He was pushing the backboard through the window. "No luck getting the door open?"

"No, the damn thing is jammed. Fuck, I wish I had more room to work in there. I'm going to need a second board. Duke is still alive."

"Who's Duke?"

She turned her flashlight so it shined on the dog, and Jeremy made a face like she'd lost her mind.

"Don't look at me like that. Duke is a soldier and a fucking good one. He gets the same treatment, and if you're going to be a medic, you better learn. You never leave one of yours behind. Two- or four-legged."

"Alright." He stood and yelled for a second backboard as she slid the other one in as far as it would go before she ran out of room. Closing her eyes, she pulled on all her old training and felt around Wolf's neck. He didn't seem to have anything broken in his neck, but until they got him into an evaluating room, there was no way to know for sure.

"Wolf, I need to move you. I have no idea how injured you are."

"Mae," he said again.

She had no idea what he was dreaming about, but there wasn't enough time to worry about it. He'd already been out here too long, and not only did every minute mean the difference between life and death, but the authorities were notified. A passerby saw the skid marks on the road and called in that someone had gone off the road.

"You need me to get in there and help?" Jeremy offered, but it was already too tight.

"No, stay there. Once I get him into position, you need to reach in and help me roll him onto the backboard. Do you have the neck collar?"

"Yup, right here." Jeremy handed in the white piece of plastic, and she set it aside.

"Okay, Wolf, here we go."

Grabbing his shoulders, she eased him forward, keeping his neck aligned. It seemed like forever before she got him stretched out and in a position where she could safely get the neck brace on Wolf.

"Gently brace his head, then we roll him toward the back of the Hummer on the count of three."

Jeremy reached in and took Wolf's head in his hands. Hands that had changed so much in five years. "Ready."

"One, two, three," she said, and with a single fluid motion, they got him on the board.

"Hey, boss, we got police and fire closing in. No more than, say, ten minutes," Judd said as he looked through the smashed windshield at her. She could hear Butch talking to Jeremy which was good she was going to need her two strongest to help carry Wolf.

"Okay, we need four to take Wolf up to the Bus, and I'll steal Jeremy to help with Duke. We will be right behind you."

Judd nodded as she tightened the last of the straps.

"He's good to go."

From the quick once-over she gave Wolf, she knew his knee was out of place and needed to be set. It looked like he also tried to slow the bleeding from a wound in his arm.

"Mae..." he moaned as Jeremy grabbed the board and pulled him through the passenger side window.

"Okay, old fella, it's your turn. How do you keep ending up in all these messes, boy? You're not going to want to hang out with us anymore," Morry said as she took the second backboard offered and slid it into position.

Duke whimpered as she moved him onto the board.

"It's okay, boy, we've got you. We'll get you fixed up. I have the best vet anywhere on my staff." Her hands worked quickly to get the straps in place to hold Duke flat and then called out to Jeremy.

"Ready."

Once more, Jeremy grabbed the board, sliding it out. Morry opened the center console above her head and grabbed everything that fell out, stuffing it all into the small pack she had flung over her shoulder. Then did the same with the glove compartment. The gun they all kept in there was missing, which wasn't like Wolf.

Weird.

She didn't have time to contemplate it now.

She tapped her little earpiece. "Lady Luck, is the A.I. information inside the Hummer I'm in still viable?"

"Most of the data has been erased."

"Lady Luck, download what you can, then shut down the A.I. in the Hummer. Access code Kilo, Yankee, Seven, Seven, Seven, Lima, Echo."

"Code accepted. Download started."

"Four minutes before they're on top of us," Jeremy said.

She gave the Hummer one last look spotting a hoodie near the back and grabbed it before heading out the window. She couldn't risk leaving anything important behind. Jeremy nodded, and they lifted Duke in one motion and ran up the steep hill.

"Cutting it a bit close," Judd commented as they slid Duke in beside Wolf.

"You know me. I like the danger. Take the service road to stay out of sight." She smiled at Judd over her stupid joke. He laughed and shook his head.

Morry turned to Jeremy, who was glaring at her. "What?"

"Nothin'," he said and stomped around the front of Lady Luck. She didn't know what crawled up his ass and wasn't in the mood to deal with it either.

Hopping behind the steering wheel, she followed the Bus, their homemade version of an ambulance. In their line of work, she and the gang needed rescue equipment, and so far, the Bus had been the best investment yet. The line of bikes followed in their wake as they turned onto the dirt road.

Morry kept her eyes trained on the back of the bus and prayed to anyone who would listen that Wolf would make it. Half an hour into the drive, she couldn't take the silent treatment anymore. She looked at Jeremy.

He was staring out the window, and even though she couldn't see his face, tense energy was clinging to him.

"What is going on? You haven't said two words to me since we left the crash site."

"I told you, nothin'," he said, but his clipped reply clearly said there was something.

"I don't get it. You've been strange lately, and you refuse to tell me what the hell is going on. Did I piss you off somehow? Are you wanting out of the motorcycle club?"

Jeremy arrived a scared eighteen-year-old kid. She honestly hadn't know if she could get him turned around—he was in a bad way mentally—but he put in the work, and now here he was five years later, one of her most trusted. She could also appreciate that he was no longer the boy he had been. His crossed arms showed off the muscle he put on his once scrawny frame. His hair was cut in a short faux hawk that looked badass. He was a man now. She would've been all over him if he wasn't twelve years her junior. She could appreciate the sexy image he made, it wasn't like she was blind.

Jeremy shook his head. For a brief moment, she thought he would finally tell her what burr was stuck in his boxers, but then he clammed up again.

"Just leave it alone, Morry. I'm not in the mood to talk about it." He closed his eyes and put the seat back. She wanted to hit that sexy chin with her fist.

Why was it that women got labeled as the difficult and emotional ones? She found men confusing, and this one, in partic-ular, gave her fits. He'd gotten too good at hiding what he was thinking from her. At one point, she knew exactly what was running around behind those incredible blue eyes, but lately, they were as unreadable as a stone.

Giving up for now, she called into the bus. Judd picked up on the first ring. "Judd."

"Hey, how are the passengers?"

"Morry wants to know how they are," Judd yelled, and she jabbed at the volume button to turn it down as his baritone voice blared through the speakers.

"Fuck, man, could you yell a little louder," Jeremy yelled, then grumbled something she didn't get before he closed his eyes again.

"The doc says they are both in need of shit done, but they will make it to the clinic," Judd said, and she could hear Dr. Henry's annoyed voice in the background.

"Pretty sure that wasn't the exact message, but it will do. See you in thirty."

They had hideouts and smaller clubhouses all over the southern and western parts of the country, and that was where she was steering the group to. It was a twelve-hour drive in good traffic to get back to home base in the Arizona desert. It was fitting that she spent so much time in the desert deployed and then weeks running for her life across it, only to come home and take up residence smack in the middle of another one. Her father always said she was a sucker for punishment.

The thought of her father had her stomach tightening into knots. He hated Andrew from the first time he met him. Maybe that was part of the reason she married him in the first place. Anything that got under the Corporal's skin was refreshing. Yet, here she was divorced from Andrew and her father not speaking to her. Not exactly a good record to date.

"Can't wait," Judd said, his voice suggestive.

"One track mind," she said and hung up the phone.

They were in Texas for business when the S.O.S. came in and was only an hour away. She thanked the stars that she'd decided to go on this trip last minute. She sent a quick message to Trev to let him know that she had the package and was safe. It was strange how she still felt she needed to report to him even though he was no longer in charge. Like so many habits, they died hard or didn't die at all.

Wolf wasn't the only one giving her fucking heartburn. She still hadn't heard from Maeve since the guys broke her out of the transport truck. It wasn't like her not to check in, and she hadn't returned to base either. There had been no chatter about her being arrested again. That was six weeks ago, and even though she had the habit of flitting from spot to spot erratically, she never went this long without communicating. It wasn't that Morry didn't trust Maeve to take care of herself, but there'd been a pit in her stomach from the moment all this shit with her being arrested happened, and now she had no idea where Maeve was.

"You plan on fucking him tonight," Jeremy suddenly asked.

Glaring, Morry swung her eyes in his direction. "What business is it of yours who I fuck or spend my time with?"

"It's not. Just need to figure out where I'm going to sleep then. Listening to you and Judd all night is not exactly my idea of a good night's sleep."

She hadn't been with Judd in weeks if not months. It was hard to remember, everything seemed to blend lately. What did it matter to him if she fucked her second? Anger simmered in her gut.

"Would you just say what you really want to say already rather than bitching at me for no reason? I already get enough of that from Andrew. I don't need you starting it, too."

"Shit, I'm just...Fuck, what's going on with Kyle," he asked. His whole demeanor changed as his eyes softened and shifted to concern.

Morry's hands tightened on the steering wheel. "He's getting worse every day, needs a liver transplant, and Andrew is being a piece of shit and won't let me see him." She looked over at Jeremy. "He's my son, too. He can't do this. It's just not right, I don't a fuck if he won sole custody the first time around. He's only doing this cause I'm fighting him for joint custody again, you'd think he'd learn that I'm never going to stop no matter how many times we have to go back to court." She hit her hand on the steering wheel. "Does Kyle think I don't care? Is he laying in that hospital bed wondering where I am and if I'm every coming to visit? I mean...Shit."

Jeremy put his hand on her shoulder, and she hated that it felt comforting to have him touch her.

"That's not right. I still don't know how Andrew won full custody. Such bullshit. It's as clear as day how much you love your son, and Kyle fucking told the social worker he wanted to live with you." He sat his seat up, and the tension evaporated.

"Yeah, well, I guess it's easy when you're a sniveling liar. Did I tell you that Andrew took pictures of me arriving at the house on my motorcycle and then said someone from my crew threatened him at his place of work? You know, none of my guys would do something that stupid. It was all bullshit, but the judge believed it because he got someone from work to get up on the stand and say a load of crap." Morry groaned and rubbed at her face. It didn't help that she'd been arrested twice for assault, but those fuckers deserved what they got.

She needed to get to the bottom of whatever was going on with Jeremy, but right now, she just wanted to feel like the entire world wasn't pissed at her. Or out to get her.

"Thanks," she said, looking over at Jeremy, then his hand. He quickly moved it and crossed his arms over his chest.

"For what?"

"Taking my side. Just, you know, being there for me, I guess." Morry gave a little shrug and looked away from those blue eyes that were so dangerous to her heart.

Lately, she'd found herself wanting to stare into them, and that would lead nowhere good. Jeremy was young, in his prime, and she...was a washed-up vet with a vicious scar on her face and a bigger one down the middle of her soul. The last thing she needed was to get emotionally involved with him when it would only lead to another scar on her heart. A physical relationship was bad enough, but Morry knew herself. There was something between them, a spark or chemistry. She couldn't nurture that. If she did, she would crash headfirst down a ravine as surely as the Hummer they just left behind.

"You don't ever have to thank me for having your back. That goes without saying," Jeremy said, and for just a moment, their eyes locked before she forced herself to look away. Her heart beat a little faster. It always did lately when he was near.

Why the world kept sending her men that she couldn't love or would end up leaving she didn't understand. Then again, maybe it wasn't the world. It was just her bad taste, timing, and judgment that kept landing her in this position. Whatever it was, she clamped down on it hard and pushed it aside as she focused on the vehicle in front of her. There were more important things to worry about than the stupidity of her heart.

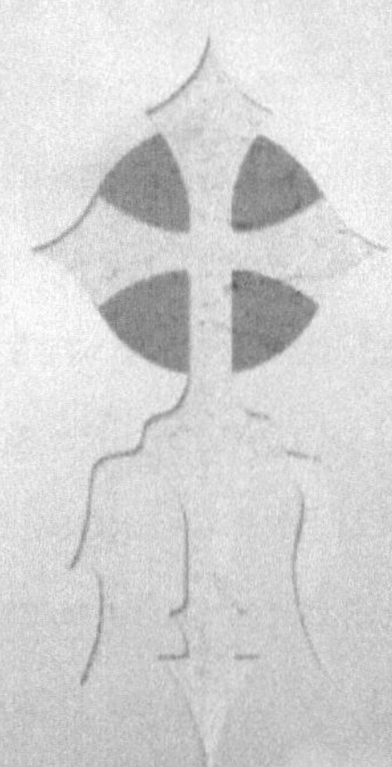

CHAPTER 3

Five Years Ago

Jeremy's eyes searched the room for any way out. He was a rat with its tail trapped in this place of fucking crazy. They were all nuts. They brought him food that tasted like poisoned garbage. Meds were forced down his throat, and he threw up as soon as they left. The cameras in all the corners managed to capture it, and they returned to force more down his throat. He was convinced they were trying to kill him or worse.

They strapped him down to a bed for what felt like days while his skin itched with the feeling of insects crawling underneath. Didn't they understand he had to scratch his arms, or the bugs would infect his brain and lay eggs? Then the insect aliens would hatch and take over. That was what they wanted wasn't it? They wanted those eyes hatch and the alien bugs infect him.

"Let me out of here." He thrashed against the straps that were holding him. All he wanted was to leave. Well, no, that was a lie. He also wanted to get high and escape it all. He shouldn't have agreed to come here. Dean tricked him and told them they would help, but this didn't feel like help. They were trying to kill him.

When the door opened, his heart was pounding so hard that it felt like it might burst in his chest. The same woman from earlier walked in with what looked like a doctor and a nurse, but he knew better. They were all aliens and they were sent to collect him for study. Yes that was exactly what was happening. He was going to end up like those cows he read about with the eyes and asshole missing. They were going to drain him of his blood and all that would be left was a dried-up husk when they were through.

"No, no, no. Get away from me! You can't have my body or my soul!"

"His blood pressure is too high. We need to sedate him, but he's so aggravated that I'm not sure if it will even work. It may make things worse."

"I said, let me out of here. Don't you understand? I want to leave. Please, please, don't cut me open. Please, don't take all my organs. I don't want to be an experiment," he said, then started to cry.

"What do you suggest?"

They spoke like they couldn't hear him. Was it possible? Was he already trapped inside a body that wasn't really moving, and he just thought it was moving? Was it possible he was already dead? No, it would be peaceful if he were dead. This was something else. He was already under their mind control and on their table.

He looked down at his body, and all he saw were dots and a white glow. Everything was white. Did he have clothes on? The skin on his arm moved, and he screamed as he watched the huge insects moving below the surface. It was too late, they'd already infected him. There were so many, thousands, and they were taking over his body, making their move to infect his brain. The lumps were moving up toward his shoulder. It was happening.

"No, get them away from me. Get them out of me." He tried to reach for his arm, ready to cut it off if needed, but couldn't. "Ahhh." He lifted his body and slammed it down onto the bed over and over.

Something warm grabbed his arm, and Jeremy's eyes snapped open. Breathing heavily, he stared into soft gray eyes that reminded him of storm clouds. The woman from earlier was talking. He could see her mouth moving. She sat on the side of the bed, and her eyes never left his. She ran her hand up and down his bare arm. Usually, he didn't like to be touched, but there was something soothing about her doing that. The bugs didn't seem to like her touch and were disappearing. Was she not one of the aliens? Was she here to help?

"You're okay, Jeremy," Morry said calmly. "I know you're scared, but no one is trying to hurt you. That is the withdrawal talking."

"But something is moving under my skin. Look," he demanded.

She picked up his hand and laid it in her lap as far as the strap would allow. She rubbed her hand over the spot where the huge insect had been.

"How did you do that? Where did it go?"

"It's gone. You're safe," she said softly. "I won't let them hurt you."

The fear started to ease. "We're going to give you something to help with the pain."

He gripped her hand hard. "Don't leave me, please."

"I'm not going to leave you. I will stay with you as long as you need me to. Okay?"

Her voice was so pretty, so calming.

"We're going to put an IV in your hand. Okay?"

Immediately, his breathing started to quicken, and she gripped his hand and rubbed circles into his chest with her other hand. "What did I say?"

"That it will help with pain," he said.

Just then, he was hit with pain that felt like his muscles were ripping away from his bones. He gripped Morry's hand as tight as he could and arched off the bed. Tears ran down his cheeks as he turned to look at the woman Dean brought him to and couldn't decide if she would save him or kill him.

"I've got you, Jeremy. Just breathe." He slumped onto the bed and then saw another with a needle in her hand. "Don't look at her. Look at me." She smiled. "I promise she is a friend of mine. Tell me something about yourself. Do you like sports? You seem like a sports guy, maybe football?"

"Baseball," he said. His head lulled to the side, and she swiped the longer strands of hair from his face. "I screwed it up," he said, and the tears came harder. "I could've had a scholarship, but I fucked that up." He found her eyes again. They felt so comforting. "My parents hate me. They hate me. I fucked up. I..." The room swam a little, and he looked at his other hand. Something was sticking out of it. "What did you give me?"

"Something to help with the withdrawal symptoms, but you're going to be okay," Morry said and held his hand to her chest.

He believed her. There was something in those eyes that felt like she could command all the demons away. The other woman left the room and closed the door, and he stared into those eyes as she softly sang a song he didn't recognize until he was pulled into the darkness.

Jeremy awoke with a start, and as he did, the pain came back. He cried out. Movement caught his eye, and there she sat on the floor beside the bed with her hand still in his.

"It hurts."

"Unbearable?" she slipped onto the bed to sit with him.

He thought about the question and assessed his body.

"No, better, for now," he answered, feeling like the pain had dropped from a ten to a seven.

"Do you mind if I go get a coffee then," Morry asked, and his hand tightened on hers as a thread of panic slithered up his spine. "You'll come back?"

"I've got nowhere else to be and nothing but time on my hands. I will, I promise." She slowly stood, and his eyes flicked to where their hands were joined.

Why did it feel so difficult to let go? He barely knew her, but his mind wanted to hang on with both hands like she was the lone rock in the middle of the ocean. Morry waited quietly until he finally let go. She moved her hand quickly, but not before he saw the indents and bruising from where he'd been squeezing.

"I'll be back. Try to get a little more rest, and then we'll take these restraints off."

She walked to the door, and he called out to her. "Morry?"

"Yeah, Jeremy?"

"Thank you," was all he could bring himself to say, and he turned his face away as the tears began to flow. The regret he was suppressing since the end of his junior year clawed its way to the surface and made him want to get high again to keep the emotions away.

"I wouldn't thank me yet. I'm sure you'll hate me soon enough," Morry said before the door clicked closed.

Chapter 4

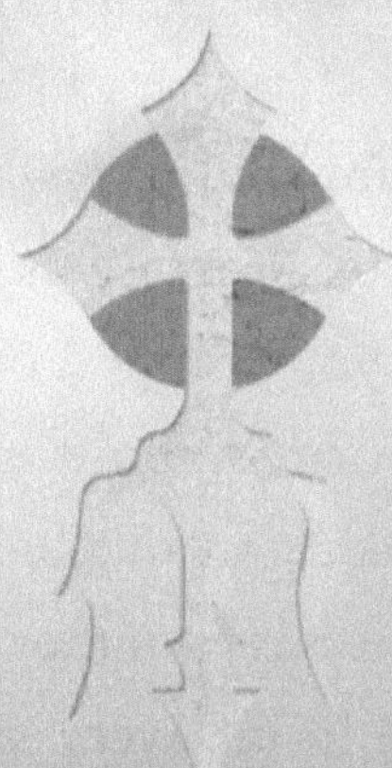

Jeremy stared at the clock on the wall, his eyes following the second hand as it made its way slowly around. It reminded him of the ones in the classrooms back in school. He looked around. Then again this was an old school so that made sense.

He'd spent many an hour staring at a clock just like this, a plain white face with simple black hands. Way too many hours watching his life tick on and feeling like he was standing still and falling behind at the same time.

He didn't dare move. Glancing at his left shoulder, he stared at the top of Morry's head as she slept. Her hand had moved and was now resting on his leg. He felt the heat through the fabric of his jeans. Moments like this were rare. Morry wasn't the type to let her guard down at any time, but they were pushing it hard on this trip, and he saw her pacing at night as she worried about everyone and everything.

That took him a long time to learn when he first arrived at The Grim Legion's rehab facility. Morry was tough as nails and acted like she'd eat you alive if you stepped out of line, but the reality was that she loved and worried about every single person under her care. Whether they were part of the motorcycle gang, were in the rehab facility, or her friends from her former life in the army, it didn't matter. She was all in on every single person. She poured every ounce of her energy into whoever crossed the threshold of her gates. It was also the first reason he fell in love with her.

The comment he made earlier about Judd was a cheap shot. The sex noises were real, but it wasn't because of Morry. It was because Judd was a slut who slept with multiple sweetbutts a night. He felt bad about it, but he couldn't break through Morry's barriers, and it was driving him mad.

Morry never saw his affection and interest in her. If she did, she never acknowledged it. He couldn't even remember when his feelings shifted. One moment, he couldn't stand being in the same room with her, terrified to be left alone. The next, he was panting after her heels, begging her to notice him as more than the fuck up and addict who'd been dropped off on her doorstep like a dog at the pound.

He lightly ran his finger over her hand. He shuddered with just that little touch. Jeremy clearly remembered how many times she held his hand all through the night as he suffered through withdrawals and again when the night terrors woke him up, screaming and begging to take something. He'd shamefully stared into her eyes and asked her to end him or give him something because he couldn't deal with the pain and the demons of everything he'd done.

All that mushed into a single event, like a distant memory and like it just happened yesterday. Jeremy was a far cry from that guy who first arrived, but no matter what he did, he couldn't get Morry to see him as anything more. Maybe the issue was compounded because of his parents. He'd tried to mend fences, and visited a couple of times, but his father would barely speak to him, and his mother only made it awkward by the over-the-top enthusiasm. It was like she was trying to be fake happy for both of them.

That wasn't a hundred percent true. Morry gave him back his freedom, and he worked his way up the ranks. Volunteered to help in the clinic or on the bikes when he wasn't visiting Dean, and most importantly, he remained clean. She helped get him clean, but now he stayed clean for himself and that alone felt like a huge accomplishment.

He was taking online medical courses. Jeremy wasn't sure what path he wanted yet, but even some training to better help in the clinic seemed like a good idea. Although, he may have bitten off a little more than he could chew by adding the mechanic course on top of the first-year medical one.

Still, that only garnered a smile and a "great choice" from her. So, his next move was to shamefully flaunt his body in front of her. He looked like a man now with the solid fifty pounds of muscle he had put on. Jeremy spent hours honing his shoulders, abs, and legs. Yet, she was oblivious to his blatant efforts to get her attention.

The first time he realized that she slept with Judd from time to time, he was tempted to slit the man's throat in his sleep. He was so angry.

Taking a risk, he flipped his hand over, palm up, and held his breath as he slipped it under Morry's. She mumbled something, and he froze, but she didn't stir, so he slowly linked their hands together.

This felt right. It was how it was supposed to be all the time. Fucking Judd. Man, he hated that guy, not because he'd gotten to fuck Morry, who he didn't deserve. No, he hated Judd because the guy picked on him from the moment he arrived. Judd was a bully. Not enough that you would say he was mean, just enough to be a fucking prick and make you want to break his nose. Judd also held seniority in the clubhouse, which meant any new sweetbutt Morry approved to work in the club, he got first. He got to choose what jobs he wanted to do and he got to choose which runs he'd have to go on. What that boiled down to was Jeremy always go the shit jobs no matter what, unless Morry requested him. Judd also strutted around the property like he was king shit.

The only redeeming quality Judd had was loyalty. Jeremy could see that Judd would lay down his life for Morry and all the other guys didn't dare say a thing negative about her. So, as much as Jeremy hated the guy and his big fucking mouth and his cock—which he was tempted to cut off—he couldn't deny that Judd being second-in-command was a smart move.

Was it wrong that he'd fallen in love with Morry? Some would say yes. She was twelve years his senior. Morry got him clean, so she was the closest he had to a sponsor. She had a son who was now fourteen and an ex who was a fucking piece of shit. Ran an illegal motorcycle gang and was a member of the same organization that Dean was part of—they were basically assassins. To say she came with baggage, drama, and constant danger would be an understatement, but he didn't care.

She found assholes no one else could or was scared to face and took them out like the fucking trash they were. It was super fucking sexy. He spent way too many nights jerking off to that very image. Jeremy always knew when she was heading out for a Righteous job. She wore an all-black, skin-tight leather outfit, with weapons strapped to her body like she was the fucking Terminator. It *always* had him hard for days. She rarely spoke to anyone about where she was going, except for the few occasions when she took Judd and a handful of the guys. That always burned his ass. Watching Judd leave with her as her most trusted. Hell to the fuck no. He'd made it his singular mission to change that.

Whenever she returned from one of the Righteous missions, Morry acted like it was just another day of business. He could admit he held her on a pedestal, but again, he didn't fucking care.

She deserved better than the shit he'd already seen her deal with, let alone all the crap she wouldn't talk about.

The thought of Dean had him wondering what the hell had happened. Jeremy hadn't seen Dean in what felt like forever. Dean hadn't communicated what he wanted Jeremy to do with the landscaping business, his and Yasmine's house, or anything else. He was simply gone.

He'd gone to work for Dean for a week or two and was coming down the street as Dean, Yasmine, and the kids all piled into a massive black stretch limo that looked like one you would see coming and going from the airports. The limo drove past him, but the windows were so dark that he couldn't see inside.

Concerned, he pulled into the house's driveway and went inside, but everything was normal—no sign of a struggle, blood, note, or anything else. The guy was a trained killer and could take care of himself. If he hadn't wanted to go somewhere, there would be a sign. Wouldn't there? Wouldn't he have called one of the other members, like Morry? It wasn't like her took his Hummer. It was still parked in the locked garage with a tarp on it, just the way Dean left it.

Shrugging it off, he figured Dean and Yasmine had planned a family trip to travel the world and forgot to tell him. He took the list of clients that needed work done and set off to continue, and that was how it remained. Every two weeks, he went to Kansas for three to four days, completed the contracts he knew needed to be done, and took any messages off the machine to answer before coming back here.

It was getting to the point where he should tell Morry. He

would give Dean one more chance, and if he wasn't there again when he visited, he would tell her and see if she was concerned.

The thing was, he wasn't sure he should bother coming back to the club anymore. It hurt to be here and see Morry with someone else. With her never glancing his way, never noticing what she meant to him. Turning down any little advance with a metaphysical slap on the wrist. His anger had also reached its boiling point. Every time the thought of someone else touching Morry snuck into his mind, all he could picture was slitting their throat and burying them in a grave in the desert. He knew all the good spots now.

Morry twitched in her sleep, and her hand tightened on his as she mumbled the word *no*. That was new. As many trips like this as he'd been on, he never saw her dream. She twitched again, and this time, she grabbed his hand hard.

"TK," she mumbled.

"Shh, you're safe. I'm here," he whispered to the top of her head before daring to kiss her. Closing his eyes, he breathed in her scent. It was sweet and feminine and always had a dash of diesel and oil mixed in. Fuck, he loved that scent. Could he bottle it and spray everything with it?

"It's okay, I promise. I'm not going anywhere," Jeremy said, and his heart swelled as her twitching lessened until she relaxed against him. Morry cuddled a little closer, and it was all he could do not to wrap her up in his arms.

He didn't know who TK was, but he felt it had to do with her time overseas. That was a topic she never talked about. It was literally a no-fly zone. She changed the subject or shut down. The only thing she would ever say was it was the place where she'd gotten the scar on her face.

Most of the time, she seemed totally at ease with the long gash that stretched almost the entire length of her jawbone to the corner of her mouth. But when she thought no one was watching, Jeremy would see her run her fingers along the scar, her face dark with pain. That look on her face was something he couldn't understand but wanted to. Jeremy wanted to understand every part of her the way she did for him, how she seemed to know when he needed a firm word or a kind touch. It was a gift...She was a gift.

Jeremy didn't even care that a big portion of her life she wasn't allowed to share. He wouldn't have known about Wolf if they hadn't gotten the emergency call. The entire Righteous organization was beyond secretive, but it was her thing, so he went along with it without question.

The metal doors at the end of the hall opened, and the sound had Morry sitting up straight like a gun went off. She looked around before finding his eyes and then looked down at their hands. He swallowed hard, expecting a *what the hell do you think you're doing* remark, but instead, she ran her thumb over his hand before pulling away to greet the doctor coming down the hallway.

He rose to stand beside her to listen in.

"So, what's the word," Morry asked.

The doctor pulled off the surgical hat he was wearing and crossed his arms over his chest. "Wolf is in a medically induced coma. He hit his head pretty good, and he had some swelling. Of course, we won't know for certain until we wake him up, but he is responding well to the medication, and I've alleviated the pressure that was building."

"How long will he need to be in the coma," Morry asked as she chewed her bottom lip.

"Hard to say for certain, but if he continues to progress well, it could be a few days, maybe a week. He does have some other injuries that are not life-threatening but should be mentioned."

"Okay, lay it on me."

"Wolf had a gunshot wound to his arm, but it was a through and through and missed the bone. He had a dislocated knee, which I've reset, but he will need rehabilitation as the muscles and ligaments were partially torn. There was bruising down the left side of his body, but so far, no internal bleeding that I could find. Three fractured ribs. Luckily, none of them broke or shifted. Also, his right elbow and hand have fractures like he was trying to hold on to something and took a blow to the area, or it was simply the force of the rolling vehicle. I would say he was lucky, but when he wakes up, he may not think so. He's got a minimum of six weeks of healing before he will be up and around."

Morry snickered. "You don't know Wolf. He'll be up and training in three tops, if not sooner, if he can get away with it. I saw him carry Duke over his shoulders and across a desert for miles with a gunshot wound in his shoulder. Trust me. The man is used to pain. He will cause us a shit ton of hassles."

"Will he remember the crash," Jeremy asked, and the doctor shrugged.

"Hard to tell. The hit to Wolf's head may not hinder memory, but everyone processes and heals differently. If it was extremely traumatic, he may suppress it or wake up screaming about it."

"Okay, when can we move him, and how is Duke?" The doctor also doubled as the Legion's vet.

"Luckily, we won't have to worry too much about jostling with the special suspension, so it's safe in forty-eight to seventy-two hours. As for Duke, he was pretty banged up, and I had to repair the bone in his right leg," he paused. "That's strange."

"What is," Jeremy asked at the same time as Morry.

"I saw the old bullet wound on Wolf, and it was Duke's left side that got hit with a bullet at the same time, I'm presuming. Now they are in a wreck together, and Wolf's right knee and Duke's right leg are injured. Just odd. You would think the two were connected." Shrugging, the doctor turned around to walk away. "Oh, and you better come with me. Duke is awake and whining. I don't think he's happy about being separated from Wolf."

Morry smirked and followed Doc Henry, then stopped to look back. "Are you coming?"

"Do you want me to?"

"It's up to you," she said, and his heart sank. Why couldn't she just say yes? Yes, Jeremy, I would like you there. It wasn't in her DNA, though. He knew she would never ask for help or anything else, and it drove him crazy.

He decided to change tactics. "I want to come, Morry, but only if you want me there. So the choice is yours, not mine."

Her eyes narrowed slightly, and she looked him up and down like she was figuring out a puzzle. She bobbed her head slowly.

"Alright. Yes, I want you there," Morry said like she was expecting him to yell, "gotcha."

He was extremely tempted, but he kept that little celebration inside his head.

As she turned around, his lip curled up. Morry was like trying to navigate a minefield, but he may have just found a new path to what he wanted on the other side.

Chapter 5

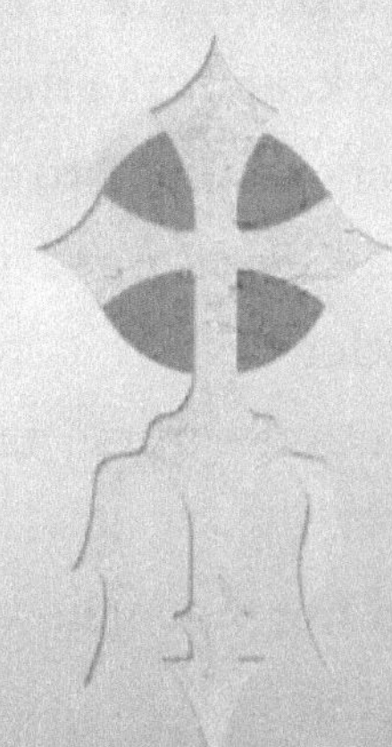

Morry walked down the hall and felt Jeremy following like a hand pressed on her back. What had she just done? She asked him to come in after waking up, holding his hand. That was not the way you kept your distance. She was wise enough to know better, yet her mouth had a mind of its own.

She looked in the windows of each door they passed. Some were empty, and some had a nurse or other staff member inside. There was a time that this place was nothing more than a dream. Now Morry had multiple locations and wondered how she managed it all. This spot was an old school sitting empty, and she converted it into a safe house with multiple rooms and one whole section set up for anything Doc Henry needed.

Henry paused and pointed to one of the rooms. "Duke is in there, and Wolf is next door in recovery. I'm going to get a coffee and something to eat. I'll be back."

She stopped outside the door where Duke was and laughed as she saw the nurse trying to keep Duke from moving around inside the room. She was obviously not used to animals, and they looked like they were dancing as she stepped in Duke's way. The dog looked as annoyed as a rattler.

"I've got this," she said to the nurse as she pushed through the door.

As soon as Duke heard her voice, he whined loudly and made to come over, his tail wagging.

"No. Wait," she commanded, and he sat, holding his right leg in the air.

The nurse seemed relieved and went to step around Morry but froze in place.

She knew exactly what the nurse was staring at or who. Jeremy could've easily been on the cover of any magazine. He was more than simply good-looking. He was downright take-your-breath-away sexy. And, just like every other time he was ogled, she pushed the annoyance aside and bent down to pick Duke up. There was no point in being jealous. They were never going to be a thing. Just because *she wanted her cake and could probably eat it too* didn't mean she should. She would only end up with a toothache.

"Hey, boy, it's been a while since I've done this, so you're going to have to bear with me," she said as Duke licked her face. "Yeah, I missed you too. I know I should visit more." She stroked his soft fur while she spoke.

This dog was more than a soldier. He was their friend. Duke was not only the last link they had to Jimmy, but he saved their asses more than once and deserved a fucking parade when they got back. Instead, like the rest of them, Duke was cast aside and forgotten about, but the group never forgot what he'd done to get them home alive.

"Ready."

He stood, knowing what she would do as she gave the command. Tucking her head under his belly, he helped as he shimmied his way over enough that she could wrap her arms around his legs.

"Damn, boy. I think you put on weight," Morry mumbled. "Or maybe I'm just getting too old for this." With a groan, she lifted Duke, who was easily over a hundred pounds, like she was squatting with weights and stood.

Turning, she spotted the cute nurse, who was trying hard for some small talk with Jeremy, but he was staring at her. She hated it when he looked at her like that. It gave her teenage butterflies. She hadn't had those for anything in years, and he fucking tried to give her hope for something that could never be.

"Can you grab the door," she asked.

There was a little thrill when he didn't even acknowledge the nurse, who was still trying to speak to him. Yanking open the door, he held it wide for her to walk through, and she turned to head toward Wolf's room.

"Where are you taking him," Jeremy asked as he walked out behind her.

"To Wolf. He wants to be with him," she said, then waited for Jeremy to open the door to the room where Wolf was.

She hated to see her friend like that. Monitors attached to him, tubes and things dripping. It reminded her that any day could be her day to end up in one of these beds or worse, but it also reminded her of her son she hadn't seen in over a month because Andrew was being a dick. Kyle was her whole heart, and she would kill to protect him, but how do you protect him from his own body? It was gut-wrenching.

Because this was one of her private facilities, the bed was twice the width of a normal hospital bed, and she slowly squatted until Duke stepped onto the mattress. As she figured, he wedged himself beside Wolf and laid his head on Wolf's chest.

Fuck, this shit was going to bring a tear to her eye. She turned away as emotions flooded her system. She stared at the ground, hating for anyone to see her cry, especially Jeremy. Their relationship was the other way around. She was his support system when he needed it.

"Hey, he's going to be okay." Jeremy's boots came into her line of sight a moment before he pulled her into his body for a hug.

She selfishly took comfort for a moment, then stepped back and walked past Jeremy out the door. The hallway was empty, and she marched along the bright white hall when Jeremy's voice growled behind her.

"Morry, why do you do that?"

She turned to look at him and wished she hadn't. He looked so fucking hot with his fists balled and his jaw set. He stalked toward her, and all she could think about was that she wanted to lick every square inch of him. She was messed up in the head. She blamed it on growing up with her father and four brothers, who were all army brats. Her mother died when she was a baby, and her father remained single, so the growling and overbearing, dominant male was what she was used to.

Subsequently, it also became what she craved. The thought of Jeremy pushing her up against the wall was fixed securely in her mind as he stopped in front of her. Jeremy's blue eyes snapped with anger that she didn't understand, but damn, he could look at her like that any time. It made her feel hot in all the right places.

"Do what exactly," she asked, putting her hands on her hips.

"Push me away like that," he said, his hand swinging back to point at the room they'd just left.

"I'm not pushing you away," she said, and one of those eyebrows of his shot up as he crossed his arms over his chest.

"Oh yeah? Then what exactly would you call it?"

"Keeping you at arm's length. I don't do hugs for support and looks of sympathy, Jeremy. I stand alone for a reason."

His face twisted in confusion. "I'm pretty sure that is the same fucking thing. You just said it like it makes you a badass."

"No, if I were pushing you away, it would mean I didn't want you near me. Keeping you at arm's length is making sure you remain on the other side of the boundary line so that our relationship stays where it should. But it's not because I don't want you near me. See the difference?"

"Oh, for fuck's sake," he growled and veered around her to march off.

Flirting and men were not exactly what she would call her

strong suit. Andrew was a fun night at a bar that ended up with her pregnant. Not the best way to start a relationship, and probably why their marriage ended the way it had. She was pretty positive Jeremy was jealous or something. She couldn't quite put her finger on it. Whatever it was, she wasn't happy about it.

She was grooming him to take over as her number two and one day be the number one when she was ready to hang up her boots. So whatever this was, he needed to get his shit right, or she needed to figure out another plan.

Judd was not a good leader. He followed orders and made sure things got done, but she wasn't stupid. The man would ruin everything she'd built. His first order of business would be to accept and fuck every woman that knocked on the door, and drink all the profits away.

Morry followed the same path Jeremy walked and pushed her way out into the bright sunshine to find him sucking face with the nurse from earlier. She ground her teeth together but turned in the other direction and marched to the Hummer. Morry slammed the door as she jumped in the driver's seat. Firing Lady Luck up, she backed up and peeled out of the parking area, punching the dash hard before shaking out her fist.

"Fuck, I hate emotions. Bunch of useless, motherfucking things that made you weak. That was all they did, made you a weak sobbing mess that left you broken," she snarled out.

She flew down the dirt road toward the main highway with no real direction in mind. Morry needed some distance from the safe house and Jeremy. Of course, she found her mind traveling back in time.

. . .

Her computer started to ring. She tossed her cards on the bed and rolled off to answer it. She hoped there wasn't something wrong with Kyle because Andrew was the only one with the link to call her, and it wasn't their designated day. She hit the answer button and was about to say hello when the screen filled with the sounds of sex like she'd flicked on a porno movie.

TK and Dean were closest and turned in her direction, smiling like she'd just put on the most exciting show on the planet. But she couldn't quite make out what the hell she was staring at. It was too close to the screen. Her mind reeled as she tried to piece together what was going on. Had her computer been hacked? Did she somehow download a porno, and it rang?

No, none of that made sense. Even as the voices registered and Morry heard her husband say her best friend's name, she tried to deny it. No way. Andrew wouldn't do something like that. Sure, they had their differences, and he hadn't been impressed that she joined the army but...to cheat.

"Yes, Andrew, right there. Fuck."

Dean stood and came over, and TK was by her side a moment later. The couple onscreen moved farther away from the computer, and that's when she realized that the computer had come on in error as Andrew fucked Lindsay on the desk. Morry's hand went to her mouth as the two people came fully into view, and her stomach plummeted through the floor.

Morry tried to form words and figure out the best thing to say in this scenario, but she only had a pounding heart and rising blood pressure. She was breathing so hard that she thought she might pass out.

"What in the ever-loving fuck." TK yelled as he slammed his hands on either side of the laptop. "You worthless piece of shit. When we get back, I'm cutting your fucking dick off."

Andrew dropped Lindsay on the bed and spun around to stare at the three faces peering back at him. The look on his face—shock that he was caught, but zero remorse—was what she would remember forever. It wasn't the sounds of the sex. It wasn't the betrayal itself. It was the look that screamed as clearly as TK had that he'd never loved her.

"Fuck, Morry. It was a mistake. It's not what it looks like," Andrew started as he rushed for the computer, but she'd seen enough.

She'd gotten good at masking her emotions. Becoming one of the guys, whether in her male-dominated home or the army. It was an unspoken code to shove your shit down no matter your gender or what was going on in your life and live solely for God and Country. That was what she'd lived by her whole life.

She marched for the door, not really seeing it as Andrew's face flashed before her eyes. She could hear TK yelling obscenities at her husband as she groped for the door, the need to escape the small sleeping quarters riding her.

Her hand slipped on the handle, and she could feel the emotion bubbling inside her as her shaking hands tried for the handle again. It was Dean who put a hand on her shoulder to steady her. His eyes were thankfully unreadable as he turned the knob and let her out. She ran across the open area to a quiet corner by the fence and dropped to her knees. A strangled gasp wracked her body as she clenched the dirt under her hands. There was so much pain, yet no sound came out. It seemed like it had been locked up so long that her body didn't know how to cry properly.

"Morry, you okay," TK asked softly as he squatted down beside her. She didn't want to be weak in front of him, but some things left a person weak and unable to fight. "Come here," he said and wrapped his arm around her shoulders, pulling her into his side.

The contact did the trick. The sound from her throat was like that of a dying animal. TK plunked himself down on the ground and pulled her into his chest, and she shamefully clung to him.

"I'm sorry," she managed to get out before she was once more consumed with incoherent sobs.

"Don't be sorry. He's the one who should be sorry. He has no idea what he's thrown away, and if he does, then he's an even bigger fuck nut than I pegged him for. You're fucking awesome, Morry, and he doesn't deserve you."

"What am I going to do? I have Kyle to think about, and...."

"Easy, soldier, one step at a time. This is not the moment to be making big choices." TK rubbed her back, and she didn't want to let go but knew she had to. He was one of her best friends, but she didn't want to burden him with this crap.

She eased herself back and wiped at her face.

"Don't I feel like the fool?"

TK cupped her face and forced her to look at him. "This is not on you. It's not your fault that he's not man enough to keep it in his pants while his wife is risking her life to make sure he has a bed to sleep in. Do you understand? This is not on you."

Not sure what came over her, she grabbed his face and slammed her lips to his, forcing him to fall back on the ground.

"*Oh fuck. Morry, you don't want to do this, not while you're this upset,*" *TK said, turning his head to the side.*

"*Don't I?*"

"*No, you don't. You're hurt, and you want revenge. I get it, but I don't want that to be our first time. I like you too much for that,*" *TK panted out.* "*But fuck, you're making this hard to turn down.*"

Pushing herself up, she stared down into his eyes. "*You like me?*"

"*At least I've managed to hide it from you,*" *he said and ran his thumb across her swollen bottom lip.* "*Yeah, I've wanted you since I first saw you, but you were married. I would never purposely try to ruin shit, and I valued our friendship too much to fuck it up.*"

"*You really like me?*" *His hands were on her waist, and she suddenly wanted to know how they would feel against her naked skin.*

"*Um, woman...No offense, but you are blind. Like, most of the single guys on base want you, even some of the ones who are taken. You're fierce and beautiful, and damn, there are not enough words. Trust me when I tell you Andrew is a fucking i-d-i-o-t.*"

She bit her lip, trying to think if there was any time she could place TK flirting with her, and she couldn't. He had hidden it well, or she was bad at seeing the signs.

"*We better get up. I'm the nice guy, but I'm starting to think fuck it, just go for it, and that's dangerous. You'll regret it, and then I'll regret it, and I don't want to regret anything that may or may not happen between us.*"

She searched his face and those light green eyes and felt like she was staring at him for the first time. How had she not known? First, about Andrew and Lindsay, and now TK? Was she really so oblivious to everything?

They pushed themselves to their feet, and she looked up at him and grabbed his arm before they made their way back to the bunks.

"Thanks, TK. You know, for being my friend, for tonight, for stopping me before I went too far."

"Ha. Don't thank me for that. I'm already kicking myself in the ass," he teased, wrapping his arm around Morry's shoulders. "Seriously, I want to get back down on the dirt again. I've changed my mind."

He smiled widely, and she gave him a hard shove. "Jerk."

CHAPTER 6

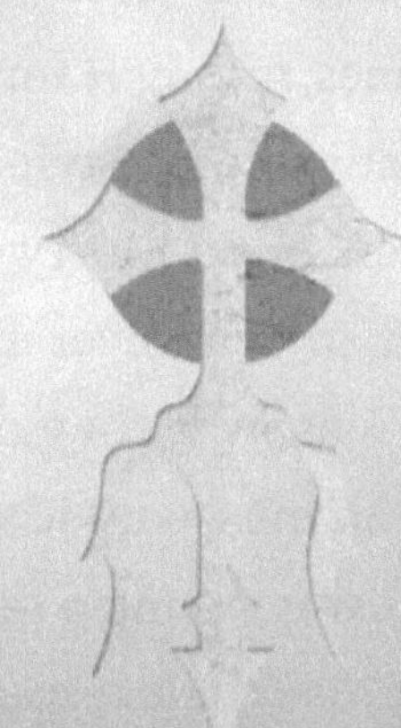

Jeremy watched Morry take off in the Hummer, pissed at himself for doing this. The flash of jealousy in her eyes was what he was after and got, but now he felt like a fucking piece of shit for doing it. It was a reflex, and Jeremy hated that he felt the need to make a point. Jeremy smiled at the nurse and excused himself.

"Can I get your number?" she called after him.

"Naw, sorry. Not into dating," Jeremy said over his shoulder and went to the bunk area.

The bikes were lined up neatly in a row, but the bikers were scattered around the sitting area with a bonfire burning even though the sun was still high in the sky. It didn't matter where they stopped. It was always the same. The guys set up camp, the girls who traveled with the group would cook food, and the story-telling and sex would start as soon as the sun went down. Sometimes the sex started before that.

His eyes traveled around the circle, and sure enough, there was a sweetbutt on her knees, giving Hammer a blowjob.

It seemed like such a strange lifestyle when he'd first arrived, and he couldn't get over how Morry wandered around the different groups, engaged in whatever they wanted, and never batted an eye at them. It was as if they didn't exist. Morry ran a tight ship mind you. No one messed with her, and he understood that she had to keep it that way. Being a female and the leader, she needed to prove herself or lose their respect. It wasn't right. She'd earned her badges ten times over, but there was always some asshole thinking they wanted to be alpha and a woman couldn't be as tough. I wondered how tough they felt when she buried their body in the desert.

First rule of the club was you never discussed club business with anyone who was not part of the club. The second rule was you never abused or sexually assaulted a club member. If you did, you were exiled with a bullet in your head, no exceptions. The third rule was that anyone who wanted to take over had to go through Morry. Jeremy watched her throw down with the men in the group more than once. Fuck. She kicked their asses. No one ever bet against her, and for a good reason.

He grabbed water from the cooler and leaned against the wall, staring at the group. They reminded him of a bunch of wild, mangy, vicious dogs. The kind of dogs that would rip your balls off and your throat out at the same time just for fun, not even because they were hungry.

"You interested in a little fun tonight," the newest sweetbutt asked as she walked over.

She was cute in her little cut-off shorts and long blond hair hanging over her shoulders. Jeremy couldn't remember her name, but it didn't really matter with this group. You could just point and yell, "hey you," and the person you wanted would eventually respond.

"What do you have in mind?"

She stepped a little closer, and he could smell the hint of bonfire coming off of her. "Whatever you want. I'm game for anything," she said, smiling.

How long since he'd been with an actual girl, not just his hand? Too long. A few months, anyway. His cock twitched at the idea of getting a decent blowy. Why should he continue to be celibate? What was the point?

"I think I could be talked into something," he said, pushing away from the wall.

"Hey, GiGinny. Get your ass over here," Judd yelled, and she looked over her shoulder. Ginny, that was her name. "Yeah, I'm talkin' to you. You promised me a lap dance. Let's go."

Ginny turned back and shrugged. "Maybe next time, the number two is hollerin'."

Of course, Judd was the one to cock block him again. It didn't seem to matter who it was. The guy was in his way. He didn't feel like hanging out with the group and decided to wander along the long building that led around back. Turning the corner, he spotted the black Hummer and looked over his shoulder. How the hell had Morry snuck back in without him seeing her?

Jeremy walked toward the Hummer parked by the small pond though he wasn't sure why he bothered. Apparently, he liked being turned down cause he kept coming back for more. He stared at the windows, but there was no sign of movement. The license plate said Lady Luck, so it was Morry, but where was she?

Jeremy made his way around the front of the vehicle and jerked to a stop as he stared down at the top of Morry's head. She was leaning against the front tire with a bottle of tequila already half gone.

"You should've fucked her," she said and took another swig of the bottle.

Jeremy never saw her drink like this. He'd never seen her drink anything more than a beer. Seeing her like this wasn't just shocking. It scared him. What was so terrible that it drove the strongest person he knew to want to get wasted?

He stepped over her outstretched legs and sat down beside her. "Which one?"

She squinted and covered her eyes to block out the sun as she looked at him. "Either, I guess."

He shrugged. "I was tempted but decided I wasn't interested," he said flatly.

He left out the part where Judd ruined his one possible bit of fun. She took another swig, put the cap back on, and set it aside.

"Not going to offer me any," he asked teasingly.

She glared at him from the corner of her eye, which made him smirk.

"You don't want to touch this shit. It does nothing good for you."

"Oh yeah? Then why are you drinking it?"

She was quiet for a long time, her face blank as she stared at the shimmering water. "To try to forget."

"Is it working?"

"No, nothing works."

"Then maybe you shouldn't keep drinking it," he said, and she snorted, her lips curling up in a small smile.

"How the tables have turned," she mocked, but her voice was dry of all humor. Morry laid her hands in her lap and stared at her palms before she curled her hands into fists. "You know I want you to take over one day, right?"

Jeremy's mouth fell open as Morry's eyes slowly turned to his. "I'm sorry, what?"

She nodded and looked away again, her head resting on the tire.

"Yeah, I thought you would've picked up on that," she ran her hand through her hair. "I don't let just anyone in on the financials or the club and clinic."

He loved her short hair, and the breeze made it stand on end. She looked rough and sexy and like she was just fucked hard. Most guys loved long hair, something they could wrap around in their hand, but not him, at least not with her. He wanted to grab hand-fuls and pull her head back while he devoured her mouth until she gasped for air. She had no idea just how fucking sexy she was.

He shifted with the sexual thoughts that went straight into his jeans and made things a lot more uncomfortable.

"I don't understand. I thought Judd would be the one to take over," he said.

She reached for the bottle and stared at the label before leaning forward and heaving it. The bottle spun end over end until it splashed into the water.

"Morry, what's going on? Has something happened that you're not telling me?" He licked his lips, not wanting to ask the next question. "Like are you thinking of retirement soon? Is there something medical going on?"

He was starting to worry that it was something serious. Morry was always so private that it was hard to know, but the fear in his gut was real. It made his heart pound harder, and not for a good reason.

"No, it's nothing like that. I always have to plan for the what ifs and Judd's not a good choice. He's great muscle and keeps the others in line like a giant pitbull, but to lead?" She shook her head. "No, he doesn't have the right balance of grit and compassion that's needed. He's more interested in..." She waved her hand around. "Everything else that's not work-related, including showing off how big his cock is." She looked over and lifted a brow. "I mean that figuratively."

He snorted as he laughed. There was no truer statement. Morry's hand was on the grass, and he grabbed it off the ground. As he suspected, she tried to pull it away, but he held firm.

"Stop it, Morry, and tell me what is going on."

"Why are you doing this to me?" She stood in a rush, jerking her hand away.

He watched as she paced, her boots thudding with each stride. Pushing himself to his feet, he tried to determine what she meant.

"What exactly am I doing to you? I haven't done anything except be a great fucking member and...." He was at a loss for the right word. Friend seemed too blasé for what he felt, but they weren't anything more. It left him floundering.

Morry turned and came right at him. He took a step back as her dark glare found his. She gave him a hard shove in the chest, and he stepped back, his body hitting the Hummer.

"You make me feel shit. You fucker. I don't want to feel anything for anyone, and here you are trying to make me feel...." She moved her hands erratically in front of her chest. "Shit. I'm all up in feels I don't want any of it, and you just won't stop pushing," she growled.

She was as angry as he'd ever seen her. His pulse spiked. It was the first admission he'd ever gotten from her that she might see him as more than the fucked-up loser who landed on her doorstep. She also just admitted that everything he'd been doing she had noticed and he felt like he'd just won the fucking Power-ball. He didn't even think about what he was doing. Jeremy snatched the front of her leather jacket and turned Morry around, so her back was against the Hummer.

"Get off me," she snarled but didn't push him away. If she wanted him to back off, she could kick his ass.

"Stop fighting what's happening between us." He slid his hands along her arms until he gripped her wrists and put them above her head. Morry's chest heaved, and he looked down at the tiny piece of leather she was wearing for a top and groaned. Fuck, he wanted to rip that off her.

"Don't say that. There's nothing happening between us," Morry said, eyes snapping with anger.

He pressed his body into hers, and his hands gripped Morry's above her head a little tighter. "Yes, there is," he growled into her ear and felt Morry's body shudder against his. "Fuck, I want you," he said. "I want to fuck you until you can only scream my name because I'm the only one you think about."

He didn't hold back as he did what he'd been fantasizing about and attacked her mouth. She tasted like tequila, the smooth bite of it mixing with her sweet flavor. Nothing had ever tasted or felt so fucking good.

Releasing her hands, he grabbed Morry's face and pressed her harder into the vehicle. He wanted to growl when she moaned into his mouth. Her hands gripped his waist and kept him in place rather than pushing him away. Oh fuck, he was going to take her to the ground and didn't care who saw them. He was so hard he ached behind the fly of his jeans. Jeremy lost count of how many times he'd fantasized about this. Now all he could think about was what she would feel like when he buried himself inside her.

Their tongues battled as he tasted every inch of her mouth. He sucked on her bottom lip and stared into her eyes which were as beautiful and stormy as her personality.

"Do you have any idea what you do to me," he asked and leaned in to nip the side of her neck.

Her pulse was pounding as fast as his own, and he never wanted this moment to end. There was a sense of urgency coursing through his body, like this needed to happen before she changed her mind.

"Well, isn't this cozy," Judd said.

Son of a fucking bitch.

And just like that, the bubble they were in burst. Jeremy didn't release Morry but glared at Judd as the thought of leaping for him crossed his mind. He'd never been this livid in his life.

"What the fuck do you want?" he snarled at Judd, and the guy's eyes widened with the tone.

"Okay, knock it off, both of you," Morry said and gave him a bit of a push on his waist.

It took everything in him to step away and not just keep her trapped for as long as he could before she decked him.

"What's up, Judd? I was kind of busy here."

"Yeah, I can see that. I thought it was only me you turned to," he said, and crossed his arms like a pouting child.

"Guess you were wrong. Now, what do you want?" Morry said smoothly.

It was total bullshit. This was the only time it had ever happened, but Jeremy had no intention of correcting it. The more Judd thought he was out, the better.

"The doc is looking for you. Wolf had a seizure."

Morry was gone like a fucking magic trick as she took off at a dead run around the Hummer toward the back door of the building. That fact she could stand and walk after down a half bottle of tequila was impressive. To see her run like she was in a marathon? He had to give mad props for that. Jeremy went to walk around the Hummer to follow her, but Judd stuck his arm out.

"I wouldn't get too comfortable, pup." Judd leaned in a little closer, and Jeremy's fist clenched tight. "She may be giving you a little bit of attention out of pity, but it's me she will always come back to."

"With you pissing all over everything, Judd, I would say you're insecure," he pushed Judd's arm out of the way. "Morry can make her own choice, and from where I'm standing, it's not you."

"You're getting pretty fucking cocky there, Jeremy. Watch your back."

Jeremy standing at six-four, turned around to face Judd and stared up at the man. Judd was taller by a couple of inches, but had no more muscle on him. Jeremy didn't know if he could take him for sure, but it didn't matter. He would take the blows to wipe that sneering grin off his face.

"You threatenin' me?" Jeremy took a step closer.

"Just reminding you that there's a pecking order, and you, boot licker, are at the bottom," Judd said and laughed as he walked past.

Everything pent up inside of him erupted, and Jeremy felt his control snap like a brittle twig.

"Hey, asshole," he growled and stomped after Judd.

The guy barely got turned around when he let his fist fly. The punch took Judd off his feet, and he landed hard on his ass.

"No one threatens me. Not anymore. I think it's time we decided who the real number two around here is," Jeremy said as Judd rubbed at the red mark on his jaw.

"You're going to fucking pay for that, kid."

Judd moved fast. Jumping to his feet, he took the cheap shot and dove for Jeremy's waist. They crashed to the ground hard, and the force pushed all the air out of Jeremy's lungs. That meaty left hook found his face, but he managed enough of a block that it was only a glancing blow. Jeremy bucked up with his body, tossing Judd forward and off balance. He landed a double blow to Judd's right side before pushing him off.

They rolled around on the ground, and Judd found a way to get an elbow across the left side of his face. The metallic taste of blood filled his mouth. Jeremy was vaguely aware that they'd drawn a crowd as they continued to exchange blows. There was hooting and hollering, and people yelled about bets, but no one interfered. This was the order of things in a biker gang. If you wanted something, you fucking took it, and you needed to earn it with your blood.

Swinging his leg back, he brought his knee into Judd's side, and the guy groaned with the impact. All he saw was Judd poking at him from the day he arrived, how he was forced to do the worst jobs, no matter what the schedule said unless Morry was around. The derogatory names bounced around in his skull with each impact of his fist. Judd, his anger, the pain, and the blood were all a blur.

There was no telling when Judd's face got all bloody or that he barely fought back until a shrill whistle cut through the angry haze. He froze with his fist in the air as he was yanked out of the murky waters of his rage. He didn't think that even a knife blade put to his throat could have stopped him faster. Panting hard, he wiped his mouth with the back of his hand and pushed himself away from Judd.

Judd groaned and rolled onto his side. Jeremy felt utterly satisfied until he turned around and caught sight of Morry's pissed-off eyes. All the satisfaction was flushed down the toilet with the steely look she gave him and then Judd.

She didn't say anything but didn't need to for him to know she would rip him a new one.

"Get him up and make sure the doctor looks him over," Morry said as she nodded at Butch. Butch was in charge of security for the Legion, and Jeremy couldn't remember the guy saying more than five words in the five years he'd been around the group.

"I don't need a doc," Judd said as he held his side and pushed himself onto unsteady legs.

"Shut. The. Fuck. Up." Morry said, and Judd snapped his mouth closed. "You'll do as I say, or I'll slit your throat right now." Judd's eyes widened as Morry placed her hand on the long blade strapped to her leg.

"But he fucking started it." Judd pointed a finger in Jeremy's direction like the piece of shit tattletale he was. It had been a long time since he felt like a whelp, but as Morry's eyes found him again, he was worried about what she would say next. Was this what got him kicked out, or worse, in a shallow desert grave?

"You and I need to have a serious fucking talk." She turned and marched away but looked over her shoulder when he didn't budge. He thought for sure Morry was going to dress him down in front of everyone, but it was worse than that. She wanted to talk to him in private. "Now."

Oh fuck. This wasn't going to be good.

CHAPTER 7

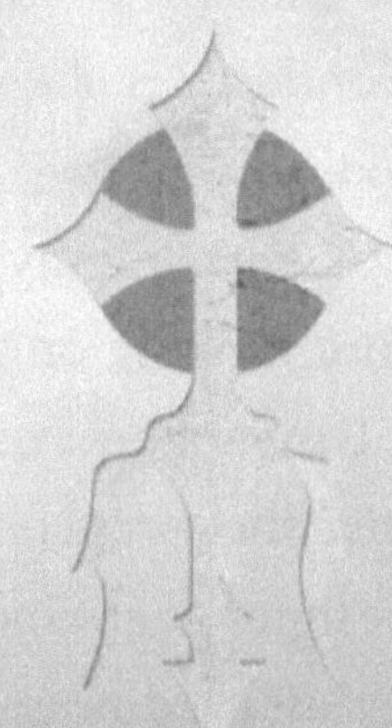

Four Years and Six Months Ago

"Hey, get up." The light flicked on in his small room. Jeremy groaned and covered his face as it blinded him.

"What's going on?" he yawned.

They had a thing about clocks here or maybe a lack of a thing. You couldn't find one to save your soul, and the only answer he ever got from Morry about it was that you should know what time it is from the position of the sun.

"I said, get up, now," Morry's stern voice bit out.

He swung his legs over the side of the small bed and sat up. A pile of clothes was tossed at his feet, followed by the thud of a pair of black boots. He jumped.

"Get dressed and meet me out front. You have five minutes," Morry said and left the room.

What happened to the woman that held his hand through the nights he was going through shit? He hadn't seen that woman in a couple of weeks, and he wondered if she was ever that nice or if it was all part of his hallucinations.

Slipping out of the sleep pants, Jeremy pulled on the snug boxer briefs and cargo pants before yanking on the socks and boots. Last was the T-shirt and hoodie. He wandered out to the hallway and realized it was very early because the entire bunk area was silent. As he neared the doors, he saw the lights of a vehicle and swallowed hard.

What the hell did she plan on doing to him this time? Had he proven to be too much work over the last six month? Was she getting rid of him? Were they taking him somewhere to dispose of his body? The worry only got worse when he stepped outside. Morry and Judd leaned against a black Hummer that looked identical to the one Dean drove.

"What's going on," he asked, shuddering as lightning flashed in the distance. The white streaks rippling through the dark clouds promised rain. He wondered if it was also a sign of what was to come.

"Get in the back," Morry said, pushing away from the Hummer. He watched Judd as he walked around to the other side of the vehicle and got in the passenger side.

He swallowed the lump in his throat as fear kicked in. The last time he was ordered into the back of a vehicle, it ended with him in the hospital with broken ribs and his ass bleeding from the abuse he'd taken. It wasn't his finest moment, selling his body for money. If his parents had seen him....

He shuddered at the thought, the look of disappointment that he was sure would be on his dad's face and the disgust in his mom's eyes.

"I said, get in," Morry ordered, firmer this time, and pulled open the back door of the Hummer.

"Are you planning on killing me?"

The corner of her lip curled up and did nothing to settle the feeling in his stomach that made him want to vomit. "That's going to depend on you. Now get in. It's time for a lesson."

Oh, he didn't like that word. He wouldn't like this, but he found himself putting one foot in front of the other and climbing into the black vehicle. She closed the door, and he balled his hands into fists on his knees to keep himself from grabbing the handle and jumping right back out.

The problem was, where was he going to go? There was nowhere to go. It was desert for miles in every direction outside the horseshoe-shaped canyon where the Legions had set up base. The first day he was allowed outside after he arrived, he realized just how secluded and off the map they really were. A large vulture had flown overhead with a dead snake in its claws, and the reality had his insides turned to ice.

They pulled out of the large metal gates, and their path took them further into the bowl shape of the canyon rather than out toward civilization. No one spoke. It was awkward, and with each passing second, his anxiety grew until his knees bounced in time to the flashes of lightning in the sky. Morry stopped the vehicle but kept it running and got out to open his door.

"Let's go. We're here."

Jeremy stared around at the vast nothingness and the darkness beyond that. He glanced back at Morry's eyes reflecting the lightning and thought he might faint. What the hell had he gotten himself into? So far since coming here, he'd been strapped down on a bed, made to scrub toilets, peeled a million potatoes, and was forced to run until it felt like his legs were going to fall off. He was in the middle of fucking nowhere with a woman who looked like she wanted to kill him, with her sidekick, who openly detested him. This wasn't good, no matter which way you sliced it.

Fuck, just get out of the Hummer. If they kill you, they kill you. At least the pain will be over.

Jeremy slipped out of the truck, and Morry closed the door. She walked around to the back of the Hummer and opened the hatch. She came back with a shovel and smirked as his mouth fell open.

"Here, take this," and held out the shovel.

"Okay, this may sound like a stupid question, but what exactly am I doing out here in the middle of nowhere with a shovel?"

Morry smiled, walked toward the front of the Hummer, and leaned against the hood between the two headlights. "Pick any spot in the beams and start digging."

"You haven't answered my question," he said as he made his way in the direction she'd indicated.

"And I don't plan to. Now start digging, or you will fail the lesson. Then it will be latrine duty for a month."

Well, that meant she didn't plan on murdering him. At least, not right now. From toilet germs, that was another story. Jeremy stuck the shovel in the ground and threw the dirt to the side, then did it again and kept digging. Right about then, he wanted to bury Dean. How could the man think this was going to help him? Sure, he was off the drugs, but the cravings were still just as terrible, and now he had to deal with the emotions and guilt he'd been avoiding. Now he could add this to the list of shit.

"How big do I need to dig the hole," he asked, his hand sore from the wooden handle. He shook out his palm and knew that blisters were forming.

"Big enough to hold a body, and deep enough to keep it there," Morry said. Judd snorted a laugh as he lit up a smoke.

Okay, maybe he was wrong about living another month. "Wow, that was fucking comforting," he mumbled just as the first drop of rain fell and hit him on the back of the neck.

Jeremy looked up toward the sky, and more hit him in the face. Great. Just fucking great. He was panting hard by the time he was done digging what he assumed was a grave. Jeremy's hands were bleeding, his clothes dripping, and he was soaked to the bone. His muscles shook, and he didn't think he could dig another scoop of the heavy, wet dirt. It rarely rained out in the middle of the desert, and they picked the one night of torrential downpours. Murphy had a fucking sick sense of humor.

His hands ached and he knew that he'd created blisters, broke them open and was bleeding on the handle, yet she wouldn't let him stop.

"Okay, you can get out of the hole now. That's big enough," Morry said.

Jeremy looked up at the tall sides, and a shiver traveled down his body. Panic and fear gripped him by the throat once more when he realized just how deep he was. The hole was pitch black, the glow of headlights only skimming the top. He spun in a circle, his heart beating harder with every second now that he wasn't focused on digging.

"Can you help me get out," Jeremy asked and held his hand up for help.

"No," Morry said. He couldn't see her expression but could picture it as clear as day.

"What do you mean, no?"

"The word no means the same thing it always has. No, I'm not helping you. Get out of there on your own if you want to live," Morry said casually. Like they were having a coffee over breakfast.

Reaching up, he placed the shovel on the ground outside the hole, then grabbed the edge of the dirt wall. Jeremy jumped to pull himself out, but the dirt gave way, and his shaking muscles couldn't hold him as he fell to the bottom.

Jeremy's heart pounded out of his chest, and he grabbed a handful of his shirt as the terror pressed in on him like something was sitting on his lungs. For just a moment, he had imagined Alice tumbling down the rabbit hole from *Alice in Wonderland*. He was pretty sure he'd already fallen and landed square in the middle of the Queen of Hearts' court.

"Please help me. I can't do it," he yelled, getting on his knees.

Jeremy held his hands together and begged her to rescue him as the demons in his mind attacked.

"Look at me," she ordered, and even overrun with terror, his eyes lifted to her dark shadow. "You can get out, and you will," came Morry's voice. "Or you'll die out here in the middle of the desert, and the birds will pick at your bones. Now move it. Get out of that hole and save yourself because no one else is coming for you. Only you can save you."

He had no idea if she was telling the truth—that she really would leave him here to die—but something told him that he couldn't take the chance. Jeremy slowly stood whimpering as the pain lanced through every muscle and making them want to seize in place. The rain pounded hard on his back as he hunched over with his hands on his knees. Each drop felt like a brick and made him wince. Everything screamed in agony, and he felt his mind wanting to shut down and give up.

A shadow moved above him in the headlight beams, and he squinted at Morry squatting at the top of the edge. "You planning on dying down there, kid?"

He glared up at her, hating every fucking thing about her and this place. "Fuck you," he yelled. "And fuck this place. I hate it. I want to go—" He stopped. He was about to say *home,* but he had no home. This place was all he had.

Morry slowly clapped her hands, and the sarcastic gesture was not lost on him. It only pissed him off more. "Well, at least you have some fight left in you. Not much, though. Maybe you were right to threaten to jump off that building."

She stood back up, her face once more hidden by the shadows.

"Look around you, Jeremy. This is where you were headed, anyway. One day, one month, maybe a year, was all you had. Begging for money, getting high, fucking strangers, and stealing...." She waited until he looked around at his dark surroundings, the reality slowly seeping in.

"You stabbed someone who had been a friend and gave you food. Did you think you were going anywhere but in the ground or behind bars for life? You're lucky you didn't kill her. If you had, Dean would've already put you in a hole just like this."

The rain chose that moment to come down so hard that he could see it bouncing off her boots. She never flinched while his body shook uncontrollably.

"You did things you never thought you would do all for the sweet, sweet score." She held her arms out wide. "Really, all I'm doing is speeding up the process because this six-foot hole in the ground is what you were secretly chasing in the first place. Wasn't it?"

"You don't know anything," he said, but she'd hit way too close to the mark.

Jeremy was so caught up in his addiction that he would've done anything—had already done things he never wanted to mention again—to get his hands on the next hit. Jeremy hated that Morry was calling him out like this. In the back of his mind, he'd already given up. He was just going through the motions until he got away from here and found his next fix. Each time there was the chance he may not wake up, and each time that he did, he was both saddened and relieved.

"Keep telling yourself that, Jeremy. Maybe one day you'll

believe it. Here's the deal, you have five more minutes to get out of the hole. If you don't, Judd and I are heading out of here. I'll give you this one piece of advice. Try using your head. You're smart. So start acting like it and stop acting like the victim. This is your life. You get out of it what you put in."

Her boots sloshed as she walked away, the sound somehow loud over the thundering rain pooling at the bottom of the hole. Jeremy turned in a slow circle, his brain on the verge of a complete meltdown. He fought the screaming in his skull and pushed it to the side. Jeremy was still circling when he spotted the shovel still sitting on the ledge of the hole. An idea came to him. He reached up and grabbed the wooden handle, his palms screaming as he gripped it tight.

Ignoring the throbbing in every part of his body, he slammed the shovel home into the side of the dirt wall and dug out a large chunk. Tossing it aside, he repeated the action a couple of feet up and again for another. He laid the shovel at the top of the hole, and this time, when he placed his right foot into the first space and pushed, he kept his footing. His left foot found the second space and then the third, and before he knew it, he was kneeling at the top.

"Fuck yeah," he screamed at the top of his lungs with the victory.

Morry walked over. He half expected her to shove him back into the hole again, but instead, she knelt and offered him a bottle of water.

"Life is never easy, Jeremy. There is always someone or something that's going to try to hold you down. You need to learn to climb and push and scrap, even when you think you have nothing left. That's the only way you will battle your addiction for good and defeat anything else that comes your way." She smiled, stood, and offered her hand. "Come on. You earned yourself a hot shower and a meal."

Clasping her hand, she helped him to his feet, and for the first time in a very long time, he saw the light at the end of a very long tunnel. It may only be a pinprick, but it was enough to feel like he could accomplish anything.

Chapter 8

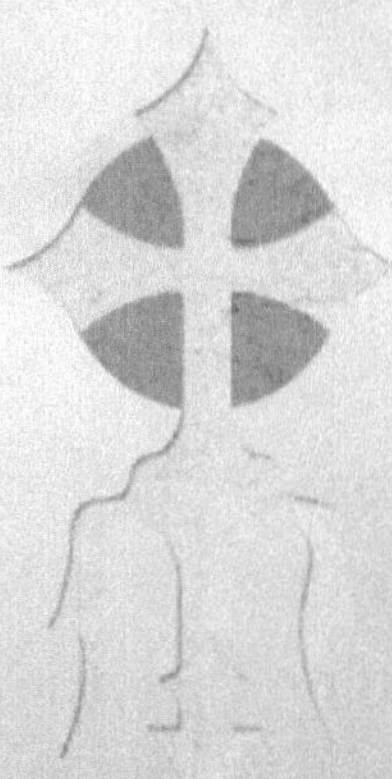

Present Day

Morry stomped into the building and down the hall — to the room she used as an office. They passed Wolf's room, and she glanced through the open door. Her worry for him spiked, which only made her angrier. The seizure was mild which was a blessing, but he couldn't be moved as soon as they'd hoped. She needed to get back to the clubhouse and find a way to see her son. Kyle shouldn't have to wonder if she loved him and if she had to break heads, arms, and rules to get in there, that was exactly what she planned on doing.

She opened the office door and held it open for Jeremy to walk through. As soon as he was over the threshold, she closed the door and stared at the handle.

"Morry, look, I'm sorry. I shouldn't have attacked Judd like that, but the guy is a fucking prick, and I'm so sick of him thinking he can push me around and call me whatever he wants."

She reached out and locked the door, then turned around to face Jeremy as he continued to explain himself.

"The guy has always taken more liberties with me than anyone else, and I'm done. You taught me to stand up for myself and—"

"Shut up," she said. "Does your lip hurt?"

He touched the corner of his mouth where there was still a small trickle of blood and shook his head no.

"Good."

Morry took off her leather jacket and tossed it on the coffee table by the couch. Jeremy stood there watching her every move, and she smirked as he tried and failed to keep his eyes on her face. They kept dropping to the bra-like top she was wearing.

Reaching behind her back, she grabbed the short zipper and pulled it down. She savored the look on Jeremy's face as she let the top slide down her arms. It, too, ended up on the table. Jeremy licked his lips, eyes wide as he stared at her chest.

Morry took a step toward Jeremy, which seemed to snap him out of his shocked state. Those blue eyes darkened, and there was the man who had kissed her outside. He lit a fire in her belly, and for the first time in years, she was ravenous for a man's touch. She needed him to exhaust every part of her body for this one time only. She had no idea why she was even allowing this to happen. It was a terrible idea, but she felt like being selfish.

"That was the sexiest thing I've ever seen you do. Seeing Judd get laid out was pretty fucking sweet. Just don't do it again unless you're defending yourself. Understand?"

"Oh, fuck yeah, I understand," he said and placed his leather cut on the same table Morry threw her jacket on. It was quickly followed by the black T-shirt he was wearing.

Holy shit, he was incredible. Morry's eyes wandered over his defined shoulders and arms first. Jeremy transformed over the last five years into a totally different person. She could hardly believe this was the same guy who Dean had dropped off.

Jeremy had the best Adonis V she'd ever seen, and she licked her lips as she followed those lines down toward the distinct bulge behind the fly of his jeans.

She had no idea why he bothered with her when a ton of sweetbutts traveled everywhere with them. They were all young and looked at him like he was their favorite lollipop. Whether it was because he wanted to say he scored with the boss or just wanted the experience with an older woman, she didn't know, and right now, it didn't matter. She would take what he offered and what she desperately wanted, then slam the door shut once more.

"You plan on keeping that promise you made outside," she asked as he wrapped his arm around her waist. Goosebumps rose all along her skin with just that simple touch.

"About making you scream only my name?"

"Yeah, that one."

Jeremy smirked, and the heat bloomed dangerously

throughout her body while her heart skipped behind her ribcage. She should stop. If she were smart, she would order him out the door right now.

"You better believe it," he said.

That reason right there was why she wasn't going to. Jeremy whipped them around and pressed her up against the cold wall, drawing a sharp breath from her. There was no time to adjust before his lips crashed down on hers. It felt like his body was somehow trying to speak to her. She could feel the need coursing through him from every spot their bodies touched. Morry moaned as she laid her hands on him for the first time as a woman. Not his boss or emotional support. Her hands ran over his skin and hard muscles.

"Oh fuck. Is this actually happening," he asked, breaking the kiss. "If it's not, don't tell me. I want this fantasy to play out."

Jeremy gripped her ass and shocked her as he lifted her up until his lips were level with her chest. There was nothing tentative about the way he ravaged her.

"Oh fuck," she moaned and grabbed his hair as he sucked her nipple into his mouth.

It was like fire against her cool skin, and she wiggled in his grasp as his tongue swirled around her sensitive bud. Jeremy's eyes closed, and he sucked so hard she knew there would be marks from his teeth on her sensitive skin. Yes, this was what she wanted. Jeremy growled like an animal as he broke the seal and immediately moved to her other nipple, giving it equal attention.

Morry dropped her head back on the wall and closed her eyes as the sensations rippled like a tide of desire through her. She shuddered in his hold as every part of her body lit up like a switchboard.

"You're so fucking beautiful," he said and pulled her away from the wall.

She tried to come up with words that made sense or at least were equally endearing, but there was nothing but static in her brain.

"Do you want me to fuck you hard? Use you? Or do you want me to fuck you slow and sweet? I want both. I intend on taking both, but what do you want right now?"

"Hard. Make me scream. Don't be nice." Morry locked eyes with him, and a sliver of the woman she used to be broke free. The person who envisioned a whole future with someone who set her soul on fire.

"You might change your mind when you see what I'm working with," he said, a cocky grin spreading across his face as he walked her toward the desk and placed her on the hard surface.

"Are you trying to tell me you're big without saying you're big?"

"Something like that."

Kneeling, he untied her shitkickers and tossed them aside, then reached for the button on her leathers. Her heart was pounding impossibly hard. She'd never felt this level of raw need for anyone before. Then again, she'd been fighting this for a while. She could berate herself later. Right now, she wanted to let herself go and enjoy the moment. There were so few real moments in life that took her breath away, and Jeremy did that for her.

She couldn't tell him that. She couldn't tell him that just

looking at him made her heart race. She couldn't tell him that she wished things were different or that she wasn't a washed-up vet barely holding her shit together. He made her feel young and beautiful, and special again. He made her feel, period.

Morry leaned back on the desk and clung to the sides as he grabbed the legs of her leathers that fit like a second skin and peeled them off her body.

"Fuck, that's hot," he groaned, making her blush as he stared at the little triangle of black fabric that was her underwear. Stepping between her legs, Jeremy placed an arm on either side of Morry's body as his face hovered above hers. "From now on, this sweet pussy of yours is mine. No one else can have it but me," he commanded, his voice deep as his intense stare bore holes into her. This was a side of Jeremy she'd never seen, and a shiver raced down her spine.

She cocked an eyebrow at him, but he gripped her chin between his fingers and kissed her hard while his other hand cupped her pussy. Jeremy pushed her thong out of the way, and all thoughts of arguing faded when he ran his fingers up and down her sex. Morry whimpered into his mouth as he sank his finger into her.

"Say it, Morry," he ordered, and it was incredibly sexy how in charge he suddenly was. "Say it. Tell me I'm the only cock that gets to fuck you. I'll kill anyone else who tries to take you from me." She shuddered on the desk. "I'm not joking. I would've killed Judd. I will slit their throats. You're mine now. Say the words," he growled against her lips. What he said was still processing as he pulled back and dropped down between her legs.

"Oh shit," she swore as she pulled her feet up onto the edge of the desk and let her knees splay open. Jeremy grabbed her clit between his teeth and gave it a gentle tug. "Fuck me, that feels incredible," Morry said, reaching between her legs and grabbing his head.

How did he know her body so well? He wasn't holding back. His finger rubbed deep, right over her G-spot, while he sucked her clit hard into his mouth. An orgasm from deep inside stormed to the surface at a pace she couldn't have stopped, even if she wanted to. "Yes, oh God. Yes, right there. I'm going to come."

Jeremy stopped moving, his finger almost all the way out and his lips hovering over her needy clit.

"Oh no, no, don't stop. Please don't stop," she begged, wiggling around on the desk in desperation.

"Then say it," he said, his voice so deep and rough it didn't sound like Jeremy. "I'm the only one who gets you from now on. You're mine, Morry. Say the fucking words and mean them. I'll know if you're only fucking saying it to placate me."

Panting, her body desperate for him to continue, she nodded. "Yes, from now on, I'm yours," she said.

She meant it, but it wouldn't matter. The promise would break the first time Jeremy fucked someone else. She had no interest in being his personal fuck toy while he screwed whoever he wanted. It would happen. He would want the next cute sweetbutt who walked through the door wanting in on the club lifestyle. But for now, she played along. The prospect of having him multiple nights until he screwed up held appeal. Why shouldn't she get a little more of this?

As soon as the words left her mouth, he pressed firmly on a spot she'd never felt. She arched off the desk, her mouth open in a silent scream. He took her clit into his mouth and sucked harder than before. With each forceful draw of his mouth, he commanded the climax out of her body. Morry gasped and gripped the edge of the desk, her nails digging into the metal.

"Fuck, Jeremy, yes." She cried out.

Morry wasn't reaching a climax. No. She was thrust over the peak in a wild rush that left her reeling.

"God, you taste good," he said as he pushed himself up to his feet and stared down at her.

Morry sagged in a state of ultimate bliss. Her muscles twitched as waves of pleasure continued to crash through her body. Jeremy gripped her hips in his large hands and yanked her to the edge of the desk.

"I'm going to fuck you with these on." He said, running his fingers over the fabric of her thong. "I fucking love the look of them."

Jeremey's eyes followed his hands over her body as he explored. Goosebumps rose wherever his hands traced lines. That look on his face was addictive. It was way too easy to want to see that look all the time and know that she was the reason for it.

Groaning, he undid the button on his jeans and pulled down the zipper to show off that, unsurprisingly, he was commando. That didn't shock her. Most of the men in the club rode that way. What surprised her was what lay behind the open flap of material. Jeremy wasn't falsely boasting about his size, and as he pulled the jeans down his ass, his full length made her swallow hard.

She licked her lips as she stared at the cock standing straight up his belly, then sucked in her bottom lip as he wrapped his hand around the thick girth and slowly stroked his shaft.

"Have you changed your mind about me doing what I want?"

She had to force her gaze off his hand to look him in the eyes before shaking her head. Fucking Christmas had come early. There was no way she was saying no now.

"All right then. Feet on the floor and turn around."

Sliding off the desk, she stood in front of Jeremy. For the first time, she felt small around him. Something about his presence pressed in on her, but not in a way that made her feel weak. It was more like she saw the magnitude of how much he'd changed and grown in five years.

She turned around and pushed the folders she had onto the floor before lying forward.

"Oh damn. That's cold," Morry said as she pressed her boobs into the metal desk.

"Don't move. Fuck, this is the sexiest thing I've ever seen."

Her first instinct was to roll her eyes.

"Don't fucking roll your eyes at me. I can feel your attitude without seeing your face. If I say this ass"—Jeremy's hand cracked hard on her ass cheek, and the sting had her moaning loudly—"is the sexiest sight I've ever seen, then I mean it."

All the crap that floated around—doubts, insecurities, and haunting memories—were suddenly silenced as she looked over her shoulder at Jeremy. There was something in his face that made her question everything she thought, her sanity for letting this go any further, and why she hadn't done it sooner.

She wanted Jeremy to make her scream in pleasure and pain, and she had a feeling he would live up to his claim.

CHAPTER 9

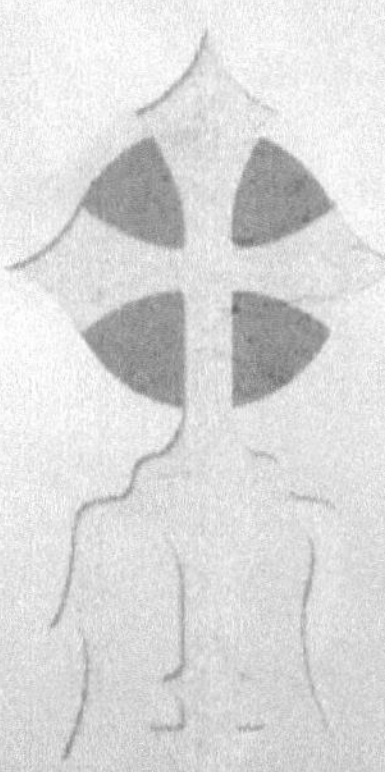

Jeremy's mind was still reeling. He couldn't believe this was even happening. He played it out so many times in his head that there was no way he was asking *why* right now. He stepped back and took a moment to appreciate the sight. She looked so fucking hot laid out like that on the desk. Morry's incredible legs were spread wide, giving him an unobstructed view of her perfectly round ass and pussy glistening wet and calling to him.

Jeremy licked his lips, savoring her taste as he stroked his cock and spread the clear precome around the head. He knew he was blessed with a cock that made most women tell him to be gentle once they saw it. Or they couldn't take him at all. It was a bit of a curse, never being able to let loose.

She gripped the sides of the table and looked over her shoulder at him with eyes that made him want to get down on his knees and crawl to her.

"You change your mind," she asked, wiggling her ass like a red flag to a bull.

He groaned, watching it sway from side to side, and already felt the churning in his gut to find his release deep inside her. He had no intentions of pulling out. He was claiming her tonight. What she did to him—the side of him she brought out—was so far beyond attraction that he worried for his sanity. Everything about this woman had been tailormade for him.

"I was waiting to see if you changed your mind. I'll ask you one last time. How hard do you want me to be?"

Her smirk made his cock surge in his hand.

"Do your worst."

"Fuck, you're tough. I'm going to enjoy making you scream my name."

Jeremy stepped in close, rubbing himself along her ass, loving the visual of his cock separating Morry's cheeks and the rough feel of the thong against his sensitive skin. He pressed her rosebud with his cock and was tempted to try, but his patience for being nice and working slowly into her tight ass wasn't there tonight. It would happen, though, one of these days, real soon.

Leaning over her, he ran his hand through her short hair, then gripped it in his fist to pull her body up off the table.

"Are we talking 'spank me gently' or 'you're not sure you're going to live'?"

Even though he already knew the answer, he wanted to hear

the words *fuck me hard* from her mouth. His hand tightened in her hair as he ran his tongue up the side of her neck. She moaned, her body shuddering against his. That sound was sweeter than candy and gave him a better high than any drug he ever taken.

"Fuck me until I'm not sure I'll live," Morry said, her voice wispy and dripping with desire.

He groaned and had to take a deep breath to collect himself. He was close to rutting her like a fucking animal.

"I'm going to fuck you until we pass out, and then I'm doing it again. Outside, you can order me around all you want, and I'll get down and bow at your feet. But in here, I'm in charge, and I say when we're done. Are we clear?"

He nipped her ear and sucked the soft lobe into his mouth to play with the little diamond stud she always wore.

"Yes."

"Yes, what?" he growled against her neck.

"Yes, Sir," she said, and there wasn't an ounce of sarcasm in her tone.

Fuck, that sounded good, and if he weren't already rock hard, those two words certainly would've had him at attention.

Jeremy released her hair and stood, once more beating back the urge to be too aggressive. He didn't even know he had this streak in him, but it had grown along with his feelings, and it didn't seem like it would dissipate where she was concerned.

Grabbing Morry's ass, he squeezed her perfect cheeks, then slapped the right one, wanting to see his handprint on it. She didn't yelp or jump. No, she moaned and wiggled slightly in his hold. He slapped the same cheek, her fair skin pinking with the abuse.

"That feels so fucking good," she groaned as his hand connected for a third time.

Wrapping the thin string of her thong around his hand, he pulled it off to the side and gripped her hip. Rubbing the head of his cock over her hot pussy lips, he made sure he was good and wet before pushing into her. Her tight walls clamped down on him with every inch.

"Oh fuck. You feel incredible," he said, unable to look away from where he was pressing deeper into her.

A sweat broke out across his skin as he fought to bury himself inside of her with a single hard thrust. There weren't adequate words in any language that could describe what he felt. It was as if every muscle was on fire while his blood coursed through his veins so fast that he was lightheaded.

Jeremy closed his eyes, and his nostrils flared as he sucked in a deep breath. Calming himself before he exploded the moment he bottomed out. Morry moaned as his pelvis pressed into her ass, the last of him finally inside of her. The squeezing of her pussy walls never lessened. They didn't relent at all. Her pussy got tighter until it felt like his cock was being choked in the best way possible. Jeremy's muscles trembled as he fought his own body's need.

He could fuck for hours if need be after he came—staying hard after a climax wasn't an issue—but he wanted to enjoy this for as long as possible. He thought he had himself under control until

Morry pushed back into him and wiggled her ass around in a circle.

"Oh fuck me," he growled, giving up the fight. Squeezing Morry's ass hard, he pulled back until just the tip was left inside of her, then thrust forward. Morry moaned loudly. He loved that sound coming from her mouth, but he wanted her to scream and call him by name. He wanted Judd, wherever the fuck the guy was, to hear that Morry was finally where she belonged. And it sure as fuck wasn't with that asshole.

"Fuck yes," she moaned as he drove into her again.

This time, the desk squeaked and moved an inch, not allowing him to get as deep as he wanted. It was like the desk was trying to prevent him from taking what he wanted. With each thrust, the desk moved again, and his teeth ground together. Frustration riding him, he grabbed the lip of the desk on either side of Morry. He lifted it until her feet were off the floor and pushed it hard until the heavy piece of metal slammed against the wall. He was so worked up that he would've picked up a car and thrown it to get at her.

Morry looked over her shoulder at him. No words could've puffed up his chest more than the impressed look on her face.

He purposely pulled out and plunged deep into her, watching her eyes flutter in pleasure.

"Yeah, that's it. You like that?"

She bit her lip and nodded as he thrust into her hard enough that their skin smacked together. Morry moaned and put her head down on the table again.

He didn't hesitate to smack that stunning ass as he pulled out and drove into her again. His hand stung from the hit, yet she moaned like he was massaging her muscles. Fuck, she was beyond hot. Wrapping the skimpy material around his hand again, he pulled it out of the way and grabbed the ass of the woman, who had tantalized him for the last three years. He lost count of how many times he jerked off to the image of Morry in his mind. Wondering what she felt like, what she tasted like. Now he needed to know what Morry sounded like when she screamed his name.

"Fuck, you've got the tightest pussy," he growled through gritted teeth as her muscles constricted around him. "So fucking incredible."

He lost himself in the rhythm. Morry's whimpering moans were the only sound breaking through the lustful fog. They spurred him on, faster and harder. He couldn't take his eyes off where they were joined. The sight of him fucking her made him delirious. The orgasm he was holding back was taking control.

"Oh no, you fucking don't," he swore at his own body.

Pulling out of her, he grabbed his balls hard in one hand and squeezed his shaft with the other like he was trying to choke it. The sharp bite of pain forced him back off the ledge he was about to tip over. The throbbing worsened, and he knew he wouldn't get away with that again. He was far too amped up. He stared at his glistening cock, screaming to come even with the uncomfortable abuse.

"Turn around," he said.

Jeremy loved how Morry's gaze went right to where he was still firmly gripping his cock to make it behave. It was weeping non-stop, the shiny drops of precome forming at the tip and sliding down his cock like it was drooling for her. A wicked smile lifted her mouth in a lopsided grin as she bent over and licked the head like it was a fucking ice cream cone.

"Oh fuck. Don't do that," Jeremy said, but Morry did the complete opposite and sucked what she could into her mouth before she met his hand.

"Ah, fuck, fuck, fuck." His body jerked as he fought his climax while she bobbed her head on the first few inches of his sensitive cock. It was aching so bad now that each hard suck sent a seductive jolt of extreme pleasure and pain down his shaft.

"Get up on the desk, now," he ordered.

Jeremy was so lost to the need that he abandoned the grip on his cock and grabbed Morry by the waist, plunking her down hard on the desk. Gripping her legs, he held them out to the side, then realized the thong was once more covering her pussy's entrance. Dropping her legs, he grabbed the material in both hands and pulled hard, ripping it in two.

"Don't bother wearing underwear anymore unless you want them destroyed." His eyes found hers as he lined himself up and rubbed on her swollen clit. "Because I plan to fuck you every chance I get."

Morry was so wet he was able to shove in harder than before. They both yelled as he slammed into her, and his balls were pressed firmly into her ass. His head fell back as his hips worked. It didn't take very long for the need that hadn't subsided to come screaming back, and his balls pulled up tight. Jeremy yelled out in agony as he tried to force it down.

"Fuck, yes," Morry cried and arched off the desk.

He could feel her inner walls constricting tighter around him, and it was too much. He would've gladly died being choked like this. Picking her hand up off the desk, where it was clenched into a fist, he put it between their bodies.

"Touch yourself. Come on me, Morry. I want to feel you come all over my cock as your pussy takes all that I can give." He unleashed himself as he stared at her breasts, bouncing in time with his thrusts. Morry did as he asked. He thought that the view of her spread over the desk earlier was the sexiest thing he ever saw—that it couldn't be topped—but that was obliterated when, a few seconds later, she came all over him.

"Jeremy, fuck yes." Morry's mouth fell open as she clamped down with the orgasm. Morry's back arched once more off the desk as she was gripped in the waves of desire coursing through her body.

"Yes, yes. That's it. Oh, God. Oh fuck," Jeremy growled as the first stream of come left his body.

Jeremy yelled her name and was almost brought to his knees. His fingers tightened on her legs to hold himself upright as each thrust drew more from his body. Coming was painful after he had held back for so long, but it was glorious.

"Keep going," Morry panted out, and he picked up the pace again as her climax continued in waves that rolled over his cock and somehow drew more from him as well.

Panting hard and spent for the moment, he lowered her legs to wrap around his waist. He wanted to collapse on her body and stay like that forever with his cock buried inside her. Every single muscle shook from the aftermath of what they'd just done. He nuzzled the side of her neck and took a deep breath before kissing her damp skin.

"I hope you don't think I'm done," he said into the side of her neck.

She laughed, and he groaned as her body tightened and released his still-hard shaft. Lifting himself up, he kissed her and hoped that what he was feeling came across. The kiss was long and slow. Jeremy didn't leave a part of her mouth unattended, and it felt like his heart would explode from the emotion bubbling to the surface inside of him.

"Is that so," she asked and ran the tips of her fingers along his shoulders, making him shiver.

"I just need to take a quick break, but I'm far from done with you."

Keeping them joined, he scooped her up off the desk and walked over to the couch. Lying down, he held her as tightly as he could to his body and wrapped his leg around hers so she couldn't magically escape. There was a small blanket on the back of the couch, and he grabbed it with one hand and shook it out to spread over her back, then wrapped his arms around her once more.

Morry'd finally opened the door, and all sorts of possibilities ran through his head. Jeremy had to make sure that he used whatever time he had left in this moment wisely. He wasn't stupid. She may have agreed to be only his, but she could rescind that anytime. He needed to convince her that he was what she wanted. Not just for the fucking incredible sex, but forever.

Morry's eyes were closed, her head over his thumping heart,

and he felt complete. He'd been so close to giving up all hope, but now there wasn't anything he wouldn't do to keep this. There wasn't anyone he wouldn't kill to have her like this for the rest of their lives.

He would give her ten minutes to rest. Then he was taking her again on this couch.

Chapter 10

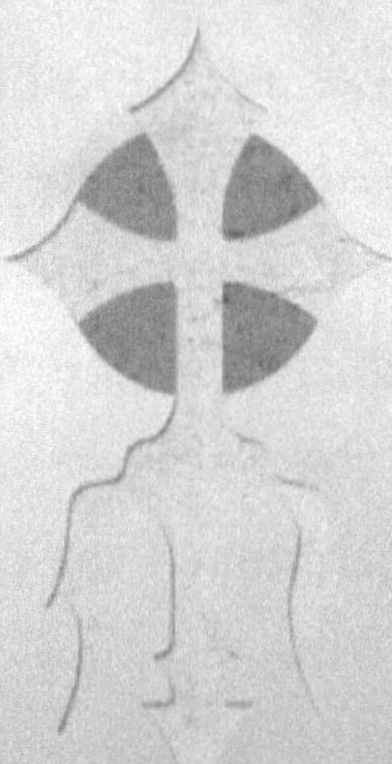

Five Years Ago

Morry leaned against the clubhouse doorframe and stared across the way at Dean, who sat beside the dying flames of a bonfire. His face was mostly cast in shadow, but she could see the stress of time etched into his handsome features.

Heading back inside, Morry grabbed two beers and walked across the open space that reminded her of overseas. Maybe that was why she'd decided on this location for the clubhouse. Not only was it formidable and easy to defend, but there was a lot she missed about being overseas. Life was simpler in a lot of ways.

"Mind if I join ya," she asked and pushed his feet off the chair to sit before he answered.

"I didn't say yes."

"I also know you wouldn't say no. Besides, I brought you this," Morry said and held out a beer for Dean.

"You always did know the fastest way to my heart," Dean replied as they clinked their bottles together. "The kid settled?"

"Seems to be, but I have a feeling he's going to have a rough few days." She turned her head to stare at Dean. "Do you ever see them," she asked, her eyes fixed on the dancing flames of the fire and the faces she saw lingering in the wavering heat. They'd lost so many, and each one of their screams had its own choir section in her mind. If only she could teach the conductor to keep them all quiet.

"Who?"

Morry glared sideways at Dean. "You know who I mean."

Dean nudged the rocks by the flames with this foot, and embers rose into the night sky to decorate it with little glowing specks. It was a beautiful, clear night, and it felt almost mystical to see the orange embers twist in the wind beneath the full moon.

"I see them all the time. Awake, asleep, in the flames, it doesn't matter. They follow me around as surely as my own shadow," Dean said. He shook his head and covered his eyes.

She knew exactly how he felt.

TK's image followed her around all the time. She would hear a laugh so similar that she thought it was him—as impossible as that was—and spin, just to find no one there. She would be doing something in her house and swear that he was there with her. She caught herself more than once talking to him like he was in the same room, and chills would travel all over her body. She didn't know if his spirit was restless or if he was still lurking and making sure she was okay. Fuck, he was the best.

Morry and Dean talked at length about the ghosts of their past. What it was like to live in the present with them clinging to their mind and bodies. It could be the smallest thing that pulled you back in time, and once more, you were living with the ghosts as they rubbed shoulders with you, as if mocking the fact that you were still breathing.

"So tell me about this Jeremy guy," she said and took another swig of her beer.

"Not much to tell. I barely know him. He robbed a friend of mine, stole her money, and left her for dead." Dean shrugged like it was an everyday occurrence, and for Dean, it probably was. He tended to collect odd personalities around him. Hers included.

"Oh, well, it makes sense now as to why you'd like him," she teased.

"Fuck off," he said but laughed hard.

"You took a real risk bringing him here. This close to your father's reach—that takes balls. So tell me, why him?" She leaned forward, grabbed a small log sitting off to the side, and tossed it on top of the embers to rejuvenate the fire.

"In a way, I guess because I get him. I see a lot of me in him. He's what I could've ended up like if I had stayed. There is real potential behind that arrogant asshole personality. I've seen it in his eyes, and the remorse he felt for what he did was real, which tells me he's not completely lost, just fumbling in the dark. Besides, if he doesn't get his shit sorted out, kill him."

After Dean left her alone at the fire, Morry couldn't say how long she sat there staring into the soft glow and thinking about her regrets. Marrying her ex was first on the list. She would've been better off having Kyle as a single mother than marrying a man she barely knew. Maybe if her mother hadn't died when she was so young, it would've made a difference, but she'd been brought up to marry the man who got you pregnant, and that was what she had done. And he ended up breaking her heart.

"You're still out here?"

She looked up at Dean as he stepped up to the fire. "I am. You headin' out?"

"Yeah. I'll grab a coffee from your mess, then shove off, but I have a favor to ask of you," Dean said and slowly sat down.

Morry lifted a brow at him. She wasn't sure where this was going but knew she probably wouldn't like it, based on the look on his face.

"Oh yeah, what kind of favor are we talking?"

"So my father took someone important from someone else, and I stole her when I ran."

Morry leaned back in the lawn chair. "Oh, I'm really not liking the sound of this already."

Dean rubbed the back of his neck before reaching into the pocket in his fatigues and pulling out a piece of paper. "This is the name I think she is going by and the last place I saw her. I'm asking you to find her and see if she is safe. If she is, don't do anything, just let me know you found her, and all is great. If not... then...." Dean looked off into the distance, and there was deep pain in his eyes. "Then please help her."

She leaned forward and took the paper from his fingers to

study. "Why are you asking me to do this? You're capable of finding her just as easily as I am?"

"I never sleep soundly, Morry. Even now, I'm still hiding from my father and his reach. I don't know if he's still looking for me, but if he is, he can't know where she is or who she is. If I'm found, and I find her, I'll lead him right to her, and trust me. He doesn't want her for anything good. Please, Morry, I don't beg often, but I'm asking you for this favor because you're the only one I trust one hundred percent. I need to know that she is okay."

Morry looked at the small paper again and the words *Maeve (Fire Station 131, Utah)*. It wasn't exactly much to go on. "This girl means that much to you?"

"Yeah, she really does."

"Are you going to tell me who she is and why she's so important," she asked but figured she already knew the answer to this question.

"No, I think it's safer if I don't."

"This is getting serious. Are you putting my place at risk by asking me this favor? Are the lives of those I look after in trouble?" Morry watched Dean's face carefully. She didn't think he would try to lie to her, but his reaction would certainly tell her the threat level clearer than his words.

"Not if the people looking for her don't find her. And not if anyone who meets her doesn't know who she is. It's why I'm not telling you. This is my cross to bear, but I don't dare do this myself."

"Dean, why the fuck can't you be like a normal guy and ask me something like, *hey, can you go pick out a gift for my girlfriend for her birthday because I suck at it?*" She crossed her arms over her chest but knew she would cave. Dean was her best friend and her brother, blood be damned. If he needed help, she would freely give it.

"Is that like a bonus I can ask for? Because I do suck at gifts," he said, making her laugh. "I made a promise to this girl, and I can't break it. Please, Morry, I will owe you one, whatever you want. You just call in. The favor is yours, no questions asked."

"Well now, that is enticing." Morry rubbed her face and had a gut feeling this was going to be a tough mission. She couldn't say why, but if she said yes, then one day, shit was going sideways. Even knowing that she couldn't say no. "Okay, fine. You know I can't say no to you. If this girl is alive, I'll find her."

"Thanks, this means everything to me." Dean stood, and she followed suit. After a brief hug, Dean got his coffee and headed home.

"Who the heck are you, Maeve?" Morry whispered as she stuffed the paper into her pocket.

CHAPTER 11

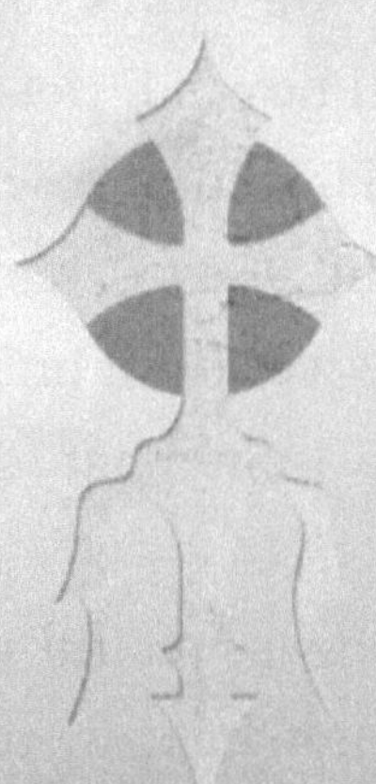

Morry's eyes fluttered open. The heat radiating into her naked body told her that what happened with Jeremy wasn't a dream. She moved slightly and sucked in a long breath feeling achy in every part of her body. It was moments like this that reminded her she was no longer twenty.

Her leg was flung over his body, and by some miraculous feat, Jeremy's cock was still inside of her. How he managed that was beyond remarkable. She flicked her eyes up to his face. He was still sound asleep, his muscles lax as he rested. It wasn't fair that he had such stunning eyelashes. She would've killed to have the length and thickness he did.

She took a moment to stare and not worry about any potential consequences. Jeremy had a great jaw, and with the stubble, she could almost pretend he wasn't as young as he was. His stamina, on the other hand, was a dead giveaway. That was the best sex she'd ever had. Mind-blowing didn't come close to the euphoric sensations he caused. Even now, all the stress she carried around on her back felt lighter and not so overwhelming.

He groaned slightly and shifted his hips, making her wince despite her pussy growing wet from only his presence. His effect on her was nothing new, but that didn't mean she should acknowledge it.

He was in one of his deep, restful dreams. It was annoying how he could pass out anywhere in ten seconds and sleep as soundly as a dead. Jeremy didn't seem to be waking up, but his hips pumped up and down slightly. She could feel the huge cock thickening as it grew hard, and even though they should get up, the gentle rocking was rubbing his hard body on her clit in just the right way. It felt fucking fantastic.

Jeremy mumbled something incoherent and licked his lips. It was fascinating, and felt delightfully dirty to let him dream about fucking while his cock slowly worked its way deeper into her body. She honestly didn't think she could take any more for a couple of days when they'd finally collapsed. Yet, she had to clamp her lips together to keep from moaning as the miniature thrusts became quicker. Reaching down, she cupped his heavy balls in her hand and loved how they felt as they relaxed and then flexed up with his movements. Jeremy let out a deep, guttural groan, his body twitching as she messaged them.

Jeremy sucked his lip into his mouth, and his chest rumbled

under her ear. The sound made Morry shiver, igniting a spark burning into a fire throughout her body. He made the same sound again as his hands twitched, then flexed on her ass before kneading the soft skin. He groaned and pushed down, forcing her to take him deeper. The extra pressure was just enough that her clit, already being teased, was now pressed firmly into his hard ab muscles. It was driving her wild.

She bit her finger hard to keep the moan silent as Jeremy continued to groan, his movements not as fluid in sleep, but fuck, he felt fantastic. She had no idea how he was still asleep, but then again, she'd seen him sleep through other things that made her shake her head. He would've done well overseas.

"Oh, Morry," Jeremy mumbled, and her stupid heart swelled to twice the size.

The fact that he was dreaming about what they'd just done sent a thrill of excitement through her body while her stomach flipped a million times. His pace quickened, and the hands gripping her ass tightened until she knew she would have his handprints there later. His body suddenly jerked, and she knew he was about to come. His muscles flexed at the same time his cock did, and with a couple of hard thrusts, he unloaded inside of her. The feel of him comeing as he groaned loudly had her cresting that intoxicating peak once more. Morry closed her eyes and bit her lip to keep from making a noise. Jeremy pressed up hard into her while his hands pushed her ass down as he continued to unload.

His body slumped, and she had a feeling that if she didn't wake him, he would continue to fuck her until they died of dehydration or the world ended, whichever came first. Running her hand up his chest, she admired the tattoo there, her finger tracing the words, *Last Chance* before she cupped his cheek. As soon as her thumb ran over his lips, he sucked into his mouth.

"Mmm, I want to fuck you again before we have to get up," he said, his voice husky as those blue eyes slowly opened.

. "I have news for you. You already did." She laughed and then groaned as her pussy clamped down on him and reminded her that she was sore

Putting an arm behind his head, he opened his eyes fully, and his brow furrowed in confusion.

"Let's just say you like to fuck while you're asleep as much as you do awake."

One eyebrow shot up. "I did? I thought I was dreaming." His cheeks grew red, and it was adorable to see him blush.

"Yes, but at least you didn't call out anyone else's name," she teased and pushed herself up, but Jeremy reached out and gripped her chin in his hand, his eyes holding none of the humor she'd intended.

"I think of no one else, ever."

Morry swallowed the dryness in her throat as she stared into those intense eyes. Unsure how to take that comment, she didn't say anything but forced herself to stare back.

"I know you don't believe me. I don't know why you don't, but it's the truth," Jeremy said and let go of her chin.

"We better get up. I seriously need a shower." She held up her finger to stop him before he could say it. "No, I don't mean a come shower," she said, and the hard lines on his face softened as he laughed.

"I was thinking that too. Fuck, that would be a sight. You on your knees, coated in my come. Yeah, I'm so doing that." Jeremy smirked, his eyes glazing over, and she knew he was picturing doing exactly what he described.

Okay, she needed to get up before he talked her into playing out the fantasy. Not that it wasn't appealing, but she had shit that needed to get done, and none of it would happen with her locked away in here. Pushing herself up, she sucked in a sharp breath as his cock slipped from her body.

"Fuck, I'm going to be walking like a bow-legged cowboy for the day," she said, and Jeremy laughed harder, his eyes shining with amusement. Making her way over to her bag with her clothes, she grabbed the straps and then pointed at Jeremy, who looked like he was about to get up. "You stay here. I'm going to go shower first. You can shower after me."

"But I want to join." His hand went to the cock, which never wanted to rest, and began stroking it.

"I can't believe I'm going to say this, but I can't take any more right now. If you fucking say that to anyone, I'll deny it. Fuck." Her legs were stiff as she walked toward the bathroom.

"Do you mind if I rub another one out," Jeremy called out as she reached the door and turned to close it.

"Knock yourself out. I want to watch another time, though," Morry said teasingly and closed the door.

"Oh, don't say that. Fuck," Jeremy groaned, and her pussy clenched with the sound.

Morry looked down. "Don't even think about it. We are not fucking him again, maybe not ever, let alone right now," she said to her pussy, which didn't seem to care that she ached in every part of her body and in spots she didn't know could ache.

The hot water was a blessing, and the soap was a miracle worker. When she emerged from the shower, she fixed her messy hair so it didn't look like she'd been electrocuted. She was about to pull on her clean thong when she remembered Jeremy's warning. She stared at the small piece of fabric like this was a debate about world peace. Put them on or not? If she put them on, then what would he do if they did have sex again? Would he rip them off, maybe punish her? The thought had many potentially hot ideas running around in her mind. Although, if she left them off and found out he was with one of the sweetbutts, she would feel stupid for ever thinking there was more between them than one hot night.

"The decision to put on underwear or not shouldn't be this fucking difficult." Pinching the bridge of her nose, she gave in to the temptation and put them back in her bag.

"This is stupid. Jeremy's going to fuck with your head, then rip out your heart, and you're playing right into his hand," she mumbled to herself as she stuffed her legs into the black jeans. "Then you'll have just one more stupid scar on your heart, like a line carved into the wall of a cell." She shook her head as she pulled on the black tank. "But you're going to do it, anyway, because, at the heart of it, you're a hopeless romantic."

Morry stepped out of the bathroom, disgusted with herself, that the first thing she looked for was Jeremy. He was in the same position she'd left him, right down to his cock in his hand. He was back asleep, but there were easily one, if not two, loads of come on his chest and stomach. Walking over, she stared down at him in astonishment. It was apparently *Learn Something New About Jeremy* week.

"Hey." She tapped the couch with her shitkicker. "Jeremy, wake up."

"Mmm, just one more round."

Shaking her head at him, she gave the couch another kick. "Up, now."

Jeremey's eyes snapped open with her tone, and he looked up into her eyes, then down at his chest and cock. "Shit, I passed out again."

"I'm not surprised, you need the rest after that many rounds." Jeremy looked down at his chest and lifted his shoulder in a casual shrug.

"I can do more."

"This doesn't surprise me. Shower is free. I'm heading to see Wolf and Judd, and then we will roll in an hour." Morry grabbed her leather jacket from the chair at her desk and laid her hand on the door handle when Jeremy called her name.

"Morry?"

"Yeah?" She looked over her shoulder at Jeremy, who was slowly sitting up and she was once more reminded of how he'd sprouted into a man seemingly overnight.

"I was serious last night," he said, laying his arms on his knees. "You're mine now. No fucking Judd. I *will* put a bullet between his eyes." He didn't wait for a response before standing and walking into the bathroom. The door closed with a click that was as dangerous as the hammer on a gun. Fuck, that shouldn't turn her on as much as it did, and it certainly shouldn't create the flicker of hope in her chest.

"Shit," she muttered and marched out the door.

Morry found the doctor in Wolf's room as he was finishing up his assessment. "Perfect, I'm glad you're here. I was just about to come and find you," Henry said.

"Please tell me it isn't more bad news, doc."

Duke's tail was thumping on the mattress, and she went over to give him some love. His soft fur running under her fingers was as comforting to Morry as her touch was to him.

"Actually, just the opposite. Wolf is responding well to the medication, and the swelling has decreased significantly. He's still not going to be able to travel for a few days, mind you, but this is positive news. Also, I think Duke needs to use the washroom. He keeps whimpering at me but won't let me separate him from Wolf."

Bending down, Morry looked Duke in the eyes. " Buddy, you have to be good for Doc Henry. I have to take off soon, and you need to let him help you, too."

Duke made noises that she would've sworn were back-talk, but it was probably a good thing she didn't know what he was saying. The choice words this dog would've had for all over them over the years would've made a sailor's hair curl.

"Come on. I'll take you out now." She turned to Henry. "Reassure him that you'll bring him back, and he'll let you carry him outside." Henry's brows rose slowly, and he pushed his glasses up his nose as he stared at her. "I'm serious. He knows what you're saying. If this dog could speak, the secrets he could tell...." She lifted her shoulder in a shrug. "Once you do it once, and he knows you're good for your word, he will be ready whenever you come by."

Henry tapped away on his tablet. "Anything else?"

"Yeah, don't bother trying to feed him kibble. He will throw that shit up in your shoes when you look the other way. If you're making steak, make him one too. Having scrambled eggs for breakfast, you might as well make a portion for him. Oh, and he likes coffee with one cream, no sugar, and don't let him talk you into more than a couple of sips." Henry's fingers stopped typing as he lifted his head, and I could see the question in his eyes. "Just trust me. Okay, Duke, you ready to go outside?"

The large dog slowly stood up on his three good legs, and she got herself into position to carry him like she had yesterday. They'd just made it out to the yard when Judd wandered over.

"Yo, Boss. You still pissed?" He stuffed his large hands in his pockets.

She didn't think he would go after Jeremy again for a while. Then again, being smart wasn't exactly Judd's strong suit. Judd was sporting a black eye and a cut lip, which was swollen up like a miniature balloon.

"No, but Jeremy and half the crew will ride with me. I'm leaving you here," she said.

"Fucking kid. This is all his fault. I should be the one going with you." Judd swore and crossed his arms over his chest.

Morry glared at her number two. "First, he's no longer a kid. The shiner you're sporting should tell you that. Second, it's only for a few days until Wolf can be transported, and I know you'll make sure he gets to the compound safely." She closed the distance to where Judd was standing and stared up at his face. His eyes went wide as she got up in his personal space. "Lastly, don't ever fucking question me. If you disagree with a decision I make, keep it to yourself, or you'll end up in the infirmary again, but I won't be as nice as Jeremy was. Clear?"

Judd ground his teeth together, the urge to talk back evident right down to his short beard twitching, but he wisely nodded.

"Good, now that we have that clear. You're here until the doc says Wolf is clear to transport."

Duke finished his business and made his way over on his three good legs, his head touching her hand as if trying to calm her down. She hadn't realized how angry she was until she took a shuddering breath and stepped away from Judd.

"Am I being demoted," Judd asked as she picked Duke up.

"Not unless you force my hand," Morry answered.

Morry didn't want to start a shitstorm by mentioning that Judd would be answering to Jeremy at some point. They needed to sort out whatever the beef was between them before she ever made that announcement, or the club would end up divided. She walked past Judd, then called over her shoulder. "Pick whatever sweetbutts you want to stay back with you."

It was a small thing, but Morry knew that an offering like that went a long way with a man like Judd. He wasn't complicated. Ride, fight, fuck, and food. Those were his top priorities, just not necessarily in that order.

She kicked the button to open the automatic door and walked inside and down the hall to Wolf's room. There was a plate of toast and eggs on the floor already, which made her smirk. At least Doc Henry listened.

Morry placed Duke down on the floor and let him eat while she walked over to the bed. Grabbing Wolf's hand, she squeezed his limp fingers and leaned over close to his ear.

"You feel that? I'm right here, and that means you need to keep fighting, soldier. You can't give up, not after all the shit you've survived. I mean, fuck, you're either the luckiest or unluckiest motherfucker I've ever met. Seriously, you would think you would have learned to stay out of trouble by now." She watched the monitors and the little line silently bouncing along that said his heart rate was strong.

"Listen, I have to leave, but I promise I'm leaving you in good hands, and Duke is right here with you. There is some family crap I need to take care of. I won't bore you with all the details. I will once you're up walking and talking, and I do expect you to be awake in a few days. None of this lying around in a bed all day shit." She smirked, picturing the look Wolf would give her if he could. He was one of the hardest working people she knew, and the concept of lying around all day in bed would be something he wouldn't even contemplate.

"Do you remember when we found that little village? The one that was mostly abandoned and nothing but rubble? Remember that boy who showed up out of nowhere all alone and told us to spend the night?" She paused as she pulled on the memory. Like so many memories from that time of her life, the ones she wished she could forget plagued her mind, while the ones she would love to remember seemed just out of reach.

"That bowl of cold slop he gave us tasted so fucking good. It was like a three-course meal. You know, I don't know if we would've made it out alive without that full night's rest." She sat quietly for a moment. "I think of him often. He was like a little ghost, came out of nowhere, gave us food, and was gone by morning. Sometimes I wonder if I dreamed him up, and then I realize I'm too scared to ask because it would mean I was seeing things." Leaning forward, she rested on the white railing and stared at the side of Wolf's face. He'd been a constant, just like Dean, TK, Jimmy, and, of course, Perez. They were her family away from home, a group of brothers who always had her back.

"I know this is going to sound crazy, but I can't help thinking he was a guardian angel sent to look out for us. I just wish he could've looked out for all of us. So many didn't come home, so many we had to leave behind." She wiped away the tear sliding down her cheek. This was why she didn't like to get together with the rest of the guys much. Not only did they have to keep a low profile from one another, but seeing their faces stirred emotions in her soul and made her heart ache.

"Sometimes, I wonder which of the guys it was. I like to think it was them, or maybe it was Mel. She would do something like that. I see them all the time. They still smile in my dreams until I wake up and realize they're all gone. Sometimes I see their images at my table, laughing and telling jokes. I hope they're happy wherever they are."

Morry cleared her throat. "Sorry, I didn't mean to get all emotional; it's just that...Well, that family stuff I mentioned is Kyle. He's sick, and I could use another angel right about now.

Well, maybe two." She looked down at the sound of Duke moving. She smiled as he hopped toward the bed. "You already have your angel," she said and bent to pick up Duke.

There were a great many things she could've used in her life, but a miracle to save her son was at the top of the list. Morry placed Duke on the bed, and she waited until he was comfortable before patting his head.

"What do you think, boy? Do you have an extra miracle tucked in your fur?"

"Hey." Jeremy's deep voice behind her made her body jerk with the sudden sound in the silent room.

Glancing over her shoulder, she took in his relaxed position as he leaned against the doorjamb with his arms and feet crossed like he'd been holding up the wall for a while.

"How long have you been standing there?"

"Long enough," he said and stepped into the room. Morry angled toward him. "Don't worry, I would never repeat anything I heard, but I would like to know more about you and your past."

Morry cleared her throat, completely uncomfortable with this whole emotional support, trying-to-get-to-know-her thing.

"Maybe one day, but we need to get going." Laying a hand on Duke and then giving Wolf's hand one last squeeze, she marched past Jeremy with her head held high and her shoulders back. "Let's go. We have ten things to do and not enough hours in the day to get them done."

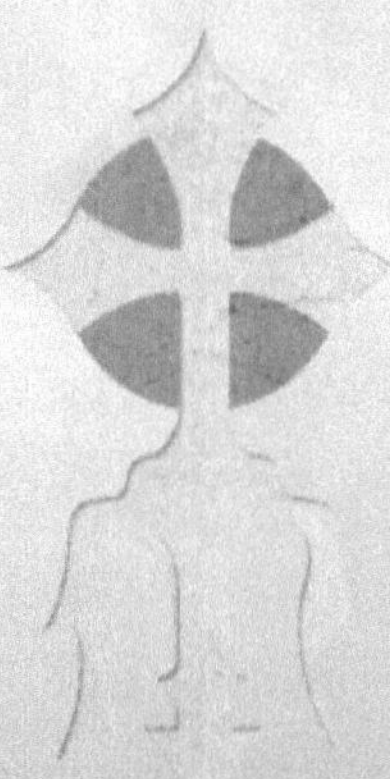

CHAPTER 12

Jeremy glanced in the side-view mirror at the procession of motorcycles following them and then to the front but didn't see Judd in the pack. He was tempted to ask, but honestly, Judd's name, even leaving her mouth, set his blood on fire with anger, so it was better to let sleeping dogs lie.

The music was on shuffle, and the next song that came on was about driving backcountry roads with the woman you love. He couldn't help looking at the woman in the driver's seat, her face calm and in control, just like she always was, but today there was something more. He never saw it in Morry before and yet appreciated it just as much as the take-no-shit side of her personality. Under all the layers and toughness, she had a vulnerable side. A side that had lived through and seen terrible shit he couldn't even imagine. And yet she dealt with it like she did everything else, and that was to kick it in the face and keep going.

"Why are you staring at me?" Morry turned her head, and even though he couldn't see her eyes behind the dark sunglasses, he could feel the weight of her gaze.

"Just thinking." He lifted a shoulder and let it drop. "About you, about the club, about us." Morry shifted in her seat like she was uncomfortable, and he wasn't sure if it was because they'd been driving for four hours or because of what he said.

"Dangerous topics," she finally said.

Shifting around, he leaned his back against the door and lifted his foot up so his knee could rest against the back of the seat. She looked over, glaring at his boot on the seat, but he didn't move it. Pushing Morry out of every comfort zone she had was now firmly at the top of his to-do list.

"Dangerous, how?" He grabbed the unopened bag of chocolate-covered peanuts and yanked the package open. Popping a couple into his mouth, he waited for a response.

"What exactly do you think is going on between us," Morry asked instead.

"What do you think is happening?" He shot back and earned another look. This time she pulled the black lenses down enough that he could see her eyes and the annoyance brewing.

"I'm not joking around here, Jeremy."

He dropped another handful of the sweet candy and nuts into his mouth and licked his fingers off for her benefit. There was no reaction in her facial features, but her cheeks couldn't lie, and they deepened in color with the heat he was creating in her. He may not have noticed it yesterday, but he sure as fuck noticed it today.

"Neither am I." He poured a handful of the chocolate into his hand and held it out to her. She glanced at his hand like a wary animal but took half of his offer. The side of his mouth pulled up in a smile, but he quickly hid it by chomping down on more snacks.

"Why are you making this difficult," Morry asked as she chewed the nuts like she was angry with them. Better them than him.

"I'm not, but I'm pretty sure you are," he said.

"What the hell does that mean?" Her tone was angry, and so was the look in her eyes. Fuck, that was hot. Was it wasn't normal to get turned on when someone was pissed at you? He must have some sort of issue.

"It means that you're probably sitting there going over what we did and beating yourself up for sleeping with me and then contemplating all sorts of shit that will end up with you deciding that it's better to stay away from one another."

Her brows rose, and she looked away to stare firmly at the road. "I wasn't doing that," she said, but the meek, deflated response said something entirely different.

"I'm pretty sure that's a lie."

"Okay, how about you stay the fuck out of my head? I didn't realize I'd become so transparent," Morry growled, her hands gripping the steering wheel so tight it squeaked.

Cracking open a bottle of water, he offered it to her first. Predictably, in Morry's eyes, he saw the inner argument before she took the water, gulped some down, and handed it back. Jeremy chugged the rest and laid his head against the window.

"I don't think you're transparent to anyone else. They don't study you the way I do," he said, allowing himself to say the things he kept to himself.

"Okay, that sounded creepy."

Jeremy smirked. "Maybe, but I also know you like it." Her eyes flicked over for just a moment before turning away again. "Look, Morry, stop overthinking everything, at least when it comes to us. I want you. I've wanted you for a long time, and that's not about to change. Just let it happen. Stop standing in the way of what we both want."

"Oh, so it's that simple," she drawled.

"Yeah, actually, it is." Polishing off the package of candy, he crossed his arms over his chest. "What are you scared of?" Scared was a taboo word when it came to Morry, and he could almost see her hackles rise as she sat up straighter.

"I'm not afraid."

"Fine. Prove it."

"What?" She flicked on the turn signal, and he realized they were pulling off at a rest stop. The bikes behind them were taking the cue to pull over as well.

"Tell me you like me and that you're going to give us a chance to work," he said.

Jeremy knew it was a dick move to put her on the spot like this so soon after finally getting through her walls. The thing was, if Morry was left to contemplate it too long on her own, she would find a reason why they didn't work. Shit, she probably had a list of a hundred reasons ready to go.

"This is ridiculous," she said, pulling into one of the spots. The Hummer came to a sudden halt as she threw it into park. "I don't need to prove anything."

"Morry...."

"No, I'm not doing this with you. I need to get a coffee. Do you want anything?" She hopped out of the Hummer and stood holding the door.

"No."

"Fine." She slammed the door and walked toward the building.

"Fuck, fuck, fuck." He jumped out of the vehicle, and his long strides ate up the ground as he headed toward the path set up to stretch your legs. Why did she always make everything so difficult? Morry was the most stubborn person he'd ever met, aside from maybe Dean. Was it a prerequisite to be part of their secret group? You needed to be as *tough as nails* and *as stubborn as an ox?*

Jeremy started walking the long loop with his hands stuffed in his jeans and his mind wandering.

He wiped off his sweaty brow and turned to see where Dean was. This was a far larger job than either of them had banked on, but part of that was due to the rain they'd been getting. It made tearing up the old stones slow. Laying the new foundation was even worse now that the sun was finally out. None of the pieces of the new patio wanted to fit together.

The sun was getting low in the sky, and everything was bathed in dark shades of pink and orange. Jeremy didn't see Dean, so he rubbed out the tight muscles in his lower back and walked to the other side of the large country home. It was a gorgeous spot and exactly the kind of location he could see himself living in someday. He was about to give up and walk around to the front of the property, figuring that Dean had gone to the truck when he spotted movement down by the water. There was a large pond down a long sloping hill at the back of the property where the owners had set up a dock and boat. Dean stood at the end of the dock, staring at the sunset.

Making his way down the hill, Jeremy stopped at the bottom. Dean didn't turn to look at him, which was so not like Dean. He would've sworn the guy had supersonic hearing.

"Hey, Dean, you all good?"

Dean's shoulders jerked like he'd just been shot.

"Yeah, all good. Just watching the sun go down."

Jeremy stepped up onto the dock and slowly walked to the end to stand beside Dean. At one time, he was terrified of this man. No amount of money could've ever made him come to work for him, that was for sure. It was funny how a few years made a big difference in perspective. Now Jeremy didn't see Dean as the monster dressed in black who hung him upside down over the side of a building. Instead, he saw him as a man, a friend, as family. He was the person who had given him a second lease on life.

"Can I ask what you're thinking about?"

"Those we lost. Time is a funny thing. In the same breath of air, I'm thankful for my life with Yasmine and my children, the work I do, and the friends I've made." Dean turned his head, and as their eyes met, he knew that Dean meant him. "But there are days when I hate that I survived. I hate that pain still grips me when I least expect it and how

those who died will never be honored as they should. They died to save the lives of people they'd never met. Politicians and staff were ordered to pretend our unit and what happened never existed."

This was the most he'd ever heard Dean talk about his past in the army, and he didn't dare move for fear he'd stop.

"So much loss, so many screaming voices...." Dean's voice trailed off. "I'm haunted by the knowledge that I lived, and before you say anything, I know that I shouldn't, and living my best life allows what they died for to be meaningful. I get all of that, and I tell Yazzy the same thing when she thinks about her sister, but it never makes it any better."

"What were they like? Those you lost?"

Dean smiled, and it lit up his whole face. "Mel, she was a ball of fire. You want to talk about a woman who made the men sit up and take notice of a woman in charge. It was her. Ringo...," Dean laughed. "Damn, that fucker could sing and would give you the shirt off his back, even if he had nothing left to give. Scooter was the quietest of the bunch but always looked out for everyone else. How he put up with Arek as a best friend was beyond me."

Jeremy smiled.

"Jimmy missed his calling as a stand-up comedian, and even with the worst shit going on around us, he would find a way to make us all smile. Perez and I met not long after I got assigned to my unit, and we became fast friends. He came from a terrible family like I had, and we just got one another, didn't have to say a word. He was scared that day. He was scared that he was going to die like it was a sixth sense, and I watched him get torn in half. I held him as he took his last breaths."

Jeremy's smile fell. He had no idea what to say to that. What did you say to something like that? "Sorry" seemed so lame. He suddenly felt horrible for ever thinking that Dean was a cold-hearted monster.

"There were a lot of people I didn't know who died too, but I think the hardest to watch was...." Dean stopped as his phone rang and dug it out of his pocket. Before Dean ever answered the phone, Jeremy knew that it was Yasmine by the smile that spread across Dean's face.

"Hello, my beautiful wife," Dean said as he turned and walked away.

Jeremy stood there and watched the sun as it finally dipped behind the far trees and plunged the world into night. He couldn't imagine what it would've been like to feel so isolated and cut off as you struggled to survive such a harsh climate while your friends were dying around you. Jeremy rubbed at his arms as a chill traveled down his spine like the dead were trying to let him know they were still there. He looked over his shoulder, but no one was there. Jeremy couldn't help wondering who Morry had lost and what had happened. Maybe she hadn't been as closed off, just like Dean, until the world decided to try and destroy her.

Jeremy was rounding the last curve in the trail when he spotted Morry sitting on a bench alone. That was normal for her, so it didn't seem out of place, but for whatever reason, he noticed the difference that he hadn't understood before. He knew she needed to be tough as a woman in charge of a motorcycle club, but she separated herself to keep control. The club needed to see Morry as the lone top alpha. Never glimpsing her fears or vulnerability. Morry was an island among a sea of sharks just waiting for her to fail. She was strong enough that she wouldn't, but she was always on guard for the next attack, no matter where it came from.

Parking himself down beside her, she handed over a coffee, and he smirked. It was so like Morry to do something nice, even when he didn't deserve it.

"I'm sorry I pushed so hard." He rubbed at the back of his neck. "I just really don't want things to go back to how they were before last night, and I know you'll try to put us back in that box."

She took a deep breath and then sipped her coffee before turning to look over at him. "Jeremy, this is what I know. I know that despite you now being very much a man, you're still young and in your prime. You have your whole life ahead of you to travel the world, fall in love, finish school and become whatever you want."

She placed and hand on her chest. "And I want all those things for you. Yes, one day, I want to hand the club over to you, but in the meantime, you should live your life carefree without the baggage I carry. So when you tell me to give us a chance...." Morry took a breath. "There is no future for me without my son, the club, the rehabilitation center, the ghosts of my past, and all the other crap I deal with. Right now, at this moment, my life, for whatever reason, seems cool to you, and that's great. I'm happy to do the friends-with-benefits thing. But where does *more* leave me and all the emotions that are sure to form when you're ready to experience the world and all it has to offer, and I'm still here?" She turned her eyes to the Hummer, and her shoulders slumped slightly.

He itched to touch her, but with the group so close, he didn't dare. She would swat him away faster than a fly.

"I don't want those things, Morry."

"Not right this moment, but you may."

"I may want a lot of things. I may decide to become a Tibetan monk or join a circus, and you could decide to leave the club behind and start your life over somewhere else. We could all be hit by an asteroid tomorrow and go the way of the dinosaurs. I know we can't waste our time worrying about what might happen. Somewhere along the way, the line between us blurred, and I know you felt it before last night."

Morry stood. "Just because I felt it doesn't make it right."

"Okay, enough of that." He stood and faced her, and the air became so tense around them that it felt like they were in their own world. "I'm no longer the guy who was dragged through your gates with an ultimatum hanging over his head. I'm my own man, and I may thank you for what you did to help me, but I don't need you to rescue me anymore. I don't need you to hold my hand from the monsters and I certainly don't need you to act like you need to parent me.

Stepping in closer, he stared down into her eyes and loved that she didn't step away. He lowered his voice. "Not only that, but you don't get to tell me how I feel or what I want."

He wrapped his hand around the back of her neck and watched the pulse jump under her skin as her eyes flared with desire. Her face may not be showing an ounce of emotion, but her body was screaming that she wanted him.

"You may not believe me right now, but I will show you I'm

who you're meant to be with, and we deserve our shot at something great. Even if you're not ready, I'm sick of waiting. It's my turn to drag you out to the desert in the middle of the night." Leaning in close to her ear, he dropped his voice further and groaned in her ear. She shivered in his hold. "What I want is you, and you better get ready 'cause I'm not taking no for an answer anymore." He softly nipped the side of her neck.

Releasing her, he turned and marched away. Jeremy smiled as he left Morry by the picnic table to contemplate. One thing was becoming very clear. Jeremy needed to take control of the situation and force her to choose him.

CHAPTER 13

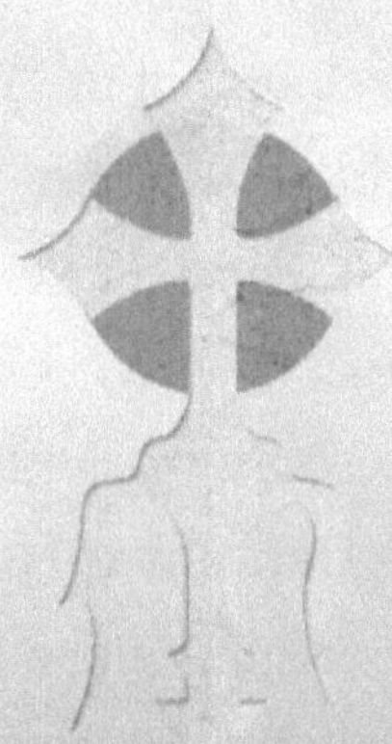

Trev's eyes scanned the latest deposition he was working on when Sally stepped into the doorway and announced he had a visitor. He quickly glanced at his calendar and didn't see anyone booked in. That meant it was someone Trev knew. No one other than those who lived here, a couple of others he trusted, and, of course, those who found him and he killed, knew where he lived. He'd also gotten into the habit of not taking the same way home twice in a row, leaving the court at different times, and never meeting in the same restaurant more than once a month.

Paranoid? Maybe. But after the last year, he didn't know who he could trust, who was watching them, or what their next move would be.

"Let whoever it is in, Sally," he said. Trev stood and smiled as Kes walked in. "I'm really enjoying this new look on you, Kes. It suits you," Trev said as he rounded the desk to shake his friend's hand.

"Well, at least that makes one of us. Technically two, since Ash seems to love it," Kes said, and then promptly undid the top couple buttons on the shirt. "I should've changed before coming. I still prefer my fatigues and a T-shirt, but apparently, that is not appropriate business attire," Kes mocked.

Trev smirked, knowing that not very long ago, Kes preferred a dirty sweater and a cardboard box for a home over where he was currently living. He was doing a lot of good in his new position, though, so it was nice to see him stick it out.

"Would you like a drink?" Trev held out his hand toward the small bar.

"Is the sky blue?"

"Depends on the time of day and the weather, but I will take that answer as a yes." Trev made his way over to the small bar and poured himself and Kes a scotch on the rocks before walking to the little sitting area where Kes was already lounging.

"Where's Arek? The house is so peaceful I barely recognize it without his annoying voice," Kes said, taking a sip of the scotch.

"Arek, Renee, and the kids are away on a family vacation. I believe one of the large theme parks, which should be highly entertaining for Renee."

Kes snorted, and Trev knew they were both picturing Renee trying to wrangle Arek from doing something like wrestling an alligator.

"My guess is that my brother is trying to get his wife knocked up again, but that's only my opinion. He seems to have taken to fatherhood in a way I never expected and suddenly wants an entire football team. Renee has not been as eager to become his player provider," Trev said, and the two of them laughed.

They sat quietly for a few moments, and Trev's expression sobered as he stared at the tense look in his friend's eyes. "How are things going in that department for you and Ashley? I'm sorry. I didn't mean to be so insensitive."

He knew it had been a tough go of it. Between her MS symptoms, balancing her medications, and the hormone treatments she had to inject herself with, it was one rollercoaster after another.

"Ash is doing okay. We're holding our breath at the moment. I'm only telling you because I know you'd never say anything, but she's six weeks pregnant." Kes rubbed the back of his neck. "But she's so high risk for a miscarriage and complications it worries me. Fuck, it terrifies me. I didn't think something could terrify me as much as what we went through, but this...." Kes looked down into the glass of scotch. "She's so happy, man. I don't want to see her go through any more pain, but there's nothing I can do other than make sure she takes it easy and is pampered to boredom. I think that's the worst part. Knowing that nothing I do could help her keep the pregnancy or make any of her issues she's going through any better. I feel completely useless." He rubbed his face, and Trev leaned forward and gripped his leg.

"I think that if Ashley were in the room, she would tell you that you're already doing everything she needs from you and to not be so hard on yourself, and of course, that you're acting like an idiot," Trev said, and Kes laughed.

"You really have been talking to her. That does sound like Ash. Although, she has a very colorful array of swear words."

"I bet she does, and she probably needs it with the likes of you," Trev quipped.

"Ouch. Your blows are low, my friend."

"It's way too easy when you and Arek are cut from very similar cloths," Trev said, earning himself a glare.

"Don't compare me to that unsophisticated, annoying, completely irrational stubborn ass." Kes looked into his whiskey and sighed. "Yeah, okay, you're right. I sound like him," Kes laughed, then tossed back the rest of his drink.

"Would you like another?" Trev nodded toward the glass, but Kes shook his head no.

"I need to drive." He placed the glass on the table and leaned back into the couch. "I came because I have news, and none of it is good."

"Well, that's ominous and not how I like our conversations to start." Trev settled into the comfortable chair and waited for the bombshell. "Has Wolf taken a turn for the worse? Last I heard from Morry, he was stable."

"I don't know anything about that. This is concerning the guns the Golden Dragons were using, the drugs they were selling that were killing thousands, and the S.O.S. call that had a hidden message that someone tried to scrub." Kes smiled wide. "But they didn't do it well enough for Zumi. She listened to it and picked up right away that something was missing from the original, and

God bless her. She hacked this random server where it had gone and retrieved most of it. Some of it was still very damaged, whether that was something with the A.I. or because they were in a bad area. Doesn't matter."

"Scrubbed? That's a lot of effort for an S.O.S. that was already received," Trev said, sipping his drink.

"I thought so too, but we will get to that. First, the guns."

All of this information piqued Trev's interest. "Go on."

"The guns the Golden Dragons were using were military grade, and we were wondering how they were getting their supply. They were coming from Morry, but I'm pretty positive she doesn't know. Every time she brought in a new shipment, they were divided up." Kes held up a finger. "To Righteous members, such as us, those from other clubs she has alliances with was , and finally, the Golden Dragons. They never purchased massive quantities, so the shipments wouldn't flag as suspicious."

"What makes you so certain she didn't know? Not that I think she would, but I'm curious."

"I found yet another shell company in the mass of companies my father had buried in our corporate structure. This one was set up to look like a sovereignty fighters group specifically targeting those wrongfully held and imprisoned by war criminals. The paperwork is incredible. I'm talking about forged docomeents, fake correspondence, and fake redacted missions. I thought they were legit at first sight, but I got a friend who owed me a favor to look into it, and it's all fake. In fact, the money that has been funding it wasn't from my father. It was none other than, dun dun dun, Dean's father."

"What?" Trev didn't get blindsided much, but this went beyond his suspicions of what was going on.

"More specifically, the cartel itself, but we both know that nothing happens in that cartel without Diego's say-so." Kes stood. "Do you mind if I get a water?"

"No, go ahead." Trev rubbed his chin as he thought about the news. The Dragons were drug runners, and more importantly, it was how they hid their human trafficking. So far, they'd uncovered a dozen major corporations, three senators, and a couple of judges that were all in on it at some level. "Do you think Dean knows what is going on?"

The mini fridge door opened as Kes grabbed a water. "I thought about that too, but I can't reach him. His phone goes straight to voicemail. I tried tracking it, and it shows him as nowhere." Kes slowly made his way back to the couch. "Not entirely unusual for Dean, but it's been like that for weeks, which is strange. He may go completely off the grid for a few days while on a hunt, but never this long."

"You're thinking that Dean is behind all of this, aren't you," Trev asked, and Kes flopped back down onto the couch.

"That brings me to the S.O.S. message. It was to you." Kes reached into his jacket pocket and pulled out his phone. "Here is the message. *Crosshairs, the bogies used to be friendlies, don't trust anyone. They are working for private sector, and Maeve is their targeted asset. If you get this and I'm....*" Kes pressed stop, and Trev stared at the black phone. "The rest is cut off. That was all Zumi could recover, but he said more, and we need to know what it is."

"Well, that won't happen while he's in a coma." Trev tapped

his chin. "Friendlies could mean anyone we used to know," Trev said, but his gut was churning. "I had that weird encounter with Miller a few months back. I told you about that." Kes nodded. "His words, *the Righteous would fall,* and how it was all a figment of our imagination still bounces around inside my head. That message keeps me up at night."

"I have too many things keeping me up at night, but I agree."

Could Dean have turned against them? Could he have gone back to his father and was attacking the Righteous members from within the cartel organization? If he was, what was his motive?

"No, I don't believe that Dean would do this. I know what it looks like, but we spent over a month in the desert with that man, and Dean was a team man. He helped drag your ass across the desert when you were at your worst, and it could've cost him his own life. That is not the type of man that turns on his unit." Trev stood and began to pace as he thought out loud. "I handpicked him because of that."

"I don't have an answer for that, and there have been so many surprises that I wouldn't even try to guess, but here is the weird thing. How did Wolf even know about Maeve?"

"That is a good question." Trev continued to pace as his brain swirled with the new information.

"He called me a couple of weeks back and said he was working a job and didn't know who to trust anymore. I told him to be careful, but he mentioned nothing of Maeve. Could she have been his job?"

"For whom? The Righteous or the Marshals," Trev asked and stopped pacing long enough to pour himself another drink.

"No idea why the Righteous would want her. You said it your-self, she has no real record that they would target, but we did help her escape going to prison," Kes said as Trev sipped the scotch.

"Do we know where she is?"

Trev turned and looked at Kes as he lifted his shoulder. "No clue. I dropped her off on the strip in Vegas, and I haven't seen her since. Morry hasn't said anything, and to the best of my knowl-edge, she wasn't with Wolf in the accident. At least she wasn't taken to the hospital or found in the Hummer."

"We need to find out where the Hummer was taken, and then we need to get our hands on it. We need to figure out if Maeve was in the vehicle, and we have to find out if she was taken or if she's hiding and still trying to reach Morry if she hasn't already. Wolf said she is an asset. That could only mean that she is important to someone."

"Sure, but who and why would they frame her for murder and then call her an asset? None of this makes sense. It's like a puzzle we're trying to solve without the image to reference."

They sat in silence and stared at one another, neither of them coming up with any answers. "Well, to start with, let's find that Hummer and pay whatever we need to to get our hands on it. Then I guess we need to wait and see what Wolf can remember once he is awake."

"I will make some calls and see where it was towed." Kes hit a number on his phone and walked to the other side of the office.

Trev pulled out his phone and tried to call Morry, but her phone went straight to voicemail. A reoccurring theme lately. He decided not to leave a message just in case it was intercepted. This was the kind of information you got in person.

Hitting end, he looked over at Kes, then at the picture on the table. Dean's smiling face stared back at him, and maybe it was naïve of him, but he couldn't bring himself to believe that Dean had gone rogue.

There were many things in this life that Trev had gotten wrong over the years, but a judgment of character wasn't one of them. It was clear that they were under attack, and at the moment, the enemy had the upper hand. The question remained, what the hell was going on?

Chapter 14

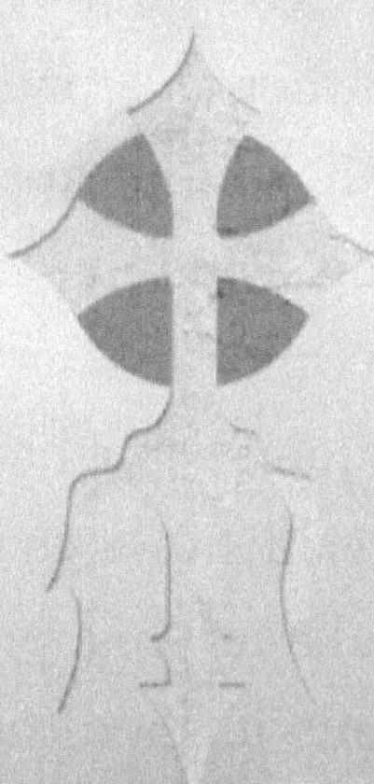

It was dark when they rolled back onto Legion property. Morry could see the lights of the buildings and the security fence in the distance. It always amazed her that she'd taken this place from a single dingy long building— that she wouldn't have let a rat eat off the floor in—to the thriving spot it was.

There were many bumps along the road, and she had scars on her body to prove that she'd paid with blood, sweat, and tears. But now there was a full-time mechanic garage for all the vehicles. A storage area for all the merch they moved, including a large bar for those in the club, complete with very large bouncers who worked the doors to keep those from the clinic out. There was a large dorm-type spot with rooms for the club guys and a separate wing for the sweetbutts. Then, of course, there was the clinic. It had surgery rooms, a full-time doctor, therapy sessions, a mess hall, mandatory classes for any degree they wanted, and a barn she built for the handful of therapy horses.

There was no slacking here, no moping or wishing you could leave. Once you arrived, either as a patient or club member, you never left the fold unless it was because you graduated out, got permission or in a body bag. Those were the only three ways, and she made no exceptions to this rule.

Morry glanced over at Jeremy, he hadn't said much the rest of the trip, but his silence said more than any words could. She wasn't sure what to make of his proclamation. It took her completely by surprise, but it shouldn't have. She opened the door, and he kicked it out of her hand. There was no one to blame but herself for this.

The gates were open before they pulled up, and Morry lifted a hand to wave as they drove through.

"What do you want me to do?"

"What," Morry asked, pulled out of her brooding thoughts.

"What do you want me to take care of first?" Jeremy said.

"Oh." Parking the Hummer, she watched the motorcycles roar past and disappear inside the long storage building and out of sight. Glancing at the time, an idea formed. "How would you like to play nurse?"

"Well, hello, straight into roleplaying. I like it," Jeremy said, reaching for the door handle.

She grabbed his arm and shook her head as he looked at her. "No, I mean, actually pretend to be a nurse?"

"I'm not following."

"I want to see my son, and I need a distraction. You are my distraction. Can you keep Andrew busy talking while I sneak into the room?"

Jeremy pulled down the visor, and she lifted a brow as he opened the mirror and the light flicked on. He stared at himself in the mirror and then nodded. "I need to shave and grab a different set of clothes, but yeah, I can do it."

Morry smiled and surprised herself when she reached out and grabbed his face to lay a hard kiss on Jeremy's lips.

"Thank you." Hopping out of the truck, she paused. "Well, are you going to get ready or what?" She barely managed to hold back the smirk as Jeremy jumped out of the Hummer. "I'll be in my office. I need to check in with the few patients and make sure the latest shipment of guns has arrived," she said as they went their separate ways.

Her phone dinged as she stepped into the office, showing a missed call from Trev, but whatever he wanted to talk about would have to wait. Walking to her desk, she grabbed the latest intake folder that had been put into her tray and flipped open the cover. Her hand and the air in her chest froze as she stared at the name of the newest patient: Stephen Kekewich.

Morry swallowed the lump lodged in her throat. Her pulse raced as her finger slid down the intake information, the year he was born, his family history, and there it was in black and white, brother to deceased Tyler Kekewich. Was it coincidence or just fucked up timing that brought TK's brother to her just as she tried to let go of some of the pain in her past? It was like the universe never wanted her to heal.

There was no forgetting the only other person she'd ever loved or watching TK die in her arms. Morry screamed and threw the folder across the room. Papers flew in all directions, then fluttered to the floor, reminding Morry of the rain of bullets that took Tyler from her.

"Run!" Trev yelled as the sound of an RPG screamed closer.

Sand exploded into the air like a torrent with a deafening explosion as the missile hit near them. They were running for their lives across the desert without any cover, needing to put distance between themselves and those following them. There was a rough path on the maps that vehicles couldn't cross, and that was where they were heading. It was their only chance of surviving, even if it added an extra week to their journey. They would be dead for sure in a matter of days if they couldn't take real cover. They were all low on ammunition and water, plus they were moving slowly, having to help Jimmy— who'd just taken a bullet in his leg— and Kes, who was delirious from the pain of his burns on his side.

The sound of gunfire broke out once more, and it was something you never got used to. The bang and whizz, then the soft thud as the bullet narrowly missed you. Each one was like a deadly game of dodgeball, but there were no timeouts. This game was for keeps, and the winner was left alive while the loser bled out in the middle of hell.

"Over here," Trev yelled again to be heard over the sound of the artillery raining down on them. It was only by some grace of God that they were not all being taken down one by one with the amount of lead that was falling all around them.

A Jeep came racing over a sand dune to the right of where she was running. She stared at the driver and the man standing at the back with his gun trained on her and knew she was dead. She had no idea where TK had come from—he'd been helping Dean run with Kes—when he appeared out of the periphery of her vision.

Bang, Bang. Two shots rang out. The man standing on the back of the Jeep fell, and the driver slumped over in the seat.

"Watch out!" Morry screamed as the Jeep careened toward the spot they were all running to for cover.

In a move that should've been on the big screen, TK ran like a man possessed and grabbed the door handle of the Jeep. Morry ran after him, unable to believe what she was watching as he pulled the driver out and somehow, without getting sucked under the wheels, got inside the Jeep and brought it to a stop.

"Get on, everyone. Get on," TK called.

Everyone diverted course to get on the Jeep. There were too many of them, with the civilians and the injured. TK jumped out of the driver's seat and told Trev to get in.

"You should go with them for as long as the fuel lasts. It will give you a chance to live," TK said as Morry ran up to the Jeep. Kes and Jimmy were being loaded into the back.

"No, I go where you go," she said.

TK looked at the Jeep and then back at those who had lost some ground but were still coming.

"Morry, please."

"Don't please me. I'm no different from Dean, Arek, or even Wolf, who will all have to run. We will protect the Jeep's ass."

He chewed his lip as the last of the bone-weary civilians were loaded into the open back area.

"Anyone else coming," Trev asked. We all looked at one another and shook our heads no. "Okay, you know where we're headed. The plan hasn't changed." Trev slammed the door, and sand was tossed in the air as the Jeep drove away.

"All right. Let's move out," TK said, and they formed a single file line and followed the tire tracks.

"Wow. Who are you planning on killing?"

Morry jumped and pulled her gun as she spun toward the door. She pointed it up as she saw the shocked look on Jeremy's face.

"Shit, sorry." Putting the gun away, she walked over to the strewn papers and bent down to start cleaning up the mess she'd made. Jeremy's hand gripped her shoulder, and as soon as he touched her, the quaking in her limbs started.

"Hey, you're shaking," he said, pulling her to her feet.

She couldn't look him in the eyes as she wrapped her arms around his waist and buried her face in his chest. The tears were flowing, and there was no stopping them as the scab on her heart covering the pain of TK's death was ripped free. Jeremy didn't say anything more while he held her, and she appreciated that.

Pulling back, she wiped away the wetness on her cheeks. "I'm sorry."

"Don't be sorry. Do you want to talk about it?"

She shook her head and turned away to collect herself and

shake off the humiliation of crying in front of Jeremy for the second time in twenty-four hours.

"I don't think I can right now. I just want to see Kyle. Can we do that?"

"Of course," he said. Morry nodded and didn't look at him as she walked to the door. "I'll clean up later."

Jeremy turned to her as soon as they were clear of the compound. She couldn't see his face clearly in the darkened vehicle, but she felt the compassion and worry coming from him.

"I get that you don't want to talk, but when you're ready, I'm here."

"Thanks. I want you to check on the new guy tomorrow, okay?" She glanced over at Jeremy, and he nodded.

"Sure, if that's what you need. You usually like to do the initial welcome chat," Jeremy said.

"Yeah, but I think it's time you took more of the reins. Especially if taking over is something you can see yourself doing." She was being weak. Morry hated that she couldn't face Stephen, but she needed a couple of days to collect herself. She hated even more that she was using Jeremy to be weak.

"Okay, I'll look at his file in the morning and then go see him."

It felt like it took forever to get to the hospital, and when they arrived, she parked as far away from the entrance as she could, near some decorative trees. The last thing she needed was for Andrew to spot the Hummer.

"So remember, Kyle has biliary atresia, and he already had one surgery as a baby, but is now in need of a transplant," she said as they made their way toward the front entrance of the hospital.

"I remember. Don't worry. I've got this. Andrew has never met me, and I can pull off the new guy act. Do you know what room he's in?" Morry marched in with Jeremy beside her.

"Yeah, two-thirteen," she answered as they walked past the reception area.

It was late, so regular visiting hours were long over, but people were always coming and going, so they didn't look out of place as they casually strolled through the hospital. A cart filled with gowns, scrubs, and other items was sitting in the hallway, and she looked around before thumbing through the sizes and grabbing ones that would fit Jeremy. Barely, but they would suffice.

"Here, you put these on and go up the elevator. I'll take the stairs." She walked off, pushing through the door to the stairwell and jogging to the second floor. There was a little square of glass, and she stared out, trying to gauge where Kyle's room was.

She would dig a hole in the desert and bury Andrew if she thought Kyle would be better off without his father. Truthfully he was a really good dad to Kyle for as shitty of a husband as he was when they were married. The elevator across the way dinged, and Jeremy stepped out into the hall.

Roleplaying had its merits. He looked fucking hot in the scrubs and doctor's jacket he'd found. He'd also found a stethoscope that hung casually around his neck while he held a clipboard and pen.

It was a little old school, but Jeremy totally looked like the new guy.

Jeremy nodded toward the door where she was hiding, then walked down the hall and out of sight. Pushing open the emergency door, she slipped out to peek down the hallway where Jeremy had gone. Morry could just make out Jeremy talking to Andrew, who was sitting in the hall. She had no idea what Jeremy said, but they walked away from Kyle's room in the opposite direction.

Jeremy had just earned himself whatever roleplay session he wanted because she would never have gotten into that room without him. Time to move.

CHAPTER 15

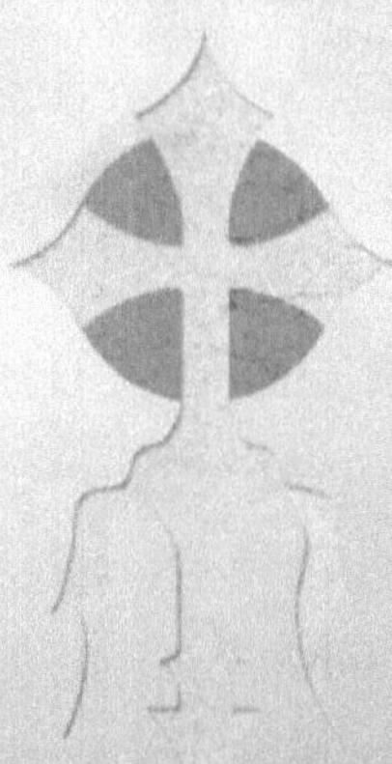

Morry marched down the hall and watched as Jeremy led Andrew into another room. She watched the numbers until she got to two-thirteen, then slipped inside, closing the door behind her.

"Morry?"

She would know that voice anywhere. Morry spun around and came face to face with the woman who was once her best friend.

"Lindsay?"

She looked the same, a little older, like the rest of them, but she was still beautiful with her ability to look like she'd just stepped off the pageant stage without even trying. Morry had always envied that in Lindsay and how guys would physically run over anyone to get at her. How many times had she been pushed into a locker because the latest new guy decided he wanted to speak to Lindsay? She became obsolete and completely invisible. Guess it was her fault for remaining friends with someone like that and marrying someone like Andrew, who was always overly friendly with her so-called best friend. She should've seen the affair coming.

"Morry, what are you doing here? If Andrew catches you in here, he'll will call the police."

Crossing her arms, she glared at the woman she thought she knew. They'd grown up together, done everything together, and yet when Morry needed her best friend the most, she fucked Andrew and helped destroy her marriage.

"Like you fucking care what happens to me. I didn't even know the two of you were still together. Andrew never mentions you."

It was a low blow, but she didn't care. The old anger Morry thought was long squashed rekindled at the sight of Lindsay's pretty face.

"I guess I deserve that," Lindsay said.

"You deserve a lot more than that. I trusted you. You were my best friend, and you took my husband, my home, and now my son from me," Morry growled, barely managing to keep her voice low.

"Mom?" Kyle's sleepy voice extinguished any anger that had been brewing.

Morry rushed to Kyle's side and grabbed her son's hand as he rubbed at his eyes with the other.

"Yeah, sweetie, it's me. I'm so sorry that I haven't been to see you." She smiled wide as she stared into her son's handsome face.

He was the one thing in the world she could say with certainty she'd done right. He was incredible and she loved him unconditionally.

He looked so different. Every week he was a little more grown up, but the sickly shade of his skin had the threads of panic making Morry's heart race.

"It's okay. I know Dad won't let you see me."

Her eyes grew wide with shock. She hadn't expected Andrew to be honest. The man didn't know the meaning of the word. "Your Dad said that?"

"No, Lindsay told me. I asked why you hadn't come by, and she said that Dad was being all weird 'cause I said I wanted a leather jacket. I didn't mean to get you in trouble mom." He lifted a shoulder, his face falling.

"No, don't you ever think any of this is on you. What your father and I argue about is only because we both love you and want what's best, we just don't always see eye-to-eye on what that is. You did nothing wrong."

Morry looked over her shoulder to Lindsay. "I'm going to wait outside and give you two a few minutes, but if Andrew comes back...."

"Yeah, I know. Your loyalty only runs so deep," Morry said.

Lindsay bit her lip but didn't say anything and slipped out the door.

"Hey, I don't have much time, but here." Reaching into her pocket, she pulled out a phone and handed it over. "Don't let your father know you have this. I even got the same cover, so if he catches you on it, he will think it's your other one, but this way, we can text."

The smile on Kyle's face made the possibility of any wrath from Andrew worth it.

"Thanks, Mom." He looked down at the phone, and his eyes were so much like an adult's. He should be worrying about things like sports and dating, and parties.

"I'm working on finding you a liver. I have a few leads out, and you know that your mother doesn't ever give up," she said.

The corner of Kyle's mouth pulled up. "Yeah, I know, but if not...."

"No, we are not going to talk about the possibility of another outcome." She squeezed his arm like she'd done to Wolf. "I miss you, and I can't wait until you're healthy and out of this place. I found this gorgeous spot near Montana that I know you'll love. Lots of fishing, and I spoke to a man who rescues bears. He has some that he said you could take your picture with."

"Really? That's sick," he said, his whole face lighting up.

Kyle loved bears from the time he was a small boy. Morry searched until she found a man who rescued bears and housed ones that couldn't live out in the wild. They were trained for movies or commercials and lived like kings on his massive country property. As soon as she saw the place and met the man, she knew she had to take Kyle there.

"Do you really think I'll get to see them," he asked, and the question broke her heart. The earlier tears threatened to make another appearance, but she didn't want to worry him any more than he was already.

"I know you will. Just how I knew that I would make it back from the desert and just how I knew that you would make captain of the baseball team. Trust in your mom. I've got you."

Kyle opened the phone and smiled. "You attached your credit card to the games? Are you the one not feeling well?"

Laughing, she smiled widely. Kyle was the one bright spot in her life, even when shit was at its worst. Morry would give up everything, including her life, to save her son. He was everything to her. It pissed her off so much that she couldn't donate part of her liver. She was his mother. She should be able to do this for him. Of all people, she should be the one to save him.

"Yeah, definitely don't tell your dad about that. I would never hear the end of it," she teased.

"Are you kidding? This is like walking into my favorite Magic the Gathering store and buying a black lotus card." Kyle lifted an eyebrow, and he looked so much like her at that moment with the sassy stare that she couldn't help but smirk. "I'm totally taking advantage of this. Something good has to come out of being stuck in this bed."

"Could we maybe take it a step down from that black lotus?" She sighed as the clock on the wall showed that five minutes had already passed. "Listen, I better go. If your dad catches me, I really will end up banned for life," she teased and made a face that had Kyle laughing.

Kyle snorted. "Yeah, Dad is a little overly dramatic, but Lindsay is chill most of the time."

"She treats you good?"

He lifted a shoulder in the typical teenage, non-committal

way. "She's not bad. She doesn't ride motorcycles, but she's nice enough."

Morry smirked and gave her son's soft dark brown hair a ruffle. She knew he hated that. "That's good."

"Mom," he complained, making her laugh.

She stood up but didn't want to leave. This was not enough time, and her heart ached to remain in the room for every second she could, but Andrew had the judge's ear. If he caught her or Lindsay said something, then her chances of winning back joint custody or at least visiting rights would never happen.

"Kyle, I know that your dad, Lindsay, and I don't always get along, but the one thing that will never change is how much we all love you." Leaning over, she kissed the top of his head. "I love you, Kyle. Don't ever forget that and no matter how scared you are, know that I'm fighting to help you every second of every day. I will not stop until I find you a liver." She closed her eyes and gave his head another kiss.

He reached up and wrapped his arms around her neck, squeezing hard, then let go and went back to the phone. He was caught in a strange limbo, and she was right there with him. He was fourteen and sometimes acted so mature that she forgot his age, and then right now, with his nose buried in a new gadget, he looked exactly how old he was. He had one good friend who still came to visit, but other than that, being sick had scared all the other kids off.

He looked up at her with gray eyes that matched her own. "Go, Mom, before Dad gets back. Besides, your staring is starting to wig me out."

She gave him a lopsided smile. "Okay, I'm going, I'm going."

Forcing herself away from the side of the bed, she cracked opened the door. Lindsay was sitting in the chair across the way.

"Mom?"

Looking over her shoulder, she stared at her son's face. "Yeah?"

He fidgeted with the blanket and looked away from her eyes. "I love you."

And just like that, her heart filled like a balloon with so much emotion and then popped with pain. She took an extra moment to memorize him. She was going to find a way to save him. This world wasn't taking Kyle from her too.

Jeremy sat across from Andrew, and as hard as he tried, he couldn't stop picturing his own father. He pretended he was the grief and emotional support counselor—his specialty. Jeremy had just enough knowledge in all areas to be dangerous. If he ever decided not to run an international gun-smuggling biker gang that had a fucked-up rehab clinic for soldiers, then he could have a killer career as an actor. He smirked at the thought.

Jeremy had Andrew eating out of the palm of his hand. He even went into a bit of his own sob story but changed drugs to cancer and his parents disowning him to them sitting vigil at his bedside. It was enough. Andrew hadn't stopped talking since they walked into the room. Jeremy's eyes searched Andrew's face, and he tried to see what Morry saw when she married this man. Andrew was a decent-looking man with a good job, but he seemed the opposite of Morry in everything. If Jeremy met Andrew on the street, he would've said his personality aligned with a wet noodle.

"I just don't know how to keep it all together anymore. There is still no word on a donor, and my son gets worse every day. Then there is my ex-wife, who is a terrible influence, and our horrible legal battle. What scares me most is that Kyle is almost at the age where he can choose to go live with her."

Anger bloomed in Jeremy's gut with the disrespect Andrew continued to show Morry. In the short time they'd spent together in this room, Andrew referenced how terrible Morry was in some manner at least ten times. It took everything he had not to get up and lay the guy out on the floor, but that wasn't going to help Morry, and that was why he was here.

"You mean if your son lives?"

Andrew's face blanched. "Oh, yes, of course. I meant when he gets out of here healthy."

"Well, Andrew, the only thing I can say from my own experience is that the more you try to force your ideals on your son, the more he will fight you and push you away."

That was all true. It wasn't just Jeremy's grades slipping and losing the baseball scholarship that started his path toward drugs. He'd felt smothered and suffocated by his overly strict parents. So when he was offered stuff at a team party, Jeremy took it, and unfortunately, that was the beginning of a terrible road. Jeremy often wondered if his life would've turned out differently if he hadn't gone to that party or had different parents, but those thoughts also seemed like an easy excuse. Jeremy was man enough to admit that he fucked up, and now he had to live with those choices.

Andrew stood and walked to the window, and Jeremy glanced at the time on the wall. Almost ten minutes had gone by.

"Did you ever act out against your parent's wishes?"

The laugh that came from Andrew's mouth was bitter. "Yeah, when I married my ex. My parents never liked her and told me it would end in disaster, but I didn't listen. I wanted to do the right thing when she got pregnant, so I proposed. Biggest mistake of my life," Andrew said.

Jeremy ground his teeth together. "So there is no hope for you to work things out as friends for your son's sake? This strain between the two of you must be difficult on him?"

Andrew spun around and glared. "Whose side are you on?"

Jeremy slowly stood and gripped the clipboard to keep himself from beating Andrew over the head with it. "I'm on no one's side. That's the point of my position. To support all in this terrible situation where your son and his illness become the priority. I'm just as much here for you as I would be for anyone else dealing with the pain of an ill child."

Andrew's face softened, and Jeremy could see his mind working. If nothing else, maybe this selfish piece of shit would let Morry visit because he knew that seeing Kyle so little was killing Morry inside.

"I need to get back to my son," Andrew said, and like the weasel he was, he darted around Jeremy and out into the hall.

Jeremy quickly followed Andrew out and called his name when he saw the door to Kyle's room open. Andrew turned, and Morry stuck her head out, spotting them in the hall. She took off in the other direction, and the woman who had to be Lindsay, the woman Andrew was now married to, followed her.

"I just want to give you my number in case you ever need to talk again," Jeremy said. Using the paper on the clipboard, he wrote down a number and ripped it off to hand over.

"Thanks, Dr. Evans. I'm sorry if I seem tense. I haven't gotten much sleep." They shook hands, and Jeremy followed along quietly beside him. Andrew veered into Kyle's room, and as he passed the door, he couldn't help slowing down and staring inside.

He hadn't seen much of Kyle in the last two years since the second round of the court battle ensued, but the kid was the spitting image of Morry now. It was uncanny how that happened. Marching on, he found the two women in a whispered argument by the stairs.

"Ladies is there a problem here," he asked, still keeping the doctor persona.

"No, I'm good," Morry said and pushed through the door to the stairwell.

Lindsay stood there, looking like she was going to follow, then glanced up at Jeremy before her eyes filled with tears, and she took off down the hall. Jeremy used the elevator, then slipped into the washroom to change. Folding the items, he kept them in case he might need them again.

His phone dinged, and he stared at the message.

M: Outside with LL

J: K, see U in a min

Walking like he didn't have a care in the world, he made his way out the door and across the parking lot to Lady Luck and Morry. She was already in the driver's seat and didn't say anything as he got in. Jeremy knew her well enough to know when not to push.

The lights of the city disappeared, replaced with stars and darkness. He never thought being this far out of civilization would be something he enjoyed, but like so many things, the universe proved him wrong again.

He sat up a little straighter as they veered off the main drive to the front entrance and toward the single-lane access to the top of the canyon. Okay, this he hated. The narrow road was barely the width of the Hummer. Plummeting off to their deaths was possible on one side, while the cliff scraping against the side-view mirror always set his teeth on edge.

He gripped the door and pushed back in his seat like that would somehow keep them from crashing. The front tire under his feet went over a larger rock, and he swore as sweat broke out on the back of his neck with the thump. Jeremy stared out the window, and it was like they were flying. All he could see for miles was the skyline and a drop to darkness that looked like a straight shot to hell from this height.

They rounded the steep curve and crested the top, and Jeremy sucked in a deep breath while his heart pounded out of his chest.

"Fuck, I hate that road," he grumbled. "Why are we up here, anyway?"

Morry put the Hummer in park and killed the lights. She stared out the windshield, silent for the longest time before she finally turned her head his way. Morry could be broody, but she was acting stranger than usual tonight, and he couldn't put his finger on what exactly had set her off.

"It's my fault that he's dead," she said, but her eyes weren't focused on his face.

"Who?"

Morry's eyes shimmered with unshed tears, but it was the terrified look in their depths that shook him to his core.

"TK"

CHAPTER 16

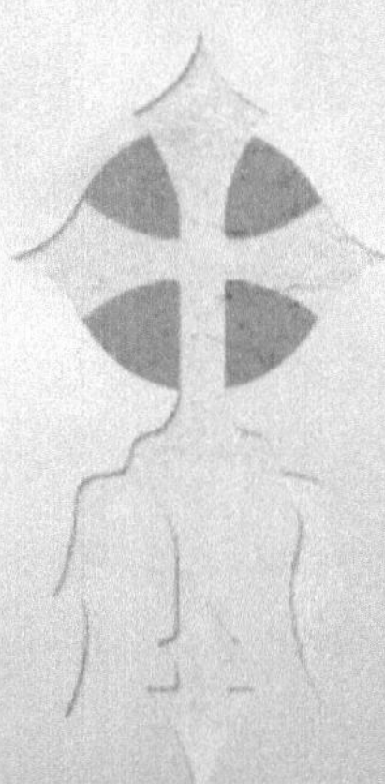

Jeremy didn't dare breathe for fear that Morry wouldn't continue. But it didn't matter. She opened the door and jumped out, slamming it in her wake. He could see her shadow moving around and knew she was pacing. Hopping out, Jeremy closed the passenger door and decided she needed to talk for her own sake. Whatever Morry kept bottled up was boiling under the surface, and she would explode if she didn't let some of the steam out.

As Morry turned, he stepped into her path and grabbed her shoulders. Her entire body was shaking.

"Tell me what's going on."

Instead of saying anything, she reached for the top of his

jeans. He gripped her arms tighter. "No, Morry, sex won't make this go away. Tell me."

She growled, and with a harsh twist broke his hold, and marched away. Jeremy may have won the award for the stupidest move ever, but he caught up to her, grabbed her arm, and spun her around.

"Let go of me," she said, her voice caught in that strange place between ready-to-cry and I'm-going-to-kill-you.

"If you want to hurt me, then hurt me, but I'm not letting you run away from whatever is eating at you again. You wouldn't have let me or anyone else who comes through that gate, and it's time you listened to your own advice."

"You have no idea what I need," she said and stepped in close to his body.

He expected her to nail him in the crotch, then leave him up here to walk back, but she reached up and laid her hand on his cheek.

"Talk to me. I only want to help. I have no ulterior motives, and we are in the middle of nowhere. No one else can hear you. You need to finally open up about whatever is eating at you."

Morry ran her hand from his cheek down his neck and chest. He was getting ready to step away when she squeezed the bulge already forming in his jeans. Jeremy sucked in a breath and groaned as he fought back the instant desire that was always there when she was around. He wondered if the sensation would ease up after the other night, but it only increased how much he wanted her. His heart pounded hard as Morry traced the outline of his cock.

"You want to know what I need?"

As hard as it was, he forced himself to step back from her exploring fingers. "I'll fuck you all you want after," he said.

"No, the other way around. Fuck me first, then I'll tell you what you think you want to know, but it comes with a word of warning."

Jeremy licked his lips, afraid to ask but too intrigued not to. "What's the warning?"

"What you're going to hear will put your life in danger for even knowing, but more so, it may be the thing you decide is too much, and you won't want anything to do with me. If that happens, you only have yourself to blame." She stepped back, then turned and marched for the Hummer. "No matter what, though, I'm taking that cock right now," she called over her shoulder. "Unless, of course, you don't want to fuck me."

That got his feet moving. It was totally unfair how Morry managed to turn the tables around on him. It had been like that from the moment he arrived. Whatever Jeremy thought he wanted, she always proved him wrong. Whatever stupid thing he went to do, she was right there to either stop him or help him up when he failed. He wanted that skill.

He followed her around to the back of the Hummer. She opened the hatch and hit a button that flattened the seats. There was a blanket stuffed in one of the compartments, and she pulled it out and laid it in the back of the Hummer with a single flick of her wrists.

"I used to come up here a lot to clear my head. I think I've slept inside the Hummer more than in my bed." She looked over at him.

"I rarely feel safe outside of this armored vehicle. Almost every moment of the day, I look over my shoulder for the bullet that will take me out," Morry said as she slipped out of her leather jacket. She tossed it in the back and then whipped the black tank top she was wearing over her head.

He shuddered at the sight of her tits. They were the perfect size. Just enough to wrap his hand around, and her pale skin with the dark areolas and hard nipples had him throbbing in his jeans. She never wore a bra. Jeremy already knew that from a rigorous workout, where they brushed against his arm and chest, and he had jerked off, fantasizing about sucking on them. Shit, all she had to do was walk by, and he was hard for her.

"I wish I could help. I don't know what to say right now," Jeremy said, his brain already misfiring as the thoughts of sliding into her took control.

"Are you going to get undressed, or am I going to have to do this all myself," Morry asked as she kicked off her boots. The jeans were next, and in a blink, she jumped up onto the bed area she'd created and sat there with her legs spread.

"Do it. I want to see you touch yourself," Jeremy ordered.

A smirk played across Morry's lips as her hand slid down her stomach. He shuddered as he watched one finger dip inside of her. His clothes came off quickly, and he tossed them onto the pile with hers.

"Don't you dare come without me," he said, hopping into the spacious area and crawling between her legs.

He knew she was using his body to wipe away whatever memories or emotions were creeping to the surface, but he said he wanted to help and if this was what she needed right this moment then so be it. Every muscle, fiber, and thought screamed one thing, pleasure her and make her scream his name as he claimed her.

Settling between her thighs, Jeremy hovered above her body. He groaned as Morry wrapped her hand around his shaft and swirled her wet finger over his sensitive cock head. Jeremy thrust his hips gently in her hand as he fought the urge to let himself go, to coat her body with his first load. The image of his come dripping from her chin was so strong that Jeremy had to blink and look at her face to confirm it hadn't already happened.

Morry made him lose his mind. Reaching up, he wrapped his hand around her throat. She moaned, and the vibration shot along his arm and down his body to his needy cock.

"When we're done, and you're nothing but a writhing mess begging me to stop, you're going to tell me what's going on inside your head." She tried to turn her head away, but he kept the grip on her throat firm. "I can always get back out and jerk off on a rock. I've done it before." Her hand tightened around his shaft, and he nudged into her pussy's entrance, so just the head rubbed around and begged for entry. "So you need to promise you're not going to change your mind. What is it going to be, Morry?"

He ran his thumb over her jawline as she thought. Even though he couldn't see her eyes well in the dark, he could feel her stormy gaze on him as if weighing his words.

"Are you threatening to withhold sex?"

Jeremy smirked as he leaned down and nipped at Morry's bottom lip. He ran his tongue playfully along the soft skin, and the moment she opened for him, he kissed her like he was never going to see her again. She moaned and gripped his shoulders hard, her nails digging in. Breaking the kiss, he kept his lips against hers.

"I'm just making sure this is a two-way relationship, and if sex is the bullet I've got, then I'm asshole enough to use it." Jeremy felt her smile against his lips. He pictured her beautiful features and the way her eyes sparkled with humor.

"Fine, you win... this time. I promise," she grumbled before grabbing his face and resuming the kiss with a fierceness that blanked out all other thought other than burying himself deep inside of her.

"Fuck, you're killing me," he groaned, pressing his hips forward enough to slip his cock inside her.

Morry wrapped her legs around his waist, and the new position allowed him to sink deeper. He groaned as she moaned in his ear—such a sweet sound.

"Fuck, you feel good," she said. "Fuck me like I've been a bad girl."

"You want me to punish your pussy, do you," he said as he started to move his hips with short jabs.

Releasing his shoulders, Morry slipped her hands between their bodies. He lifted up enough to give her access to rub at her clit or slip a finger into the mix, but she took him by surprise as her hands wrapped around his cock and her finger slipped under his balls.

"Oh damn, that's incredible," he growled. The new sensation was better than any cock ring. Her finger slid along the sensitive skin leading to his ass. "Woman, you're going to make me come too soon," he said as he slammed into her harder. The blanket under them slid with his movements, and with only a few thrusts, her head was touching the front seat. "Fuck, what is it with shit sliding around on us?"

Grabbing Morry by the waist, he lifted her off the bed of the Hummer and rolled over so she was on top. The ceiling was low, but it didn't stop Morry from picking a rhythm that had him burning up. He was torn between grabbing the sexy tits bouncing in front of his face or her ass. Gripping her ass helped her keep pace, so he leaned up the short distance to suck on the nipple, teasingly brushing against his cheek.

He wanted to know every little thing about Morry. One thing he learned was that she had the sexiest little tell when she was close to coming. Her body would shudder, and she would close her eyes as she bit her lip. The pure pleasure written on her face was something that he never wanted to forget.

A soft whimper escaped her, and Morry's movements became erratic as she drew close. He shouldn't be this pent-up, but he was ready to come when she did.

"Come for me, Morry," he said, releasing the nipple he was teasing to get a better grip on her ass and stare at the rapture on her face. He didn't want to miss this. If she let him, he would fucking take a photo of this moment and keep it forever as his screen saver. "Yeah, that's it right there," he growled and thrust up hard into her.

She was incredible. There was no other word for it. Her moans were so close together it sounded more like one long one than a bunch of smaller ones, but with the first twinge of her thighs, Jeremy knew what was coming.

"Oh fuck, Jeremy," Morry yelled, and like a stunning piece of artwork, she froze and arched her back until her head touched the roof as her fingers dug into his pecs.

Jeremy realized that, somewhere along the line, he'd fallen in love with her. It was dangerous, but this intimate moment between them drove home just how deeply he felt. He'd seen the dark side of life and could be dead tomorrow. So whatever time he had left, he wanted to spend it with Morry.

Giving her a few moments to enjoy the orgasm on its own, he held still. But then he let loose and hammered his hips into her as he claimed her. She was his. He didn't give a fuck who joined the Legions or who popped up from Morry's past. If another man looked at her in a way he didn't like, he would break their face and bury them six feet under.

"Fuck me, Morry. Fuck," he yelled through clenched teeth as his back arched off the makeshift bed.

He held her hips down hard onto his cock and felt himself bottoming out. And yet, it never seemed like enough. The powerful orgasm gripped Jeremy in a chokehold stealing the air from his lungs. He tried to yell but couldn't. Wrapping his arms around Morry's back, he pulled her down so they lay skin to skin as he continued to pound into her until he was spent, and both were panting.

Jeremy held her snug to his body and never wanted to let go. He almost blurted out how he felt when she cuddled closer, sighing and rubbing her cheek on his chest. That would've been a stupid move, and he had to bite his cheek hard to keep those three little words from slipping out. There was no doubt in his mind that she would've run for the hills.

"I don't think I ever loved Andrew," she said. Jeremy didn't say anything. He just let her talk. "Did I ever tell you how we ended up married?"

"No."

"To say my house was strict would've been an understatement. I was allowed to do three things growing up: school, more school, and learn to fight. I have four older brothers. My mom passed away when I was five, so between my brothers and my father, I lived in a home of overprotective males. I loved it and hated it."

Jeremy kissed the top of her head and then grabbed the edge of the blanket, pulling it over them.

"I was accepted into the army as a cadet at nineteen and decided to celebrate with others who made it through. Andrew was there partying with all of us. We'd been dating by then, but it was typical teenage dating with movies and hanging out with friends or the odd party." She sighed.

"It was supposed to be a fun night, and we were both hammered. One moment of forgetting to use a condom later, and you get the idea. God, I was so terrified to tell my father I was pregnant. It took me weeks to build up the courage, and I only said something when I decided that if I wanted the child, I needed to tell my commanding officers and drop out until I could reapply." She sighed and wiped her face. "I've never regretted a single day with my son, but I wish every day that I'd never married Andrew when he proposed."

"Let me guess, he did it to be noble and do the right thing," Jeremy asked, barely managing to hold back the snort of disgust as he thought over what Andrew had said to him.

Marrying someone just because you got them pregnant was destined to fail, even if it seemed right. Jeremy had seen it so many times with his friends at high school. Every other day, it seemed like one of them came to school saying that their parents were splitting. The one thing most of them had in common? They'd gotten married too young or got pregnant and married to do the right thing for the child.

They never seemed to ask how good that decision was when it all fell apart, and the kids were reeling from a separation that could've been avoided.

"Yeah, you guessed it. I knew that was why Andrew proposed, but I was desperate not to feel alone in the decision to keep Kyle. My father and all my brothers were overseas, and none of them were married at that time. I would've been barely twenty when he was born and alone. Stupid reason to marry someone, but Andrew wasn't a bad guy, or at least I didn't think so. I don't know anymore."

"That piece of shit cheated on you and then tried to steal your child from you. He had no idea what he was letting go of, and he certainly has no idea who he's dealing with."

Morry lifted her head and laid her chin on the back of her hand on his chest. Their eyes locked, and he could see the softer side of Morry shining out. The side that, as far as he knew, no one ever saw. It made him feel warm all over and more protective of her.

"The problem is, he's not entirely wrong. I'm a damn good mother, and I love my son with every breath. I would kill anyone who tried to hurt him, but I'm the leader of a notorious gun-running motorcycle club. Although I only sell to those doing good, and the crew and I also do jobs for the Righteous and I have the rehab clinic for vets. All Andrew can see is a bunch of criminals hanging around his son, and of course, Kyle loves the bikes and leather, and he's at the age where everything about my world and what I do is cool. Andrew is a banker and has a cubicle in an office. He lives a very different lifestyle of golf and chardonnay. Kyle detests golf."

"But you weren't that person when he cheated," Jeremy said.

"I can't argue with that."

"So if you never loved Andrew, have you ever loved anyone?" He couldn't believe he had asked that question and held his breath to see if she would respond. What answer was he hoping for, he had no idea, but he needed to know.

"Yeah, I did once. His name was Tyler, but we all called him TK. I didn't even notice myself falling in love with him. One day we were friends and then friends with benefits, and the next, bam, I realized my feelings had shifted. He'd always liked me, but I was married and coming off a very painful and embarrassing breakup, so I apparently took longer to come around."

Jeremy bit his lip but smiled. There was a sliver of hope for him yet.

"So what happened? You said it was your fault he died. I don't believe that."

"I stood up," she said and then stopped. She was quiet for so long that Jeremy didn't think she would explain.

The lack of water and long, hot days of physical exertion were beginning to take its toll on everyone. They ran out of water two days ago, and although Wolf was incredible at finding spots to dig and find pockets of water buried under the hot sand, there was never enough for more than a handful or two for each of them.

Her legs were screaming, the muscles seizing and aching so badly she couldn't hold still. After hours of steadily jogging under the sun, they met up with Trev and were surprised to see smoke coming from the small camp. Trev hated for them to have a fire for very long. There was a ring of boulders that he'd tucked everyone behind. She dropped to her knees and wanted to cry at the sight of the food. Rodents larger than rats but smaller than rabbits were on multiple spits set up over the open fire. There was enough cooking for them to have almost one each.

"Here, drink this, just not too fast," TK said, holding a canister.

Taking it, Morry thought she was dreaming about the weight. Staring inside, she could see the liquid sloshing around.

"Where did you get this," Morry asked, thinking she must be having some sort of delusion.

TK sat down beside her. "Take a small sip, and I'll explain."

"Always with the negotiations," she teased.

Hand shaking, she lifted it to her lips which felt like moving a mountain on her own, and she moaned as a bit of water touched her dry tongue. She didn't even care that her lips were cracked and hurt with the touch. The water tasted that sweet.

"That's enough for now," TK said and took the canister from her. She wanted to growl at him and fight over the water, which told her exactly how dehydrated she was. She knew she needed to listen to him, or she would throw all that preciousness back up.

Shifting around, she sat on her ass and leaned her head against his shoulder as she took in the ragtag group that had managed to survive the race with death. The screams of those who died echoed in her head, and she jerked when a hand touched her shoulder. She didn't remember falling asleep, but the fire was out, and everyone around them was quietly eating.

She couldn't help wondering if they would ever talk or laugh again. It was always 'remain as quiet as possible,' and everything was done or said in hushed tones.

Trev was kneeling in front of her, and TK held out one of the perfectly charred food offerings. She didn't want to know what they were eating, and her stomach growled with the same understanding. It didn't matter. You eat it, or you die.

"How much farther?" She hadn't asked the question before, terrified to hear the answer.

Trev looked over his shoulder at the injured and then at the handful of civilians before shaking his head.

"Hard to say for certain, but I have enough fuel to move the civilians another half day, maybe, and then we are all back to our feet. I'm thinking someone else can drive tomorrow. I managed to rest my legs driving." She nodded. "My best estimation, at the rate we are traveling, is three hundred and thirty-six hours. Make sure to drink more water and give me the canisters. I found a spot inside a narrow cave not far from here. Once it's dark, I'll sneak off and fill all the empty ones."

"Thanks, Trev," TK said as he popped a piece of meat into his mouth. "I know you don't think we'll get out of here alive."

She turned her head to look at TK as he pulled the food apart and offered her pieces to eat.

"What makes you say that?"

He shrugged his shoulders, a motion that was so him. "Because I see the dark clouds in your eyes, and they are troubled. You've lost your faith."

"How can you not have doubts," she whispered, then took another sip of water with the next bit of food.

"Because when we get out of this place, I plan on marrying you. That is reason enough to make sure that we never stop putting one foot in front of the other."

She smiled. "Marrying me? Is this your formal proposal?"

"Oh no. I have a grand proposal planned. You'll be so embarrassed, but you'll smile and blush and love every moment of the attention you claim to hate," he said. Little butterflies took flight, and her heart felt lighter as TK continued. "I was thinking of a wedding on your dad's property. Do it right with a big old tent, and we'll invite all these assholes." TK nodded toward the group that was at different stages of eating or already sleeping. "Oh, and I was thinking Kyle could be the ring bearer. You'll look stunning walking down the runway in your sexy little mini dress and combat boots."

She stifled the laugh. "Okay, I think you've entered fantasy land."

TK smiled as he stared into her eyes, and slowly, they became seri-

ous. Reaching up, he ran his thumb over her cheek. "You don't even realize how beautiful you are. You steal my breath away."

She touched the large bandage covering the wound where shrapnel had hit her cheek. "Yes, I'm sure having your wife looking like she tried to pull the Joker on her face is exactly what you always dreamed."

TK grabbed her hand and linked their fingers together. She couldn't have stopped the swelling of her heart if she'd tried. They'd been friends for two years before Andrew pulled his porno act and announced his cheating to her and those closest to her. They'd remained friends for another year before they caved and started sleeping together. She realized before this mission that she was in love with TK, and it terrified her. Everything in her gut told her not to fall for him, but her gut and mind had no control over her heart, and it thumped hard for him.

"This scar should always be worn with pride. No, scratch that. All the scars from over here, whether we can see them or not, should be worn with pride, and never forget that." He leaned his forehead against hers. "I love you, Morrianna Waters, and when we get out of here, I am marrying you and never letting you go."

"I love you too."

The sound of something scratching woke her up. You didn't just wake up in the desert. You woke up prepared to fight. Her eyes snapped open, and even though it was still dark out, she could see the two camel spiders sitting on her chest. One of them was scratching at her top like it was trying to get at her stomach. Normally she could keep her shit together, but instead, she squealed as the second stepped up her chest toward her face. Morry jumped to her feet in a flash, and the relatively harmless spiders dropped to the ground and scurried away.

A hand grabbed her shoulder, and she jumped at the sudden

contact. "Morry, stay down. What are you doing," TK asked, his voice hushed.

She looked over her shoulder at his worried expression. "Shit, TK. Did you see that?" She pointed to the spot where the spiders had taken off. She looked back the way they had gone and shivered, rubbing her arms from the creepy sensation of having them sitting on her.

The whizzing sound was subtle, but the wet sensation that hit her in the back of her neck was not. Whipping around, she stared into TK's eyes and the hole in his neck. He grabbed at the wound as he went to his knees. She dropped to her knees with him.

"No, no, no...TK. Trev, I need you. Wolf? Anyone?" She placed her hand over the hole and pinched off the wound as best she could. Everyone stirred and came rushing over. "Don't you dare die on me. Don't you do it. I can fix this...I just need my bag. Trev, get me my kit," she ordered as TK grabbed her arm. His hand was bright red with his blood, and he squeezed her arm.

"Don't look at me like that. You can't propose and then die on me, dammit."

"I. Love. You."

The tears streamed down Morry's face, and her body shook as she tried to get the story out. Jeremy's eyes stung with unshed tears as the pain of her loss filled him as if it had been his own. He held her tight and let her cry it out.

"I stood up," she mumbled through the tears against his chest. "You don't stand up." Morry lifted her head, her eyes found his, and Jeremy's heart broke for her. Grabbing Morry under her arms, he pulled her up to kiss her lips, trembling and wet from her tears.

"It's not your fault, Morry. It's not your fault," he said.

"The universe is punishing me for getting him killed," she said as she gulped in a breath.

"Trust me, I don't think it works that way, but why do you think that?"

Morry wiped at the tears on her face like she was angry with them. "You know that new kid I asked you to take a look at tomorrow?"

"Yeah."

"His name is Stephen Kekewich," Morry said.

He still wasn't making the connection and waited for her to fill in the blanks. Running her hand through her hair, she sighed, and it sounded like the weight of the world was sitting squarely on her shoulders.

"TK stood for Tyler Kekewich. Stephen is his younger brother."

"Oh, damn."

"Yeah, oh fucking-damn."

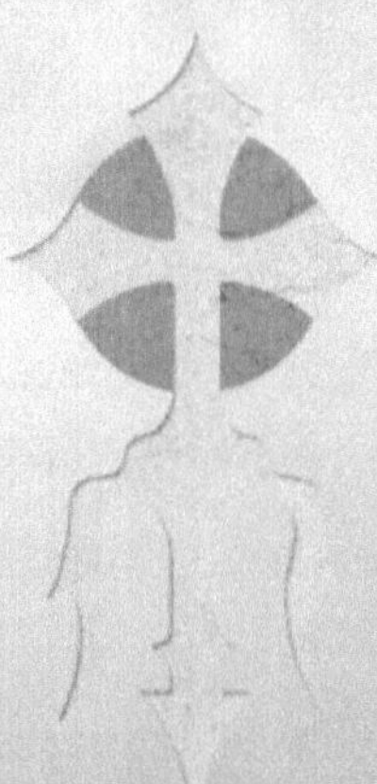

The sun shining in her eyes woke her up. Morry sat up straight and realized that, at some point, Jeremy had gotten them back to the Legion and put her in bed. She glanced around the room and didn't see any sign of him. She swung her legs over the side of the bed and reached for her phone. Holy shit, it was eleven in the morning. The worst part was that she wanted to lay back down, cover her head, and stay there.

If it weren't for all the people counting on her, that was what she would've done. Unfortunately, she wasn't the type of person who could slack or let her responsibilities slide. Last night had been all the moping she could afford.

Standing up, she stretched and grabbed a clean change of clothes before heading into the bathroom to get cleaned up.

Jeremy had definitely been here. The shower was still wet unless he managed to wash her without her knowing. Anything was possible last night.

She was stepping out of the shower refreshed when her door opened, and Jeremy stuck his head inside.

"Hey, how you feelin'?"

It was terrible, but she couldn't look him in the eye after crying all over him. She felt humiliated for allowing herself to break down like that. It never should've happened.

"I'm good. I've just been really tired, but I'm ready to get back at it. Any word from Judd?"

Jeremy stepped into the room and closed the door before leaning against it. She really didn't like this new, annoying, undeniably sexy, self-assured version of him. They were ground level, so she could just step out the window, but that seemed pretty extreme, even for her.

"What? I'm serious. I'm good," she said and tucked her tank top into her jeans.

"Is that so? Then why are you avoiding my eyes?"

Yup, he was definitely annoying. "I'm not avoiding," Morry said.

"Yeah, you are."

"Oh, for fuck's sake." She met Jeremy's gaze. "There, see. I looked you in the eye," she grumbled, looking around for her shit-kickers.

"They're in the closet," Jeremy said, and she stared at him over her shoulder.

"What are they doing in the closet?"

Jeremy crossed his arms over his chest. "My best guess, sitting there, but I could be wrong, and they decided to hold a kegger and invite some frat boys over. Boots these days." He smirked. She wanted to hit him and wipe that look off his face, but her body had other ideas as it lit up with his sarcastic wit. She was so fucked in the head.

"I like my boots by the bed," she mumbled as she opened the door and stared at the boots that were not only put away but were as clean as the day she got them. Peering around the door, she looked Jeremy up and down. "Did you scrub them?"

"And polished. I have this big hardass for a boss who likes shit to look clean, or I thought I did until I saw her room." He stared around her room like she had clothes thrown in every corner when there was only a single sweater that was out of place. She raised an eyebrow at him.

"Thanks." Grabbing the boots, she sat down and felt him coming closer. It felt like little tendrils of energy skimmed over her skin with each step he took. Jeremy sat beside her but didn't try to touch her, which was good. Something about him made her want to drag him back onto the bed, and she already had too many other excuses for hiding from the world.

"I know you're embarrassed," he said, her hand stilled while tying the knot in her laces.

"No, I'm—"

"Don't lie to me, Morry."

She finished tying her boots and then glared at Jeremy. It was much easier to be angry than accept these emotions. She didn't even know what to do with them. They were as foreign as learning a new language. It was like finding something old and dusty, and even once you got rid of the grime, you still had no idea what it was or how it worked.

"Fine, I'm a little embarrassed," she admitted and went to stand from the bed, but Jeremy grabbed her hand. "Jeremy, we have work to do."

"The shipment came in on time, and I double-checked the inventory. Everything arrived as ordered. I went and introduced myself to Stephen and told him that I would be his go-to for now and that you would be by soon to meet him. His drug of choice is oxy for pain, but I couldn't see an obvious wound. I did a sweep of his room to make sure that he didn't sneak anything onto the property, and he's currently helping peel potatoes."

Her eyes went wide as Jeremy continued and slowly pulled her so that she was standing between his legs.

"I called Judd to get an update on Wolf and Duke. He wasn't too happy it was me calling, but he was surprisingly more pleasant than normal. Duke is more lively, and Wolf should be cleared to travel tomorrow. Before you ask, I inspected the two rooms available in the medical wing and made sure one was set up and ready for their arrival. Oh, and there is a new prospect that Butch wants you to talk to before he gives the green light to bring him into the fold."

He slid his hands around her waist until he could grip her ass. "I also make a fucking mean coffee, and it just finished percolating. Have I told you how much I love your ass? God, it makes me so hard."

Morry was at a loss for words. Bending over, she cupped his

upturned face, and a flood of emotions continued to poke their heads from the sand in her heart. She loved that he had seemed to perfect the exact sexy amount of five o'clock shadow and that his eyes always begged her to kiss him. Morry dropped her lips to his, and a shiver traveled down her spine. It made her warm all over.

"Thank you. For letting me take a moment to breathe."

Jeremy reclaimed her lips and groaned as he pulled away and slowly stood. "If we don't leave the room now, there is a good chance we won't for a few more hours."

"Never heard of a quickie?"

"Not with my cock."

"Ohhh, I see."

They broke into laughter, and it felt so damn good to laugh. Even to smile had felt like another lifetime. When was the last time Morry truly let her guard down?

"You ready to face Stephen," he asked as the laughter died.

"If not now, then when? Let's do this, and then I need to make a few more calls about Kyle." She went to step away, but Jeremy wrapped an arm around her waist and pulled her back into his body.

Bending low, he whispered into her ear. "You never need to be embarrassed in front of me, not ever, no matter what." He laid his lips over the jumping pulse in her neck and then walked past to open the door.

It amazed her how he managed to soothe the snarly and untameable thing inside her. It was a feat that Andrew had never mastered, but TK always had the same effect.

"Oh hey, we were just coming to see you. What are you doing this far away from the kitchens," Jeremy asked.

Morry stepped out into the hall, and there he was, TK's brother. If she wasn't ready, too bad now. The meeting was forced down her throat. Stephen looked worried or strung out as he wrung his hands together, and his wide eyes darted around. She almost expected him to turn and run. He certainly wouldn't have been the first to try it, and she was positive he wouldn't be the last.

"Oh, I...ah, um...I was looking for the washroom, and then I kinda got lost. And then...."

"You thought you might come to this wing and see if you can find where we store the meds. Maybe some oxy, perhaps," Jeremy asked.

Morry glanced up at Jeremy. Not long ago, he skulked around the halls, looking for a way to escape in more ways than one. Now his eyes were firm but kind, and Jeremy had grown into a man who had found his inner strength. It shone through in everything he did, which was why she would have him take over in a few more years. He was a natural-born leader.

"What? No, no, I wouldn't. I..." Stephen tried, but by the look on his face, he knew he'd been caught with this hand in the proverbial cookie jar. She knew Stephen was around ten years younger than TK, but he looked barely older than Jeremy.

"Let's set some ground rules, Stephen," Morry said.

When Stephen's eyes found her, he rounded his shoulders and put his hands in his pockets. He looked defeated. It was a look she hated. You would never survive this world if you curled up in a ball and hoped all the bad stuff would disappear.

"So, the first rule of being here is that you don't lie. Lying gets you punished, and trust me. It's never something you'll enjoy. The second rule is that you don't wander over to the Legion Club House unless you want your clock cleaned and maybe your cock cut off. All the bouncers are professionally trained and would love a reason to eat you alive." She took a step closer.

"Lastly, and this third rule is very important. We are a no-tolerance facility with stricter rules than the world you left behind. If you're caught stealing or somehow find a way to get your hands on product, and you take it, then you'd better be prepared for the next ninety-six hours of your life to be worse than if you'd died and were strung up in hell. If you thought the Army was bad, you'd better think again. I've thought up worse things than they would ever dare to imagine." She stepped forward, and Stephen straightened his back, his hands going to his sides. That was a much better posture, and it was good to see that he hadn't lost the will to fight yet.

"Do I make myself clear, soldier?"

"Ma'am, yes, ma'am."

"Don't call me ma'am. It makes me sound like an old lady," Morry ordered.

Stephen didn't look much like his brother. He was at least four inches shorter than TK, putting him just a little taller than herself. They both had brown hair, but Stephen's was a softer color than the dark rich locks his brother had. They had almost identical jawlines, but the biggest difference was the hazel eyes staring back at her. TK had eyes similar to Jeremy's. So blue that it seemed impossible for them to be real, and TK always held every emotion he felt in their depths. He couldn't hide anything to save his soul and sucked at poker for the same reason. She loved how she could see what he felt when he looked at her.

"Sir, yes, sir," Stephen said.

She stepped forward and got right up in his face so that their noses were touching. This would've seemed aggressive to the outside world, but they were honed and fine-tuned to understand, crave, and need authority. Even though the Army turned its back on her when they returned from the mission that had stolen her soul, she couldn't help craving orders and hearing someone yell her name. It was stupid things like the random checks of their rooms, making sure that her shit was in order, to wearing a uniform every day that she'd missed.

"Is that all you have, soldier?"

"No, Sir," he said louder.

She looked over her shoulder, and Jeremy lifted a shoulder, then held his hand up and wiggled it, showing that he thought the effort was okay but not great. "One more chance, soldier. Do you understand me?"

"Sir. Yes, sir."

"Very good. I'm Morry and Jeremy here, or I will be your living nightmare until...well until you're ready to leave with a fresh start in life or in a body bag. There is no in-between. Mess is that way. Get back to work."

"Sir, yes, sir."

"Dismissed."

She waited until Stephen was halfway down the hallway before calling his name. "Oh, and Stephen?"

He spun around like she'd physically pulled on an invisible line.

"If you're ever caught where you're not supposed to be again, oxy will be the least of your concerns. I want to make sure I'm very clear about this with you. If need be, you'll never see outside of this compound again."

She could see his Adam's apple work as he swallowed, and the fear in his eyes was real. Good, he better be scared. If he was afraid to die, there was hope for him.

"Get out of my sight."

Stephen turned and marched away so quickly he might as well have jogged. Putting her hands on her hips, she took a deep breath. One of the things she hadn't wanted to do today was out of the way—time to take on the others. Jeremy had wandered over and casually leaned against the wall, staring at Stephen's receding back.

"Was I that transparent and pathetic when I arrived?"

"Worse." She snorted and smiled. It really did seem like forever ago now.

He slowly turned his head, the corner of his mouth pulling up. "Ouch, but fair. I did spend my first week here in solitary, screaming about aliens."

"Oh, the aliens were real," she said, and they chuckled.

His face grew serious. "I'm not sure I've ever really thanked you for what you did for me, but...."

"No need to thank me. It's why this place is here. Besides, it's Dean you should be thanking."

"Trust me, I have. Speaking of Dean...." Jeremy stopped as her phone rang, and she pulled it out of her pocket to see her lawyer's name.

"I have to take this, but we will talk later." She took a couple of strides toward her office and looked over her shoulder. "Keep an eye on him. I have a feeling he's going to be trouble. Call it a hunch." Giving Jeremy a wink, she hit answer.

"Carson?"

"Hello, Morry," her lawyer said.

She wasn't sure what it was about lawyers, but they all had the same tone. It wasn't quite as bad as accountants, where you were sure some sort of soul-sucking creature had come along and stolen all of their personality, but it was pretty damn close.

"I'm assuming if you're calling, you have good news?"

"I'm afraid not. The fight is not lost, but we had a surprise that didn't help our cause." Carson sighed, and she knew that whatever was coming wouldn't be anything she liked.

"Is it true that you stayed at the Wellness Springs when you got back from overseas for six months?"

Morry swallowed hard and slowly sat down. Mentally she hadn't been in a good place when she arrived home. Morry wasn't proud of her actions, but it was years ago, and she wasn't the same person who'd tried to take her own life. There was a reason why Morry connected so easily with the demons that lived inside those who came here. She'd suffered her demons and fought them every day when the faces of those she loved and lost would toy with her mind.

"No one was supposed to ever find out about that. I didn't even tell Andrew," she said, and she could almost feel the glare through the phone.

"Well, it would've been nice to be prepared, Morry. We looked like idiots in front of the judge today."

"Where did the information come from?" She couldn't stop staring at the picture of Kyle on her desk. He was dressed in a T-ball uniform and was smiling for the camera with a tooth missing.

"The defense says that it came from an anonymous source, but they did their research and found out that you stayed there for attempted suicide and PTSD episodes that caused violent hallucinations. As I'm sure you can imagine, they didn't paint you in the best light. They now have that you are a dishonorably discharged vet who is the leader of a motorcycle club on the FBI's watch list for gun trafficking, and now this. You are not helping me win your case, Morry. I need something positive. I need things to combat these allegations." There was the sound of feet and more sighing, and she could picture the older man perfectly. He sounded just like her father did when he was disappointed in her.

"Like what? I can't say what happened overseas, or I'll be up on charges with the Army because we were all sworn to secrecy. I run a motorcycle club, and I won't tell you what we do for plausible deniability, but it's not to give candy to those who shouldn't have it."

"Candy? Really?"

"You know what I mean. As for Wellness Springs, I did go there because of the shit that I went through overseas, which I also can't tell them about, but needing help is not a crime, and I shouldn't be looked down on because I had to get help for what I was going through." She gripped the frame of Kyle and held it to her chest as she walked over to the window. "I'm a good mom, Carson, and I do a lot of good for this world, including now running my rehab clinic."

"Which is unlicensed. I don't even dare bring that up. Look, I have four days to come up with a new plan of attack, but Morry, I need some ammunition. Like real bullets here."

"Are you telling me to shoot him," she teased, but there was no laugh from the other end of the line. "Okay, that might have been a bit dark, but can you blame me?"

"I'm doing my best, Morry, but you're not making my life easy. Right or wrong, Andrew looks better on paper. It's really that simple. Now you could wait the two years until he turns sixteen, then Kyle can apply for emancipation."

"No, no, no. Carson, for fuck's sake, Kyle is sick. He may not even live through the next six months, let alone wait two years, to be able to see my son. He needs his mother, and...shit, I need him. I'm not settling for waiting two years. I can tell you that," she growled into the phone as her anger over this entire situation burned in her gut.

"Morry, don't do anything stupid or that you can't come back from. There are just some things I won't be able to defend."

"Trust me, Carson, if I decided to do something stupid, no one would ever know," she said.

"Well, hasn't this been a comforting conversation? I don't

want to know. That's all I'm going to say. In the meantime, get me anything you think I can use to help you. It has to be legal, and it has to show your character as a good mother."

How had it become that she needed to defend being Kyle's mother? No one could ever say she was a terrible mother, not even Andrew. He didn't like the environment, but he hadn't been able to drudge up one terrible thing she'd ever done to Kyle. She really hated the justice system sometimes, especially since it was run by stuffy old men who sided with other men. She was behind the eight ball before this fight even started.

"Fine, I will see what I can come up with."

Morry hung up and leaned against the window frame to stare outside. Without even thinking about it, she dialed Dean's number. It rang that standard four times and went to voicemail.

"You have reached Sandbox Landscaping. We are busy at the moment but leave your name and number, and we will get back to you."

Beep

"Hey, Dean, it's me. Listen, I need to talk to you. I...I don't know what to do and need an ear that knows all the shit of the shit. Can you call me back when you get this?"

Hanging up the phone, she gripped the photo hard to her chest. No one was keeping her away from Kyle. If she had to take drastic measures to keep her son—then she would do whatever it took.

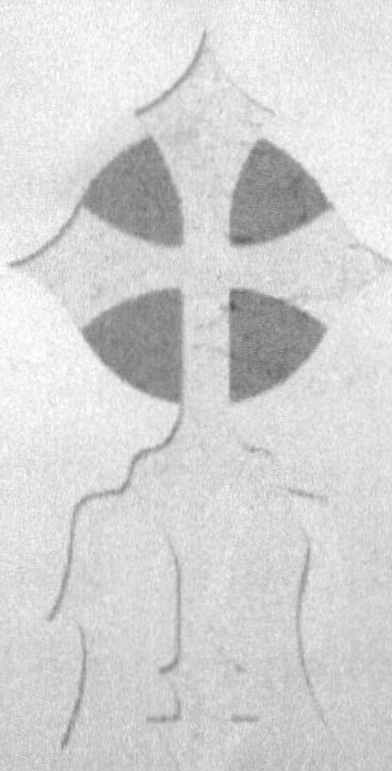

CHAPTER 18

Morry followed behind the small group of runners as they trudged over the hot desert sand. There were record highs today, and two of the four patients were lagging. One of those two happened to be Stephen. She watched him run and had no idea how he made it through Bootcamp, let alone all the other daily drills. From the moment Morry brought them out to Buzzard Point, he looked like a lame dog.

He slowed to a walk, his hands on his hips, then bent over and threw up. Stopping the Hummer, she hopped out and went to check on Stephen. The other three paused and looked back, but she waved them on.

"What's wrong, soldier?"

"I'm having trouble breathing," he said, but Stephen wasn't wheezing or gasping. There wasn't even a rattle or gravelly sound.

She narrowed her eyes at Stephen. "What was your injury, soldier?"

"What," he asked and stood up straight. Morry watched his chest rise, calculating his breaths in her head.

"You heard me. What was your injury? Your intake form says that you were injured in the line of duty, and that's how you got hooked on oxy. Unless, of course, that's a lie." She crossed her arms over her chest as Stephen stepped back and looked from side to side. He was definitely a runner. The question was, what was he running from exactly?

"Why would I lie about that," Stephen asked, his voice rising with anger.

"I'm not sure yet, but something isn't adding up. If you're not lying, then show me your wound."

"No, I don't have to do that," he said.

Just like the night Jeremy arrived, she acted. Morry was on him before he knew what was happening—with a maneuver that would have impressed Macho Man Randy Savage—she picked Stephen up and slammed him down hard on his back with her knee on his chest. The knife she kept in her boot pressed firmly to his throat.

"Maybe I didn't make myself clear when we spoke earlier, and this will be the last time I talk to you about manners. I have a three-strikes-you're-dead policy, and you're already on number two. I must say, that is a record." His hand flinched, and she glanced at the fist he made. "I wouldn't do that if I were you unless you like dying by choking on your blood."

Stephen's eyes were wide but angry. There was more going on, and she would bet everything she had that he washed out. He washed out because he was using and probably had been before he even stepped foot on the army base. There was no way this guy had completed Bootcamp unless they'd lowered their standards, which she highly doubted.

"I know you're lying to me. One look at your face tells me all I need to know. So how about we start with the truth, and then I'll decide what to do with you." She leaned close to his face, and the anger shifted to fear as she stared into his eyes. Her gaze never wavered. "I'm not joking when I say you'll leave in a body bag. The vultures around here are used to me leaving them bones to feed from, and they conveniently carry parts of the bodies away to their nests. Doesn't that sound fun, to become a bone for a bird's young to shit on? You wouldn't be the first who thought I played by the rules. Out here, Stephen, there are no rules."

He winced as he swallowed, and the knife scraped against his throat.

"Yes or no. Are you really Stephen Kekewich?"

"Yes."

"Did you join the army?"

"Yes."

"Were you taking drugs when you joined? Maybe your parents sent you, hoping to straighten you out?"

He swallowed again, and that was all the answer she needed, but she waited for him to say the words.

"Yes or no, Stephen."

"Yes."

"Did you really get injured, or did you wash out and get sent packing?"

His eyes flicked away from hers. "Packing."

She lifted the knife slightly from his throat.

"Bonus question. How did you find out about this place or me? It's not exactly like I advertise."

His eyes met hers again. "Everyone on the base knows about you. They didn't know where you were but knew the place existed. It took me a couple of months to find you."

Morry pushed herself up and off his chest, removing the knife, and stepped back until she could lean against the Hummer. The blade spun in her hand and glinted in the bright sunlight.

"Why come find me? If you really wanted to get clean and sober, you should've stayed in the Army."

Stephen slowly sat up and rubbed at the spot on his neck where her knife had been moments ago.

"I had a brother, and he was in the army. He was all my parents ever talked about. They literally have a shrine built. At least, that's what it felt like. When shit got bad at home, I decided to join too. I don't know, maybe to make them proud or maybe to feel close to my brother again." He draped his hands over his knees and looked down at the sand.

Morry wanted to tell him she knew his brother and what Tyler had meant to her, but she kept her mouth shut. There was no telling what Tyler had told his family about her. She'd never been around when he talked to them, and it was best to keep powerful knowledge like that to herself for now. Just because he was Tyler's brother didn't make him Tyler or trustworthy. So far, Stephen had proven to be anything but.

"My brother died overseas, and they didn't even bring his body home. He was just left there like disposable trash. It devastated my parents, but they were so proud of him. Tyler, the hero," he mocked.

She so badly wanted to say that he hadn't been left like trash, that he'd been loved and he was mourned over and they said prayers and cover his body as best they could. She still had his dog tags in her jewelry box. But she couldn't say any of those things.

"I was in the army less than six months when they kicked me out, and I just couldn't go home. I'd heard about you and thought maybe this place would set me straight."

Morry laughed, and Stephen gave her a confused look.

"It's not the place or the people that set you straight, Stephen. It's you. If you're looking for some miracle way to stop using without putting in the work...." Pulling her gun, she fired.

Stephen yelled and jumped as the bullet whizzed past him. He turned around and stared at the spot she'd just shot, blinking as he stared at the massive scorpion inches from his hand.

"Then you better think again. Everything out here wants to kill you and rip the flesh from your bones, including the men in the club and me. You want to survive? You want a new lease on life? Then you, Stephen, better be prepared to work harder than you've ever worked before, or next time, the bullet will be for you, and I'll let the scorpions have you."

"Can I ask where you got that nasty scar on your face?"

Morry's eyes narrowed on Stephen. She was used to people asking about what had happened and then doing the *oh, you poor thing* or exclaiming how scary that must have been. She'd also caught people staring, but to have someone ask and be so blatantly rude was new.

Turning her head to the side, she ran her thumb along the long scar. Every time she touched it, she was reminded of the pain, forced to sit still while Wolf sewed her face back together. She could still feel the sharp prick of the metal piercing her skin. No matter what she did or how hard she tried to forget, the scar on her face was a constant reminder of what had happened.

"I got this playing pinochle," she said and shrugged.

"You got that playing a card game?"

"No, but it's also none of your fucking business." She lifted a shoulder and let it drop.

Morry pushed away from the Hummer, and the sun had shifted enough that she was casting a long shadow over Stephen. "Now get the fuck up and start jogging again."

She had to give him some credit when he jumped to his feet and began jogging without another word. Morry strolled to her open door and jumped inside just as the phone in the Hummer rang.

"Call incoming from a secure line, Crosshairs," Lady Luck said.

"Answer call." The phone connected with the standard click, letting her know they were indeed on a scrambled line. "Hey, Trev, I have no news on Wolf."

"Hello, Morry. Although that is good to hear, it is not why I called." His tone was serious, even for Trev, which couldn't be good.

"What is one more crap thing on the list of crap things? Lay it on me. What bad news do you have?"

"There are a couple of things we need to discuss, but I'm unsure whether it is safe to talk on the phone."

That made her raise her eyebrows. Since when was a secure line not good enough?

"Okay, then why call at all? Why not just show up?"

The line went quiet, and she checked the dash to see if she was still connected.

"Fine, I will ask what I can. Did you just receive a new shipment of goods?"

She glared at the dash like he could see her. "How the hell do you know that? I mean, I know your stalking skills are impeccable, but that's impressive, even for you."

"It brings me no joy to tell you this, but the customer those were supposed to go to is no longer in business. Technically, they were never in business, at least for what you thought they were in business for."

"Trev, just tell me what the hell is going on. I hate it when you turn things into convoluted guessing games."

The snicker on the other end of the line was a dead giveaway that he was amused. Trev was one of the nicest men she'd ever met, with a dry wit and scary smart. He was also so hyper-focused that it could become a bit much.

"Very well. World Deeds is not the company you thought it

was. It was a shell corporation for the Golden Dragons. At first, I thought they were just a gang, but they are far more sophisticated than that. They run drugs, guns, and people. They have everything from judges, police officers, doctors, politicians, you name it, involved for different reasons. The point is that the goods you've been selling them have been hitting the street and not going where you thought."

Her mouth fell open, and she had to let go of the gas pedal, or she really was going to run over Stephen.

"I'm sorry, what the fuck?"

"Yes, it was quite a shock as well, but that isn't even the best part," Trev said.

Her mind was still reeling from the first lot of information. She couldn't comprehend more of the same.

"Once we traced the company back to the original roots, we came up with two other overseers. The first is Kes's company or his father's old company. The second is a cartel, but more specifically, one in particular. One which we happen to know the leader's son."

"Are you fucking with me right now, Trev? If you are, this is not very nice."

"I'm afraid not," Trev drawled.

"So you're telling me that all this time I've been selling goods to the bad guys, and then to top it off, the asshole who made our friend's life a living hell is behind it all? What are the fucking chances?"

"Yes, my sentiments exactly. I do not believe in coincidences,

Morry. I never have. I think we are all being played, but I'm just not sure who is pulling the strings. Also, you should know that I'm having Wolf's Hummer towed to a special compound where I'll have a team go over the vehicle."

"That's smart. I wish I'd thought of that, but I was more concerned about getting away from the scene before we were caught there."

"Let me ask you something. Did you see anyone else at the site other than Wolf?"

Okay, that was an odd question. "No, why?"

"I'm not comfortable sharing that when we aren't in person. I'll be out as soon as I can, and hopefully, I'll have the results from the Hummer as well."

"Trev, you really need to work on your fun, lighthearted calls," she said. Trev laughed before hanging up.

Well, that meant no fucking income this month. Morry needed to find someone else wanting weapons that wouldn't let them end up on the street. Not that the club technically needed it. Morry was very strategic with the money over the years, and they had millions stashed away, but it took a lot to keep a place like this running.

Morry couldn't help wondering if Dean knew what his father was doing. She was positive he would be pissed and out for blood if he did. Dean hated that man. He'd only ever told her bits and pieces of what was done to him, but even that was horrific and terrifying.

It was well past dark by the time Stephen finally made it back to the property's gates. Morry had watched him slowly weave between the Hummer's headlights for the last few miles like he'd been out drinking all night. The question became, what should she do with this guy? He was technically ex-military and Tyler's brother, so Morry felt compelled to help him, but she could tell he was used to lying and getting what he wanted. That was a dangerous combo. You could never fully trust chronic liars. And now she felt like she would have to do a deep dive just to make sure that anything he told her was the whole truth.

This was the last fucking thing she needed right now. She felt like throwing her hands up in the air and saying, *not my circus, not my monkey*, then walking away. The large gates opened, and the guards on duty nodded as she passed with Stephen, now walking and dragging his leg like a zombie. Once the gates were closed, she veered around him and parked.

"Lady Luck, lockdown."

"Lockdown mode initialized."

Placing two fingers in her mouth, she whistled a loud shrill sound that had everyone looking in her direction.

"Avery and Jeff, get over here," she called as Stephen collapsed to his knees and then landed face-first in the dirt.

"Boss," the two chimed together like a pair of parrots.

"Throw Stephen here in the showers and make sure he's moderately rinsed off before putting him in his room. You know the drill." She looked down at the guy, who was breathing but very clearly passed out at her feet. "Tomorrow, I want him working in the gardens all day," she said, marching toward her office.

Morry paused, looking over her shoulder to see Avery and Jeff pick up Stephen under the arms and drag him away. Just before they made it through the doors, she would've sworn that his eyes opened and met her own. Then they stepped inside, out of her sight.

Too many problems. She had way too many fucking problems.

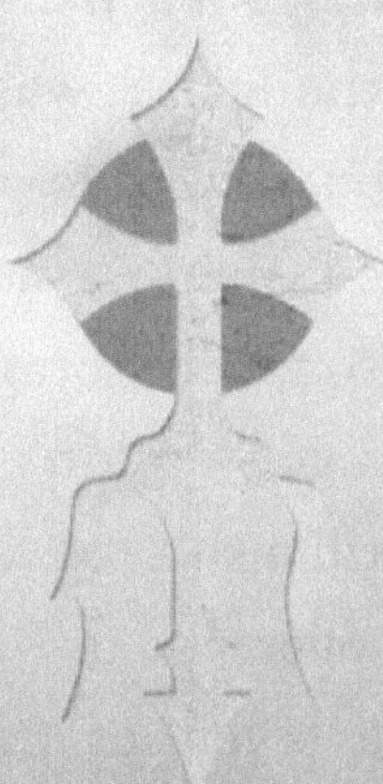

Chapter 19

Like the day before, Morry woke up, and Jeremy wasn't in bed. Even though she hadn't invited him, he managed to talk his way into her room last night. If Morry was being honest, it hadn't taken a whole lot of talking when he showed up with no shirt on and a bottle of her favorite wine.

Morry could hear the motorcycles before stepping outside, and it filled her with joy. The deep rumble always felt right and sent a shot of adrenaline through her veins. Of course, Judd was riding in front with the newest sweetbutt sitting behind him like he was the king of a parade. All he needed to do was lift his hand and wave to complete the look.

She nodded to the men as they drove past and waited for The

Bus to pull up. It was black, like everything else she owned, and she had to admit it looked fucking fierce with all the additions.

It had massive ramming bars on the front that were welded right to the frame. The side panels had all been swapped out for bulletproof metal, and the glass was army-grade. Very few weapons could stop this bus, exactly what Morry had been after when it was outfitted. The inside was as good as a hospital room when needed. It only had so much storage space for essentials like blood or medications, and you couldn't operate if you needed to keep moving, but it was still a shit ton better than what they had been using when she took over.

The old leader had a seventies Cadillac. He would throw people in the back seat and hope they made it to wherever they were heading, usually some veterinarian, to have the guys stitched up. She burned that Caddy with the old leader in the trunk.

The bus hissed as it came to a halt, and the doctor opened the back door as she walked around to greet him.

"How are the patients," she asked as Duke limped toward the door. He was putting a little bit of weight on his leg now, and she smiled widely at his furry face.

"They are both doing better," Henry said, hopping down from the bus as two nurses unlocked Wolf's stretcher from the holders in the floor. "Duke, as you can see, is starting to get around better, and his appetite has increased. I swear he could chow down as much as a horse." She smirked at the statement as she picked the dog up and set him on the ground so he didn't have to jump. "I've stopped administering the drugs that were keeping Wolf in the coma, and he should come around at some point today. The drive last night was long but smooth."

"Why are you here so early? I didn't expect you until later this afternoon."

"No, you unhook it over there and then flip the lock to the side," Henry barked at the guy, still fumbling with the lock on the stretcher. Shaking his head, he turned his attention back to her. "Judd said it was safer to travel at night. Less traffic and fewer people to remember a large procession of motorcycles passing."

The nurses moved Wolf's bed to the back of the bus, and she gripped a corner as Henry grabbed the other side. Between the four of them, they got the stretcher on the ground. Wolf looked much better with the extra days of rest and meds. His coloring was back to normal, and his hands were clenched into fists like he was already pissed off and ready to jump from the bed, even while he slept.

"I have his room ready in the medical wing. You can head on in. I need to go speak with Judd," she said, squeezing the doctor's arm before she left.

It was going to be another hot one. It was barely eight, and Morry could feel the heat pressing down on her as she walked to the Legion clubhouse. She could hear the deep laughter of the men who had returned. The music was already blaring, and she knew that by the time the clock struck noon, they would all be hammered and lying around the clubhouse or having sex against a wall.

Usually, women weren't allowed in church, and she definitely shouldn't have been allowed in the clubhouse when they were busy partying with the sweetbutts. Morry'd laid out the men who tried to tell her that tits didn't make her as much of a man as they were.

Morry walked through and never batted an eye at the shit they got up to unless some idiot brought drugs onto her property. She'd shot people for less, and they all knew it. They could drink all they wanted, smoke all they wanted, and fuck whoever they wanted—other than patients—but don't ever bring drugs onto Legion property unless you wanted to be gutted alive.

Pushing through the door, she spotted Jeremy near the bar, talking to Butch while a couple of the newer girls worked at getting his attention. He turned and smiled at them. She was too far away to hear what was said, but it didn't matter. The rage and jealousy were instant and burned like she'd stepped into the middle of a boiling pot of acid. He held up his fingers, signaling the bartender to get two drinks for them, and that was all she could stomach.

Andrew had ruined her. She'd barely been able to find it in herself to trust TK, and it only happened because he spent every waking moment with her and walked by her side through the literal bowels of hell.

She'd known that this was inevitable. She knew it, and she still made a move, so she had no one to blame but herself for the stab of pain she felt in her chest. Marching across the floor, Morry pushed through the first large door and then the second that took her into the bike storage and mechanic's area. Judd was helping the driver of the bus back into place. Waiting until it was parked, she walked over, and he smiled widely.

"Hey, sexy boss lady." He wrapped his arm around her shoulder and gave her a one-armed hug. "I hope you haven't been too lonely without me," he said. This was his standard line to all the women. The only difference was that he added *boss* to her title.

"I need to speak to you over here for a minute." She nodded toward the back of the shop area as a couple of others milled around to work on their bikes.

"Oh, now we are talkin'," he said and slapped her ass.

She glared up at him. "Don't fucking do that again," she growled through her clenched teeth.

There was no reason to feel bad. Jeremy had decided that she was not enough, but she couldn't just fuck someone else for the sake of it when she had emotions involved. Stupid fucking emotions. This was why she didn't want to get involved. There was no time to worry about relationship drama in her life.

"Sorry, bad habit," he said, but his tone was way too jovial for an apology.

Leaning her shoulder against the wall, she waited until he mirrored her position and stopped waving or winking at whoever wandered into his line of sight.

"Earth to Judd," she drawled, her voice dripping with sarcasm.

"Oh, yeah, sorry. I need a coffee, way too much sex, and booze."

"Too much info. Look, I need to ask you for a favor," Morry said, and of course, Judd's face lit up, and he put his hand on her shoulder.

"Of course. Where do you want it?"

Morry glared at his hand, and he quickly removed it.

"Not that kind of favor. I swear you have a one-track mind sometimes." She sighed and crossed her arms over her chest. "I need you to head out tomorrow on a mission for me."

His face sobered. "Mission. What kind are we talking?"

Judd knew what she did for the Righteous, though he didn't know their names or who was involved. She'd taken him for a few tougher jobs that needed a wall of muscle and a mouth that would stay shut. Those were two things Judd was good at despite his other shortcomings.

"Not for my other job. This is a personal favor. Remember Maeve?"

"Um, I remember hot ass better than anything else. I'm still pissed I couldn't get inside her pants. That girl has the perfect bubble butt that I want to...sorry, too much info. Yes, I remember. Go on."

She lifted a brow at him. At least he had the decency to look somewhat embarrassed as his cheeks reddened.

"I need you to go to Vegas and see if you can pick up her trail."

"What?"

"Look, she was supposed to be back weeks ago, and it has been radio silent. Maeve can handle herself, and I know she tends to go off the rails and party too hard, but this is different. She never misses this many check-ins, and I'm concerned."

Judd rubbed the back of his neck. "Shit, boss. Are you just trying to get rid of me? I promise to play nice with the kid."

"His name is Jeremy, not kid, and that's not the reason."

Morry pictured what Jeremy was most likely doing inside the bar with those two sweetbutts and her hands clenched into fists.

She needed to wipe the idea that Jeremy was more than a few nights of amazing sex, or blood would be spilled. Pinching the bridge of her nose, she wrangled in the out-of-control rage. Judd placed his hand on her shoulder again. When she looked up into his eyes this time, all she saw was concern.

"You okay, boss?"

"I will be. Look, this would alleviate a shit ton of stress for me. I know you've got friends all over the place, and I could use someone I trust on this." She sighed, and Judd's hand slipped from her shoulder.

"Okay, but I can't leave tomorrow. Remember, I have a meeting with the Desert Devils, and I'm booked to have...you know...that test you need to have done every couple of years," Judd said, his voice no more than a whisper.

"You mean a physical?"

"Shhhh, don't say that too loud. Don't need the guys thinkin' I have shit wrong with me." He puffed out his chest and grunted to one of the guys pushing his bike to the service area.

"I doubt very highly they'd think something was wrong with you, but fine, I'll keep it on the down low. I actually forgot about the Desert Devils, and that meeting has to happen. Okay, let's aim for the day after tomorrow, then."

"All right, boss. I'll take a small handful of guys with me, and we will see what we can find."

"Thanks, Judd." Morry pushed away from the wall, and before she knew what was happening, Judd grabbed her and hugged her.

"Woman, you take on way too much shit," he whispered in her ear before letting go and walking away.

Her eyes followed Judd as he marched off across the concrete floor. Then she saw Jeremy, who had stepped inside the shop area. He was glaring at Judd and then at her. Good, let him think whatever he wanted. Morry headed for the other end of the long building, away from Jeremy.

Jeremy stepped into the shop, looking for Morry. He was pretty sure that she'd come through the bar. It had taken him forever to pawn the new girls flirting with him off on a couple of the other guys without being rude. Other guys would've just walked away, but his mother had been big on manners, and despite the shit that went down between him and his parents, those lessons stuck.

Of course, he walked in to see Judd pull Morry into a hug and for her to go along with it like old times. His hand went to the knife at his hip. He was going to murder Judd. Jeremy could already picture the concrete red with Judd's blood as he slit his throat open. The embrace was brief, but that didn't matter. The man had touched what was his, and Morry had let him. A rumble escaped his chest as he swore under his breath. Judd didn't head to the bar, which was a good thing. He was way too amped up and would've at least removed a body part—such as the cock between his legs—if he'd come any closer.

Jeremy looked back to the wall where Morry had been standing, but she was gone. He scanned the large building as the far door opened, letting in bright sunlight. Morry's silhouette was like a beacon before the door closed in her wake. Oh, hell no. He stomped outside and felt like a fucking stalker as he walked across the wide-open area that divided the Legion club from the rest of the property. She made him feel crazy.

She slipped between two outbuildings, and Jeremy knew she was heading for the breezeway that took her to her office. He started jogging and left Morry's trail to head her off instead. Sure enough, as Jeremy pushed through the door that led to the far section of the building, he could hear Morry talking on her phone. He stepped into an alcove so she wouldn't be able to see him.

"Get me all the information you can on that group Liberte and send it to my email asap," she said.

He waited until she walked past and grabbed her by the arm, yanking her into the small space with him.

"Jesus. Fucking. Christ," she swore as he pushed her up against the wall trapping her. "Jeremy, what the fuck? Are you trying to give me a heart attack? And what the hell are you doing slinking around—"

He didn't let her finish and dropped his lips to hers. Gripping her hands in both of his, he lifted them above her head as his other hand untucked her tank top and slid up her body until he could roll a nipple between his fingers. He gave it a rough squeeze, and Morry sucked in a ragged breath.

"I thought I told you no more Judd," he growled against her lips.

She glared at him, her eyes fierce with steely anger in her gray eyes. "And I thought I told you no more sweetbutts. Just get away from me, Jeremy. I don't have time for this." She gave his hands a hard push, but he held firm. If she really wanted to break his hold, she would have to hurt him 'cause he wasn't letting go.

"I already told you. I don't want them, and I wasn't the one feeling up Judd."

Her eyes narrowed at him, and for a moment, he thought she would follow through and hurt him.

"I wasn't doing anything like that, and I do have to speak to him. He is still my number two. Why the hell am, I explaining myself to you? I wasn't the one who was letting sweetbutts paw me up while ordering them drinks."

"I didn't let them touch me, and I got them the drinks and got out of there only to find you with Judd."

"Okay, this is stupid. We're arguing around in a circle," Morry said, and he agreed.

"Yeah, but fuck, you're hot when you're angry and jealous." Jeremy nipped at her ear and felt her resistance dissolve. Grabbing her hand, he pulled her from the shallow alcove and around the corner to the storage closet.

"Jeremy, what the hell are you doing," Morry asked as he closed them in and locked the door.

He cupped her mouth and kissed her hard as he pushed her to the back of the deep storage area. It was dark, but he could still see her well enough from the light shining in the narrow window at the top of the door. Jeremy broke the kiss to pull his T-shirt off and toss it on one of the racks. He did the same with Morry's and loved that she lifted her arms for him.

"We don't have time for this, and I'm still pissed with you," she mumbled before he attacked her mouth again.

No matter what words came out of her mouth, he knew she wanted him. He could taste her need on her tongue and felt it in her fingers as they raked over his skin.

"You have no reason to be pissed with me." He grabbed her short, sexy hair and pulled her head back, exposing her neck for him. "I'm not Andrew. You need to stop dragging that baggage with you and dropping it at my feet." She panted in his hold as he nibbled and licked a wet line up the side of her neck. "I only want you," Jeremy whispered in her ear, and fucking loved it when she shuddered against his body like the words physically touched her.

"I'm trying, but you need not be jealous of Judd. I made a promise, too. I keep my promises."

She did have a point. Jeremy hadn't seen her once break a promise she'd made to anyone. But he still wanted to punish her. "True, but you let him touch you. I told you I would kill him if he touched you again. So you can get on your knees and suck my cock, or I hunt him down. It's your choice."

"When did you become such an asshole," she asked, but there was no anger in the question, only heat.

"I always have been, but I had a very special teacher who helped me reach my potential." He kissed her hard, his tongue tasting and exploring her mouth. He loved that she tasted like her morning coffee and minty from brushing her teeth. Jeremy released his hold on her hair.

"Now, get on your knees."

Morry stared at him for a moment, and he couldn't decipher

the look in her eyes. And even though he'd ordered her to do it, he was still shocked when she grabbed the button on his jeans and sank to the ground. There was no stopping the shiver that traveled through his body as she released his hard cock from the confines of his jeans.

"Oh fuck," he groaned as her hot mouth teased the end of his cock.

She slid her lips over the head, then drew back, releasing him from her mouth. The feel of her tongue swirling on the tip had his hands finding her hair once more.

"Don't tease me. I just...Oh, fuck yes," Jeremy mumbled, as inch by inch, he slipped into her mouth.

He was stretching her mouth wide, and she made little gagging sounds when he reached the back of her throat, but the sound was such a turn-on that he pulled out and thrust back into her mouth until she made it again.

Gripping her hair he fucked her mouth, and growled having to hold back enough that he didn't hurt her, but god damn she felt so good. His pace quickened as he took all his pent-up anger out on her sweet mouth. Morry suddenly pulled free of his cock, and he almost growled at her like an animal, except she dipped lower, and he gasped as she sucked his tight balls into her mouth while her hand stroked him at a blinding pace.

"Oh fuck, oh fuck, oh fuck," were the only words he could get out as the orgasm churned.

Jeremy was ready to blow, and as he opened his mouth to warn her that he was seconds away from coming, she pulled her mouth back and gripped him hard with both hands. It was the final straw. He leaned against the wall and groaned as he came hard. His cock unloaded like it had been weeks and not just hours earlier that he'd fucked her until he couldn't stand.

"So fucking good," Jeremy panted and opened his eyes to look down at Morry. "Oh God, you look stunning like that," he said as he took in the streams of come sliding down her chest and over her tits. "Can I take a picture?"

One eyebrow rose. "No fucking way," she said.

Jeremy smirked. One day, he would get his picture.

Reaching out, he grabbed a towel and handed it to her to clean herself off. Luckily, a dirty laundry bin was in the corner, and he tossed it in when she was finished.

"You planning to finish the job," she asked, and he knew exactly what she meant. He never left her unsatisfied, but this wouldn't be much of a punishment if he did that.

"Nope. You have to stew about what you did," Jeremy said as Morry slowly rose to her feet.

He softly tweaked the hard nipples, begging him to stay here a little longer and fuck her. He was beyond tempted, but he corralled his desire. He was never satisfied very long before he wanted more of her.

"Now you can sit in your wet panties for the rest of the day, aching for my cock to be inside you." He dropped his head to her nipple and sucked it into his mouth, making her moan. "Don't make me punish you again. Next time, I just might pummel that tight rosebud of yours until you're screaming for me to stop."

Stepping back, he grabbed the tank top off the shelf and handed it over.

"Jerk, I'm not wearing any panties," she mumbled, but she was smiling as she pulled the shirt on. "You ordered me not to remember?"

"Oh fuck that's even hotter." He rolled out his shoulders and had to think about anything other than her pantiless pussy.

Oh, he definitely was,a jerk and he just realized how big of a jerk he could be when he wanted something, and that something was Morry.

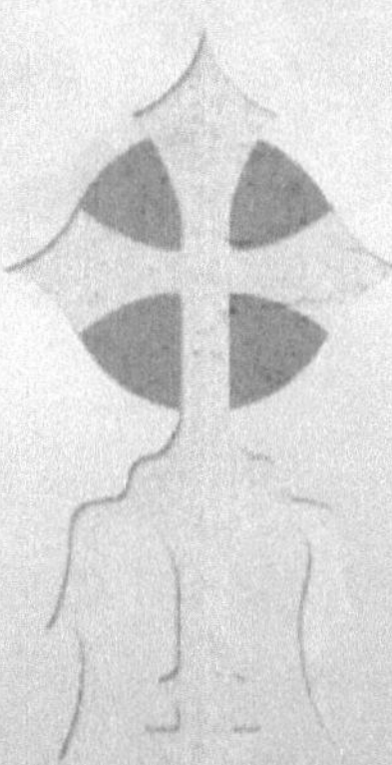

CHAPTER 20

Today was a lineup of shit things she didn't want to do. There were many days like that in general, but the two phone calls on her agenda this morning were especially shitty. The phone was on the third ring, and she was ready to hang up when Lindsay's cheery voice filled the line.

"Hello, this is Flare for Beauty and Hair, Lindsay speaking. How can I make you look glamorous today?"

It was a voice that had once made her laugh. Now, it only made her want to reach through the phone and smack the woman. They never should've been friends. They'd always been complete opposites, yet somehow, they managed until she and Andrew fucked it up. Literally.

"Hi, Lindsay," Morry said and felt like punching herself for making this call. It burned her ass like a bad case of hemorrhoids that she needed to ask anything from this woman.

"Oh, hi there. One moment, I just need to get to an area where I can hear you better," Lindsay said. Morry could hear her walking, and then a door closed. "I needed to get to the family sitting area so Andrew didn't hear me."

"Thanks for taking my call. I'm just checking in on Kyle to see if there is any news."

In truth, she'd been happily texting her son on the new phone she left him, but when Morry asked how he was doing, all she got was the patented teenage response of, *fine.* That response was highly unhelpful, so she resorted to calling Lindsay.

Surprisingly, Lindsay had handed over one of her business cards the day Morry snuck into the hospital. Morry never planned on using it, but then again, she would call and make a deal with the devil himself if she thought it was possible. Anything to save her son.

"He's a little worse." Lindsay sniffled, and instead of feeling bad for her, Morry had to force her voice to remain calm.

Lindsay was her only shot at getting any information about Kyle. The hospital staff wouldn't take her calls or tell her anything, and Andrew was being a grade-A dick.

"The doctors said he needs a transplant in the next few weeks. Now that his native liver has started to fail, it seems to be doing so rapidly."

"I'm surprised he managed to go this long without needing the transplant," Morry said.

When Kyle was born, he needed surgery to fix his bile ducts, which were inside out. The doctors predicted that he would need a transplant before he turned eight. Kyle managed to live a relatively normal life, but they'd watched over him day in and day out like a pair of hawks.

When she decided to re-enlist in the army, she'd only done so because Kyle was doing remarkably well, and the doctors couldn't believe how healthy he was or how his *native liver*, as they called it, had been holding up. They hadn't felt he would require surgery for many more years, and they were right. But now that the time had come, they couldn't find a match, and her son was getting sicker with each passing hour.

"Lindsay, does Andrew ever leave the hospital for a few hours? I would really like to visit Kyle again," she said, trying not to sound as conniving as she felt.

"Well, he does, but I don't know if I should get any more involved between the two of you."

"Please tell me you're joking. If you put yourself any more in the middle of us, we would be sister-wives and fucking Andrew together. You literally fucked him the entire time I was deployed, then smiled to my face when I was home to visit and proceeded to marry him the moment our divorce was final. You now live in my old home with my ex-husband, playing mommy to my son. Do you see the irony in your statement?"

There was silence on the other end of the line, then Lindsay sighed. "Fine, I will text you the next time he takes a break and goes home, but only if you listen to my side of the story. You never let me explain what happened."

Morry bit her tongue to keep from snapping back. She had no

interest in listening to anything this woman said, but Kyle was the only thing that mattered.

"Fine. Tell me what you want to say."

She plopped down in her chair and prepared not to let the last nerve she had for this woman snap. She never had a very long fuse when it came to assholes, but now she found that people, in general, pissed her off. Maybe it was her age. They say you get more miserable and irritable the older you get. Was thirty-five too young to start hating everyone and swatting them with canes? It had an amusing appeal.

"I never told you this, but when we were in high school, I always had a huge crush on Andrew. He was so handsome and smart and not like the other football guys, but he asked you out before I got up the nerve to ask him or tell you I liked him. The two of you started dating, and I let the idea drop, but the feelings were always there. I was a supportive friend for your first two tours, but the third one was when things changed."

Morry opened the bottom of her desk, wanting a drink, but the bottle was gone. She narrowed her eyes at the blank spot. Lindsay stopped speaking, and Morry realized she must be waiting for a response.

"I'm listening," Morry said, not sure what else she was supposed to say to that. *Congratulations, you were a good friend until you saw an opening to get what you wanted.* Maybe she should have a big fucking trophy made for Lindsay.

"Well, that was the tour my mom died, and then Kyle was hospitalized for a few weeks, and we ended up just hanging out more. I'm not really sure how it happened, but we just started calling and talking about life and our fears, and a conversation led to coffee and...."

"Yes, I know where it ended up." Morry rubbed her face and was surprised she was going to admit this aloud. "Look, Lindsay, I don't like or condone what you did. I was happily married at the time. At least, I thought I was until...Fuck, I'll never get that image of the two of you fucking on my desk in my room out of my head. The thing is, I don't know if we would've stayed together or not, but that's not the point. You were my friend, or again, I thought you were, and you threw it away. I meant nothing to you. Did you even feel bad for sleeping with my husband in my bed?"

"Oh my god, yes. I'm so sorry about that. I wouldn't speak to Andrew again until he came over and said you two were getting a divorce. I was mortified that we'd gotten to that point, and then that was how you found out, I...."

Morry bit her lip and stood to pace. "It is what it is now, Lindsay. The point is, the two of you seem happySo, in a strange way, I'm happy for you, but that doesn't mean I ever want our friendship back. I need you to understand that. You can't come back from what you did. Also, I like that Kyle seems cool with you and that you're good to him, but you're not his mother. I am. If you want ten kids with Andrew, go for it, but Kyle is my son. I'm happy he has so much love, but don't let the lines blur in your mind, no matter what venomous shit Andrew spews."

"You're right, I know. Look, I can't force Andrew to let you see Kyle or drop the case to keep full custody. He's been so angry about it and you. Honestly, he won't see reason, even when Kyle argues that he wants to see you. Sometimes, I think he is just doing it to spite you now, but I...I don't know."

Morry stopped at the window and stared out at the compound and bikers sitting outside, taking in the sun.

"I'm not asking you to fight Andrew for me. All I need is for you to let me know whenever he leaves for a few hours or half a day. I mean, he is still working, so he has to leave at some point, right?"

"Yeah, he does."

"Okay then, shoot me a text and just say, 'beauty appointment booked' with the time he is leaving. That's it. I will do the rest, and he will never know what you are doing. If you were ever really my friend, help me with this until I can get Andrew to back off." She rubbed her forehead. "I'm asking you to help me, Lindsay, please."

"God, Morry. I wish we could get back to where we were. I miss you. I really am sorry. I was in so much pain when my mom died and...I know it's not an excuse, and you've told me how you feel, but maybe one day, you'll find it in you to forgive me."

Morry closed her eyes and shook her head. "You never know, Lindsay, maybe one day," she said but had no intentions of putting any work into that.

If it happened, it happened, but even if she and Andrew were headed for divorce, a real friend wouldn't have gone there until the bed was cold and would have at least had the decency to ask. Best friends didn't do what Lindsay did. They just didn't.

Lindsay's tone suddenly changed, and Morry knew that Andrew must have walked into the room. "Yes, that sounds fabulous. I can't wait to meet you and work on your hair. A wedding is so exciting. Thank you for choosing me. Take care."

Lindsay hung up, and she had to admit that was pretty slick. Then again, she had a lot of practice at lying. Okay, one call down. One to go.

She really could use a drink for this one. Morry stared at her phone and cringed as her finger hovered over her father's name.

"You can do this. It's for Kyle."

Steeling herself, she hit call on the one that read, The Colonel. Her hands immediately began to sweat, and her leg wouldn't stop shaking. She hadn't spoken to her father since she took over the Legions. He understood about the mission and was one of the few who had been read in, so he wasn't upset about that, but she couldn't tell him about The Righteous any more than she could tell Andrew. He hadn't said anything when she told him that she was the head of the motorcycle club, but the look of disappointment in his eyes had been enough.

They had strategically avoided each other for every family holiday since then. Emmitt was the eldest of her brothers, and he was pissed that they still weren't speaking. He tried to trick them into sitting down and talking more than once.

The line clicked, and her father's deep voice came on the line. "Colonel Waters," he said, his voice brisk and to the point, just like the man himself.

She opened her mouth and closed it again. It felt like she was paralyzed and couldn't speak. Why did her father always make her feel so small? Like a tiny little bit of dirt. He didn't even know it was her, and she felt like he was judging her.

"Is anyone there? I don't have time for this. If you're there, speak up, or I'm hanging up."

She tried again, but still, no sound would come out.

"Fine, don't call this number again."

"Dad," she managed to spit out. Her heart was hammering out of her chest. The phone was so quiet she wasn't sure if he'd gone ahead and hung up. "Dad? I...I need your help," she said and closed her eyes.

"Morry, what's happened?"

"It's Kyle. Can you come see me? I know you don't approve of what I do, but...."

"Of course, I'll come. When and where?"

"As soon as you can. It's important. I wouldn't ask if it wasn't."

The deep rumbling sigh on the other end of the line sounded tired. "Two days?"

She didn't expect the tears, but they slowly trickled down her cheeks as she covered her mouth to keep from breaking down. Her father had always been tough, and they'd always been so close until that one conversation changed everything. She was so focused and kept busy with a million things that she hadn't noticed how much she missed him until now.

"That works." She swallowed back the ache and pain lodged in her throat. "Thank you, Dad."

"Anything for my grandson." Just like that, her heart broke all over again. "I'll see you in two days, Pumpkin."

The phone clicked dead, and Morry stared at it in shock. He'd called her by her childhood nickname. He hadn't done that since before she married Andrew. That was the first thing she'd done against his wishes, and their relationship only became more unstable until it completely disintegrated around her.

A knock at the door made her look up and wipe away the remaining tears. Morry didn't know why she was crying so much lately, but she really wished it would stop.

"Come in."

Judd stuck his head in the door. "I'm off to the meeting," he said and stepped into the room.

"How many men are you taking?"

"Twelve and three of our cutest sweetbutts." Morry raised an eyebrow at him. "I know what you're thinking, but it's not going to turn into an orgy fest or anything. Well, it may, but only if we have a deal to celebrate."

"Uh-huh, well, whatever gets the deal signed. Try not to kill anyone or stick your dick where it doesn't belong."

"Why? You miss it? Want me to stop by later? I'm sure I could get it up again."

She narrowed her eyes at him.

"Like fuck you will," came Jeremy's angry growl as he stepped into her line of sight.

Oh great. Jeremy had either the best or worst timing. She hadn't figured out which.

Before anything could get going, she interrupted the cock strutting and let out one of her loud whistles. It echoed, and Judd cringed. "Enough. Judd, get going and get the deal done. We need them as an ally. Jeremy, I need to speak to you, and both of you knock it off, for fuck's sake."

The two glared at each other as they passed, like two stallions eyeing one another up. Morry knew it was only a matter of time before they went for round two. Jeremy stepped into the office and closed the door.

"I need you to cut it out with Judd," she said.

He crossed his arms, his jaw clenching so tightly she could see the muscles twitch.

"Look, here is the truth. You don't have the experience yet to do everything Judd does or even take over. I know he can be a jerk, but he's good at his job, and it causes me more headaches when I have to worry about the two of you throwing down all the fucking time." She stood and placed her hands on her desk. "So here is the deal. You either leave him alone, or we stop what we have going on because I can't deal with the worry of you two killing one another on top of all the other shit."

His arms fell to his sides. "Are you serious? You'd drop us?"

"I don't want to, but if you force my hand, I will. I have a son who is dying, a motorcycle club that needs to find a new buyer for the millions of goods we just brought in because the people I was selling to are not who I thought." She held up her fingers. "I have a brother lying in a hospital bed, still in a coma, even though he should be fucking awake. Maeve is still MIA, and now I have four people here for treatment—Stephen being one of them. I just heard that I stand to lose my son on Thursday and had to break my soul to call my father to ask for help." She slammed her fist off her desk. "You are the one bright spot in all the dark in my day. So do I want to give you up? No. Fine, I said it. No, Jeremy. I want you, but I can't take any more bullshit."

His lips curved up in a small smile as he slowly made his way around the desk. Jeremy wrapped his arms around her and hugged her, kissing the top of her head. It felt so good to get that off her chest and be held like it would all be okay. He made her feel like shit just might work out. That was dangerous, but she couldn't help hoping as she wrapped her arms around his waist and hung on as if her life depended on it.

CHAPTER 21

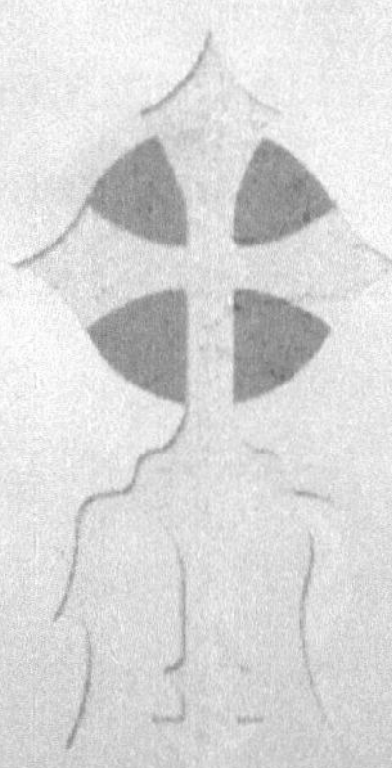

Jeremy finished tightening everything back up on the bike from the oil change he'd just done. He wiped his forehead on the back of his arm and wished the stupid air conditioning hadn't conked out. That was something on his list of shit to learn how to fix 'cause waiting for the maintenance guy to show up was painful.

The shadow outside the large bay door announced the presence of someone coming before Stephen stepped into view. The guy didn't see him tucked back in the far corner by the bike, giving Jeremy a few moments to watch him. There was something off about him, but he couldn't put his finger on what it was. He said all the right things and, after the first couple of days, had stayed out of trouble, but it felt like an act. It felt like it was too perfect of a change and what he was saying was what he thought we'd want to hear.

Not that every person who came through the doors needed to be a screaming basket case like he had been, but there were certain things all addicts had in common, and the biggest was the addiction part. How was it that Stephen needed to come to a super strict facility to get clean but, from what Jeremy could tell, had no withdrawal symptoms? The ones he showed seemed forced or overdone, like he didn't really know what it was like.

Jeremy could be totally off the mark, but he didn't think so. He just didn't want to say anything to Morry until he was certain that the guy was up to no good. Stephen stepped inside the storage area and ignored all the amazing shiny bikes closest to him. Instead, he scanned the building itself, like he was looking for something specific. Stephen's eyes lingered a little too long on the tall stacks of crates in the back, but his facial expression didn't give away what he was thinking. When Stephen's head turned in his direction, Jeremy lifted an arm in a partial wave, then continued to wipe the grease off his hands.

Stephen froze like a mouse caught in a trap, then put his hands in his pockets and walked over. Oh yeah, whatever Stephen had going on was an act, and he wasn't winning any Oscars. That was the worst transition from snooping asswipe to sad, puppy dog face Jeremy had ever seen. Even at his most high, Jeremy could've done a better job.

"What are you doing in here, Stephen? Pretty sure Morry said that the Legion was off limits." He set the cloth down on the long bench and picked up the torque wrench. He intended to use it on the bike, but it was also better to be armed.

"I was coming to see you. I saw you come in here earlier, but you hadn't come back out yet." He shrugged. "Just needing an ear."

Okay...Jeremy didn't believe a word of that but leaned against the bench and pretended he did. "Yeah, busy working." Using the wrench, he pointed to all the vehicles. "It's maintenance time. So what did you need me for?"

"I'm trying to figure out how to be more helpful. Morry has me in the garden and kitchen, but that's not really where I'm best utilized."

Oh, this ought to be good. "Okay, and what do you think you'd like to work at?"

"I'm good with numbers and keeping track of orders. I could do something like order supplies. When I was in boot camp, I cleaned weapons. I'm really good and fast at that, too."

"Mmhmm. What makes you think we have more than our own personal weapons?"

His eyes grew wide. "Oh, I just meant anything used for training purposes or if someone wanted their weapon cleaned and didn't have time."

"You've been here less than a week but think you have proven yourself enough to take over ordering all the supplies?" Jeremy kept an amused smile on his face, like this was funny and not something he needed to file away.

Morry taught him a lot, but the one thing he'd always excelled at was reading people. Jeremy knew the moment he laid eyes on

Dean that the man wasn't joking. Dean would've dropped him off that building if he hadn't chosen correctly. Just like Jeremy knew that this guy was flying by the seat of his pants on his quest for what he was really after. The twitch of Stephen's hand and shifty eyes told Jeremy he was looking for a weapon in case he saw through him. Jeremy did see through him, but he didn't intend to call him out. It was better to play along.

Stephen's shoulders lifted and dropped with a dramatic huff. "I just thought I could put my skills to better use."

"Well, we appreciate the offer, but it's too soon for either of those things. If you think of anything else, be sure to let me know, though. I'm always happy to hear new ideas." The tense muscles flexing in Stephen's neck relaxed, and he nodded and smiled. "You better get on out of here before Morry sees you. She's very strict with her rules."

"Yeah, she seems like a real hard ass. Must be hard working for someone like that all the time. Then again, I guess for you, it would be different."

Jeremy lifted a brow at Stephen and stood up straight but said nothing.

"I didn't mean to offend you. I mean, if I could get inside that, I would too." Stephen laughed, and Jeremy fought his instinct to leap over the bike and pummel him to death.

Jeremy hadn't counted on the guy saying this, and he wasn't sure if Morry wanted anyone to know they were together. In fact, they didn't touch in public, except in the alcove the other day, but no one was around. He only went to her room late at night and was gone before everyone was up in the morning. So how had this fucker known they were sleeping together? Fucking creepy much?

"Not sure what you mean by that."

Jeremy stood there staring into Stephen's eyes, and there was this moment when he knew that Stephen wasn't guessing. That was troublesome for several reasons, and none of them were good.

"Oh, no disrespect or anything. I just mean that if I could, I would. She is total MILF material."

"It would be wise not to say such things around here. Unless, of course, you want Morry to kick your ass?" Jeremy stepped close to the bike and pretended to be looking it over. Like he pretended what Stephen said wasn't making him dream of murder. "You're late for your group therapy session. You'd better get going, or it will be more vegetable prep."

Stephen seemed disappointed. His face was shadowed in confusion.

"It's out that way. Head toward the garden. That's where they'll be today."

Jeremy squatted, effectively dismissing Stephen. As the guy turned and walked away, Jeremy watched him closely. It was like watching a sped-up version of the movie *Usual Suspects*, where at the end, you realize that the guy with the limp didn't have a limp and was the leader of the gang the entire time. Stephen's back straightened, and he pulled his hands out of his pockets. This guy had serious issues, and none of them were related to oxy. Jeremy would bet on that.

Jeremy was finishing up for the day in the garage when he heard the distant rattle of the gate and the rumbling of vehicles. He stepped up to the door and shaded his eyes from the late day sun to see a large black SUV pull up and Morry stepping outside to greet whoever it was. He took in everything about the tall man in the crisp white uniform.

Whoever this man was, Morry seemed both happy and unhappy to see him, and Jeremy's curiosity was piqued. Did he really want to be an ass? Jeremy waited until they went inside to her office before closing and locking up. He hadn't been invited into the meeting, yet he found himself marching to the closest entrance and making his way to the office.

The door was closed when Jeremy arrived. He was going to turn away and be the person who didn't invade Morry's privacy but fuck it. He needed to know. Grabbing the handle, Jeremy opened the door.

"Morry, we're out of...." He looked up and froze. Morry stared at him from behind her desk, and the man before her turned in his seat. Holy fuck, the man was her father. She never talked about him, but he'd seen the family photos. "I'm sorry. I wasn't paying attention, didn't realize you had company. Are you...Are you Mr. Waters," he asked, and Morry bit her lip.

"Colonel Waters," her father said and stood to hold out his hand.

Jeremy took the invite and came into the room, closing the door before gripping the outstretched hand in a hard shake.

"Excellent to meet you, Colonel. Morry talks about you all the time," he smoothly lied.

"Does she now?" The Colonel pointedly looked at Morry.

Jeremy could see Morry giving him the death stare from the corner of his eye when her father turned back in his direction. If there was one thing he knew how to do well, it was kiss ass, and everything about this man screamed that he was used to everyone kissing his ass. Morry wasn't going to do it. She would never do it. But something told him that whatever the reason was Morry had called him, it was important. So why not give it to the man?

"Yes, all the time. You and her brothers. She's always saying how much she misses seeing all of you on a regular basis. This place takes a ton of work, and there is everything with the Righteous."

"The who?"

Morry stood from her desk. "Jeremy, that's quite enough."

"You mean he doesn't know," Jeremy asked, knowing he was pushing his luck, but he was genuinely shocked that Morry hadn't said anything.

"Is that what you're mixed up in," Colonel Waters asked as his eyes turned to Morry. Jeremy had never seen Morry look intimidated by anyone, but the harsh stare of her father had him shrinking back and his hackles going up. "Morianna Marie Waters, don't you dare lie to me. You told me that you were the leader of a motorcycle gang."

"I am," she said.

"As a cover?"

She swallowed, and her eyes flicked over to him. Suddenly, Jeremy wished he'd thought before he opened his mouth. The tension in the air was building, and it felt like it would erupt into a full-on war at any moment.

"Shit. Yes, as a cover," she blurted and stood up straight as she crossed her arms over her chest like she was preparing herself for the ammunition coming her way.

Jeremy started around the desk, but she held up her hand. He stopped moving. Fuck, this was not good. He'd really put his boot in a pile of dog shit this time.

"Why the hell didn't you tell me this before?" The Colonel leaned on Morry's desk. He looked intimidating, and Jeremy couldn't imagine growing up with a man like this for a father.

"I couldn't tell you. No one is supposed to know. He's not supposed to know." Morry held her hand out in Jeremy's direction. "But he was brought here by another member years ago."

"So all this time, you never left the desert. It's like you never came home. You went away for an undercover op, and that is exactly what you came home to. That's called PTSD, my daughter. It's called running from your past by staying squarely in it."

Morry looked away from her father's eyes, and Jeremy felt compelled to go to her. He took a step in her direction. Shit sometimes he wished he'd think before he spoke. Why hadn't he showered and waited to see her later once he was gone?

"It's not like that," she said, but she didn't sound convincing, even to him.

"Oh really? So what is it like, then? Tell me." Her father

demanded. The Colonel squared his shoulders and crossed his arms over his wide chest. Even at his age the man looked like he could bench as much as Jeremy could. Now he wondered what her brothers looked like. Fuck four older brothers and a father like this. So many questions answered.

She shook her head. "How do you know about them, anyway?"

"They're supposed to be a myth, but we all know the organization exists. We simply turn a blind eye. Besides, they do a lot of good."

Morry's eyes flicked up to her father's. "So...what does that mean?"

"It means I'm fucking pissed off that we just spent all this time barely speaking because you couldn't be bothered to tell me the truth. Fuck, Morry. You think I don't understand undercover ops?"

"Not illegal ones, no. How did you expect that conversation to go? Hey, Dad, just wanted to call and talk about the weather, and oh yeah, I'm part of a secret military organization that kills people. So have you gotten out golfing much? It really flows off the tongue," Morry bit out sarcastically, and for the first time since Jeremy walked in, Colonel Waters smiled.

He sighed and sat down. "Fine, but there has been so much missed time."

When Morry sat as well, Jeremy felt completely out of place. "I'll just excuse myself," he said, but Morry called his name.

Turning around, she waved him over. "Dad, I might as well get this out of the way, too. This is Jeremy, and we are...What would you call us?"

Jeremy shrugged. "Dating? I don't really know."

"You're a little young for my daughter, aren't you?"

"Did you just call me old?" Morry glared across her desk.

"No, just seasoned."

"Pretty sure that's the same thing."

Jeremy wrapped his arm around Morry's shoulder, not giving a fuck anymore if she wanted him to touch her or not. "Age doesn't matter. Not really. My heart and soul match your daughter's, and I'll never hurt her and will fucking die for her. So no, I don't care that I'm younger than her in the slightest. I'm lucky and honored that she's giving me a chance to be in her life."

Morry's body relaxed against his, and he could feel her eyes on his face, but he never looked away from her father's intense stare.

"Very good. I'm going to hold you to that. Now, Morry, you were about to ask me for a favor to do with Kyle?"

"His condition has worsened since you saw him on his birthday, and Andrew has re-opened the case for sole custody."

"He what?" The Colonel slammed his fist on the desk. All the items jumped, including Morry. "Have I told you today how much I hate that fucker? You never should've married him. He was a weasel then, and he's still a weasel who never deserved to marry my daughter."

"I know, Dad, but that's all in the past. I can't change it now. Look, I wouldn't ask this of you, and it makes me sick to my stomach to do it, but I need your help," Morry said as Jeremy grabbed a spare chair and sat down. He gripped her hand and linked their fingers together. "This judge really doesn't like me, and

Andrew is fighting dirty. He found out information about the club and is using that against me. I can't say what we really do, and now they've found out about my stay at Wellness Springs. He's saying that I'm unstable. Dad, my lawyer thinks I'm going to lose my son."

"Over my dead, cold body that's happening. I'm glad you called. Who's the judge?"

"Dad...."

"Judge's name, now."

"Judge Michael Patterson," Morry said, and her father stood.

"I need to make a few calls. I'll go out to my truck, but we're doing dinner tonight." He already had his phone out and was dialing someone. When he reached the door, he turned back and looked between them. "No more secrets and lies, Morry. Life is too short."

Morry sat perfectly still and stared at the closed door. "Did that really just happen?"

"Which part?"

"Is he really okay with what I do? Would he have been okay all this time," she asked, but she seemed to be asking the universe, not him.

"Look, I'm really fucking sorry I barged in here and blurted out your secret. That was an asshole thing to do."

Morry squeezed his hand, her head slowly turning in his direction. "No, don't be. I mean, yes, normally, don't fucking do that, but in his case, don't be sorry. I didn't know if we would ever speak again, and I think your loose tongue may have inadvertently repaired our fractured relationship."

They sat quietly for a short time until he got up the nerve to ask. "What is Wellness Springs?"

Morry's eyes dropped to their joined hands. "Let's just say that I understand all those who come through this place because I've had to battle my own demons."

That information only made her seem stronger. She was a woman who fought for everything in a world that wanted to beat her down because she was a woman, and here she was, still standing.

"I love you," he blurted out, then held his breath.

Morry slowly looked up from their hands and stared into his eyes. He couldn't help feeling like he was being swept away by her stormy eyes. He cleared his throat.

"You don't have to say it back or anything. I just...I needed you to know."

Morry opened her mouth when the door burst open with a bang. Judd was standing there, breathing hard, while blood poured from a cut on his cheek. "We're under attack. The Desert Devils had no interest in creating an alliance. They thought you were coming with me and had set a trap. Three are dead, one is wounded, and they are hot on our heels like a swarm of wasps. I'm not sure how many of us made it out alive."

Morry burst from the table and grabbed her cell off her desk. "Get the men ready and protect the gates. No one takes our fucking home," she growled.

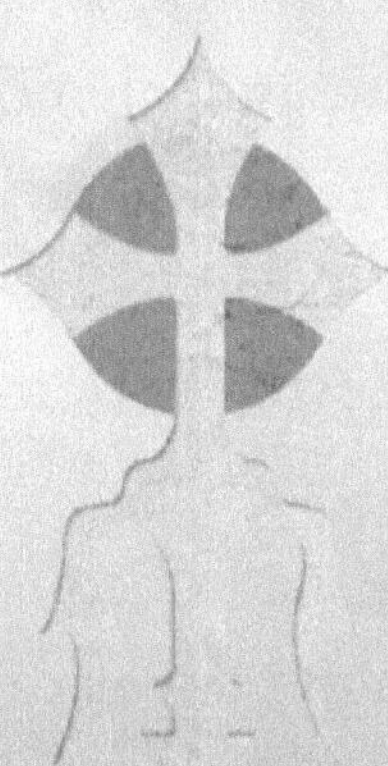

CHAPTER 22

"What's going on," her father asked as she ran to the truck he was sitting in.

"Go into my office and stay there. If need be, there's a safe room in the closet. Fucking use it. If not for me, then for Kyle. You're my only hope for keeping Kyle in our lives, and you can't be seen in this fight." She could tell by the look on his face he was going to argue. White shirt or not, he was a soldier first and an officer second. "Dad. Please. Kyle can't be cut out of our lives. Even if something happened to me, he still needs you. He deserves to know the truth about me one day."

"All right, stop right there, soldier. You're not dying today, I won't allow it. I'll go hide out in the fucking closet. God, I hate this shirt some days."

She smirked as he hopped out and ran into the building. Morry turned to Jeremy, already standing by her side with a gun in his hand. "Come with me."

They jogged over to Lady Luck, and she pulled open the back door to grab a couple more guns, handing them over to Jeremy. "Hopefully, we won't need to use these."

"What's the plan," he asked as he ran around the Hummer and jumped in, the door closing with a bang as the first sound of gunfire rang out.

"Well, I'm hoping that Lady here will be able to beat them back before they get through the gate, but it will depend on how many they have. No matter what, there are gonna be a lot of graves to dig later."

"As long as it's their graves and not our people, I don't care," Jeremy said.

She used to have that same outlook, but once she'd killed, it hadn't taken long to realize that the person you were forced to shoot was just like you. They thought they were fighting the good fight and on the right side. Whether that was right or wrong didn't matter when you were staring into someone's eyes as the life drained from their body. They had a family and people who loved them, and for every person who cheered that they were dead, someone shed tears.

She punched the gas, and the powerful vehicle revved and shot forward. "Lady Luck, arm weapons."

A soft whirring started as the gears that controlled the guns and small missiles locked into ready mode. "Battle system ready."

"Battle systems? What the fuck?" Jeremy said as they closed in on the gate.

"Open gate," she ordered. She'd strategically attached the Hummer to everything. There wasn't a single thing on the base that she couldn't control from the Hummer if need be. It was only for emergencies, like now.

"Holy fuck," Jeremy mumbled as they shot through the gate that was barely open enough for them to fit. "I think you missed your calling as a race car driver. Fuck me," Jeremy said, making her smirk.

"Close gate." She checked the rear-view mirror, and sure enough, the gates were closed. The gunfire they'd heard earlier came into view as they crested the first sandy rise. A couple dozen of their men were backed into one of the small rock faces they called Lookout Point. They were pinned behind large boulders as a mass of bikers and dune buggies raced around.

"Did we just drive into a fucking movie? It looks like a scene from *Mad Max* out here."

He wasn't wrong. It was mass chaos as the gunfight continued, and the lines of bikes and ORVs came down the road. The men were an issue, but the trucks set up with heavy artillery on the back were the bigger problem.

The sight of those trucks and Jeeps tried to stir old memories, and she could hear the sound of the sand hitting the metal as the engines revved and gunfire filled the air.

She shook her head and tightened her hands on the wheel. "You're gonna want to put on your seatbelt," she said as she stopped the Hummer on the high rise that gave her a perfect vantage point.

"Why am I equal parts terrified and fucking excited?"

"Because you've never seen the carnage before outside of video games," she said softly. "Lady Luck, lock on to artillery trucks."

"Locked," the Hummer said. No matter how many times she heard the robotic, emotionless voice say it was ready to kill, it always gave her chills, and not the good kind.

"Fire."

A dozen small missiles designed specifically for her Hummer flew from the launcher. The missiles were no bigger than a foot long and packed a lethal punch. Lady Luck had been programmed to hit either the engine, gas tank, or take out the wheels, depending on the distance and angle of the threat. The miniature *Death Dealers*, as she called them, could render an armored vehicle useless. These trucks, painted with fancy flames and large wheels for looks, didn't stand a chance.

Everything slowed down as she watched the *Death Dealers* sail through the air. No one paid attention to the lone Hummer sitting on the hill or the possible danger they were now in. Lady Luck was designed for this. The things the boys did with their Hummers in the cities were nothing more than child's play compared to the damage a lone one could do when outfitted with all the toys. She had Lady Luck stacked with every ounce of killing power she could. Now she couldn't help wondering if she'd subconsciously known she would need it one day or if it just made her feel better.

As the first missile hit, she gasped as she was forced back in time. The image before her didn't change, yet the memories in her mind were a wheel of destruction.

She could hear Trev's pain-filled wails over the ringing in her ears as they all realized what had just happened to Mel. She clutched Dean's pack as he sat in the middle of the street, stunned and holding onto Perez's head. Perez's eyes were blank, and his body was torn in two. She pulled Dean back to safety just as another RPG hit, and the shrapnel sliced open her face. They all watched as Scooter begged Arek to kill him and how he'd soothed his friend before pulling the trigger. The exploding building and raining rumble as they were pelted with chunks of rock. The look on the man's face as he took his own life trying to kill them with a bomb. Blood and flesh smattered them. His tear-stained face was stuck firmly in her mind. The sound of the helicopter coming down and how she and Trev managed to save Kes while Ringo screamed for them to save him. He reached up from the flames, begging for help as the pain-filled wails clogged her ears. The look in Jimmy's eyes when he said he didn't want the antibiotics, and how he'd held onto her hand as if saying goodbye. Then TK's final words of love spoken with his dying breath.

She shuddered and sucked in a deep breath as the images bombarded her like a horror movie that would never end. She could smell the smoke and hear the guns as loud in her mind as the terror-filled screams of friend and foe alike. Morry's hands tightened on the steering wheel as she swallowed the panic and forced her mind to return to the present.

The explosions took everyone by surprise, and the men sitting on bikes or taking shots at the trapped men turned to watch their trucks flip and fly through the air. One by one, vehicles erupted into flames and were tossed around with the combination of the sudden impact and momentum.

"Holy shit," Jeremy said softly, his tone conveying that he hadn't expected this level of destruction. It was so different seeing it in person.

One of the trucks flew sideways and landed on the men and their motorcycles, which set off more explosions, killing them in horrifying fashion. Black smoke rose into the air like the devil himself was trying to signal that shit was going down. Once more, the wrath of humans brought destruction, doing his bidding.

"How many did they bring," Jeremy asked as he looked at the long line of motorcycles still coming into view, along with a few more trucks.

"Looks like two...maybe three hundred," she said as those in the lead peeled away from the fun and raced along the packed road toward the compound. "Hang on," she said.

Punching the gas, Lady jerked forward off the rise and raced across the sand toward the mass of men. This wasn't just the Desert Devils. Mixed in with the black and red cuts of the Devils were cuts from at least two other motorcycle gangs. They thought they could waltz on in, overpower them, take their spot, kill their people, and steal whatever they happened to have. That wasn't happening, not if she had anything to say about it.

The motorcycles fanned out, maybe hoping to deter her from ramming them. She charged them at top speed. Beside her, Jeremy pressed back into his seat.

"This is not going to be pretty," she said, turning the wheel hard.

Sand flew into the air. There was a crash as one of the bikes clipped her back end. The Hummer barely moved with the impact. Turning the Hummer around, Morry stared at the multiple motorcycles and riders spread over the ground.

"I don't get it. What just happened?"

Peeling away, she hit the computer pad, and the windshield changed, giving her an aerial view of everything in a one-mile radius. Fuck, there was a lot of them. How had they hidden this many coming into the area? A problem for another time.

She glanced over at Jeremy. "They lined up all wrong. They're like dominos. As soon as one swerved into the next, it started a chain reaction. The sand blinded the ones in front, and we sent one flying."

"Like a pile-up on a freeway in the winter."

"Exactly. Holy shit." Morry swerved as an RPG came out of nowhere. It exploded behind her, but the blast shook the Hummer and rained sand down on the roof.

"What the fuck?" Jeremy looked at the small crater behind them. "Jesus Christ. That would've killed us."

"Lady Luck, who shot the RPG?"

"Boogie at two o'clock." Morry looked to her right, and sure enough, a dune buggy was parked on one of the sand hills but low enough on the far side that she barely saw his roof.

"Do we have any more missiles?"

"No, all twelve have been used."

Morry smacked her hand on the wheel. "Shit. Okay, Lady Luck, guns ready. How much ammunition do we have?"

"Five hundred rounds."

"Is that going to be enough," Jeremy asked, sitting forward to stare at the map on the windshield.

"Hopefully," she answered as the next wave got close enough that bullets began pinging off the side of the Hummer.

Morry weaved her way around the vehicles that seemed to have a death wish, her eyes fixed on the guy on the hill who was having issues reloading the weapon.

"Lady Luck, lock in on...." Morry tapped the screen, and a small circle appeared around the guy on the hill. "Fire as soon as we are within reach."

"Locked on target."

"I had no idea Lady could do all this," Jeremy said, then swore as a bullet bounced off his window with a hard bang.

"I prefer no one ever knows the full extent of what this vehicle can do. She would be very dangerous in the wrong hands." Turning back to the target, she counted the yards and watched him shake the obviously clogged weapon. That's what you got when you bought cheap crap. The man's eyes went wide as the Hummer caught air coming over the dune where he was parked. His hands stilled as he stared at the black vehicle, and the next moment, he lay dead on the ground.

Morry cranked the wheel and raced back down the hill toward the group of bikers closing in on the gates.

"Shit." Jeremy ducked as another bullet hit the window. This one left a mark.

Morry touched the windshield. "Lock guns on these targets."

"Locked. Firing range in five seconds, four, three, two."

"Fire."

The gun firing rattled the Hummer as she raced around the front group. They couldn't travel as fast as the Hummer on the softer surface. Bikes, ORVs, and people looked like game pieces as they flew off their vehicles or slumped as the bullets found them. She touched on another area, focusing on the biggest threats.

"These ones next," she said and veered the Hummer off in their direction.

Some chased them, and the bullets sounded like stones as more tried to stop the Hummer's rampage through their ranks.

She looked over at Jeremy. "We only had a live person to do this before the tech advanced. The tech in this Lady is what makes her so deadly. One day, I can see the movie *Terminator* coming true."

"Fuck," Jeremy yelled as a motorcycle ran into his door with a loud thump. The Hummer shifted sideways as the bike and rider flew over the roof while blood and other liquids hit the window. Jeremy turned in his seat and stared at the carnage left in their wake.

Morry shook her head as if to physically rid herself of the old memories as they clawed at her. "There will be a place in my heart," she sang. "Where your tears carved a mark. There is a place beside me that will never be filled." She wheeled around more bikes and more bodies were left behind. "I wish I could care." She hummed the rest of the song that Kes and Ringo had written. She was on autopilot, visualizing where to go next and how to get there without getting trapped.

"I like that," Jeremy said.

She looked at him as she spun the Hummer in a tight circle for another pass.

"What's that?"

"The song you were singing. I don't know it, but I like it."

"It's called 'I Wish I Could Care'. A couple of the guys in the unit wrote it. They were always singing."

"Ammunition reaching critical lows," Lady Luck said.

"How many rounds are left?" Morry stared at the screen, still showing way too many. There were more than a couple hundred. They must have been amassing this for a long fucking time. Cops, FBI, and all the other acronyms didn't like it when large groups of bikes moved around. This would've ended up on her radar.

"Fifty rounds left."

"Shit. How many targets?"

"One hundred and sixty-four unwounded, sixty-one wounded, and twenty-seven critically wounded. One hundred and eight deceased."

"Jesus Christ, this is a bloodbath," Jeremy mumbled as they stopped and stared at all the bodies strewn about the sand. "The cops are going to show up. Someone has to have seen or heard something, even out here."

"No, they won't."

Jeremy looked over, and she lifted a shoulder slightly.

"I pay the local cops to turn a blind eye, and this spot is blank on the satellites."

"Yeah, okay, I don't even want to know how you did that."

She would have to tell Judd to order the guys to ride. They needed to keep the group from breaching the compound. There were too many places to hide and a ton more weapons for them to get their hands on. It seemed a little too convenient that they decided to attack just when a new shipment of guns had arrived. They had a fucking rat. It was the only explanation that made sense.

Morry opened her mouth to order the call when the built-in C.B. inside the Hummer crackled. "Yee-ha. Motherfuckers."

She smirked and then started to laugh as Arek's annoying as fuck voice blared through the vehicle. Sure enough, two little blue dots appeared on the screen a moment later.

"Hogging all the fucking fun again, I see. When are you gonna learn to share, Morry?"

"What are you bitching about? I left you some."

"Ignore Arek. Where would you like us?"

She hadn't realized how much she needed to hear Trev's calm voice and took a deep breath. She stopped the Hummer and placed her head on the steering wheel.

"You decide. I've got about seven men hiding by the east rock wall. The rest are for the taking."

"Good to hear your voice again," Kes said, her eyes filled with tears.

There was something about them being here when she needed them the most that made her emotional. It was like they'd known that of all days, today was the day she couldn't take one more thing going wrong.

"Hey, Kes. God, it's good to hear your voices."

"Fuck, is she gonna cry? Did I finally make Morry cry? Fuckin' yes," Arek yelled and followed it up with a whoop just as the two Hummers burst over the giant sand hill at the same time.

"I would never cry for you, jackass," she said.

"Ouch, that hurts my pride, Morry. Seriously, you wound me."

"I doubt that, Arek."

She hit the mute button as Jeremy reached out and grabbed her hand. She smiled, gripping his hand tight. "That's my boys."

"Like the other guys, I'm not supposed to know about?"

She nodded and locked eyes with his beautiful blue ones. They captivated her. She stared into those blue depths, despite the world burning down around her, and she never wanted to look away. He cupped her cheek, and she leaned into the warmth of his thumb running over her cheek.

"Kiss me," she ordered, but her tone was teasing.

"Whatever the boss wants, the boss gets," he said.

She met him halfway.

Jeremy had been tapping at the steel door she'd placed around her heart and soul for safekeeping. She had leaned against it to keep him out, but she was weary of the fight.

"Awe, she's making out in the Hummer. Why won't you make out with me?"

Morry unmuted the CB, glaring at the other Hummer.

"If you even try to kiss me, I'll cut out your tongue. I'm pretty sure Renee would consider it an upgrade. I know I will."

"Jerk."

She laughed and turned back to Jeremy. "Before you ask. Yes, Arek is always like that. So just prepare yourself."

"Come on, Morry. I wanna race you to the compound," Arek said as he drove circles around her, creating a massive dust storm.

"He does realize he just killed a bunch of people?" Jeremy watched Arek hang out the window like they were kids at bumper cars.

"Oh yes, he knows, and sadly, he used to be worse. Here is the thing about Arek he will always have your six and would step in the line of fire any time. When that is all you can count on, it becomes all that matters."

"I'm already wondering how you didn't kill this guy," Jeremy said as Arek threw his shirt at the hood of her Hummer.

"Trust me. We've all thought about it more than once. Feel bad for his wife. That's all I'm gonna say."

"He's married? Brave fucking woman she is," Jeremy mumbled, making her laugh.

They had a lot of cleanup to do, and she wasn't looking forward to that, no matter who these guys were or what they wanted. But there was no denying that her heart felt lighter with the three of them here. Now all she needed was for Wolf to wake up, Dean to call her back, and her son to be okay. Then the world would be right once more.

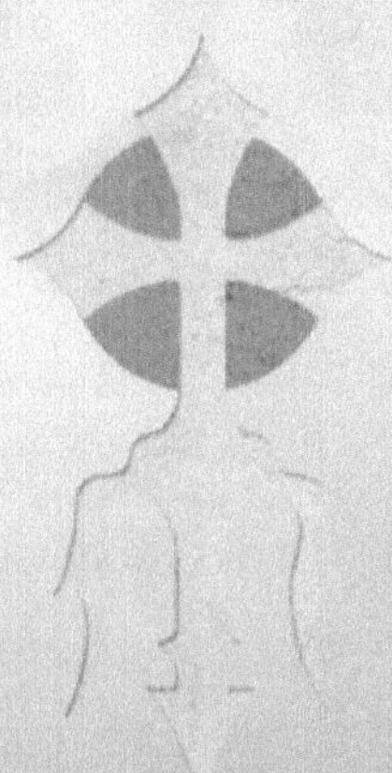

CHAPTER 23

Jeremy stared around the fire pit at the new arrivals, the men Morry called her boys. She explained it was just another term for brother and even though they weren't blood related they were to her.

"I gotta tell you, I didn't expect to find the Colonel here. He looked super pissed to see all of us," Arek said and laughed.

"Gee, I wonder why?" Kes snorted.

"It's worse than the whole mission thing. He knows now," Morry said and rubbed her face as all the guy's mouths dropped open.

"Are you sure he doesn't plan on having us all arrested? Should I be planning our defense?" Trev looked worried.

"How did he even find out? Shit, I can't go to jail. I have a baby on the way," Kes said.

Everyone stared at Kes.

"What the fuck? When were you going to tell us? You jerk," Arek swore and then stood, pulling Kes to his feet to hug him. "You're going to fucking love parenthood. I know all the cool clothes and toy shops now. I'll take you."

Morry was next to hug him. "You don't look very happy about it," Morry said.

Kes shook his head. "I'm thrilled but terrified. Ashley is crazy high risk, and she could miscarry from sneezing too hard." He waved his hand. "Okay, that was an exaggeration, but honestly, it's just too soon to get excited."

Morry gripped his shoulder. "I have a feeling it will all work out." They sat back down, and Morry glared at Trev. "You fucking knew, didn't you?"

Trev didn't say anything one way or the other but lifted a shoulder.

"You fucking ass. You knew, and you didn't tell your own brother?" Arek acted hurt.

"Of all the people in the world, you're the last person I would tell if I wanted to keep something secret," Trev said.

"Jerk. See what I have to live with?" Arek sulked and crossed his arms over his chest.

Jeremy thought it would've been more difficult to tell the brothers apart and granted they looked the exact fucking same, but the moment they opened their mouth there was no question as to who was who.

"Anyway, I didn't mean to get us off track. How did your dad find out?"

Jeremy swallowed hard. "That would be my fault," he interjected. "I thought he would know. I actually thought that was why they were not on great speaking terms." He glanced at Morry, and she stared into his eyes. "Sorry, guys. I didn't mean to create a huge pile of shit."

"Ha. Trust me, this is nothing compared to some of the piles of shit we've all created at one time or another. Do not worry about it," Trev said as Morry linked her fingers with Jeremy's. She squeezed his hand and winked at him.

"And no, to answer your question. My dad was actually happy in his weird way. Said he wished he'd known sooner so that he wouldn't have been embarrassed by me running a motorcycle club. It's not like he can tell anyone, so I'm not sure how this makes it better, but I'm not going to argue. It feels like splitting hairs."

"That sounds like the Colonel," they all said together, tapping their beers.

There was a long silence, and Jeremy's mind relaxed as he stared at the dancing orange flames, reveling in the warmth of Morry's hand in his.

"What was the song you and Ringo would always sing?" Arek interrupted the quiet.

A ghost of a smile lifted the corners of Kes's lips. "Ride the Lightning."

"Yeah, that's the name. I still hum that sometimes," Arek said as he sipped his beer. It was the first time Jeremy had seen the guy sit still since he arrived.

"Do you remember when TK called everyone out to the flag-pole just before we left for that last mission?" Arek started to laugh.

"Oh my god, I'd blocked that from my memory." Morry blushed and rubbed her forehead.

"I wish I could wipe that memory. Seeing TK pretend to be a stripper in nothing more than his boxers is a nightmare I'll never be free of," Trev said, and even though he smiled, it still felt reserved, like he never let his guard down.

"He did a pretty good job, too. I didn't know you could point your toes that well in shitkickers," Kes finished, and Jeremy snickered at the image as the rest of them roared at the memory.

He sat back and relaxed into the chair as he watched the small group continue to laugh and talk about times that he wasn't a part of, and for the first time in a long time, he felt out of place. Morry hadn't excluded him and had even introduced him to the group as her boyfriend, which was a massive step in his mind. They were all very welcoming. Well, Kestrel, not so much. Kes had squeezed his hand tight but hadn't said anything as he looked Jeremy up and down. Arek had hugged him, and Trev was extremely polite.

No one had asked him to leave, but he couldn't contribute to the conversation. They talked about people he didn't know and experiences that hurt to hear as he sipped his drink. On the one hand, he was happy to learn so many new things about Morry's past. On the other hand, it confirmed how little he knew about her life before this place and what shaped Morry.

He scanned the newcomers, and his quick assessment screamed that Trev was the leader. Morry hadn't said anything, but the way he carried himself, how everyone spoke to Trev, and how Morry's mannerisms changed ever so slightly, told him it was the truth. Trev's twin, Arek, was the clown. Any other time, he would've been pissed if someone picked Morry up and swung her around, but their dynamic was family, even if they weren't related by blood. Kes was the hardest to read. He was broody and quieter than everyone else. His eyes continuously scanned the dark to the point that Jeremy kept looking over his shoulder for the boogeyman.

Yet, this was the most relaxed he'd seen Morry in forever. She was smiling and joking around, and he wished he made her feel that at ease. Then again, he couldn't compete with surviving what they had.

"I'll be back," he whispered to Morry, and her face sobered.

"Is everything okay?"

"Yeah, I'm gonna go check on Butch and the guys on cleanup," he said.

He kissed her before standing and walking toward the gate. He did want to check on the progress, but he also wanted to give them time together. Once upon a time, he had friends he thought he was close to like that. Maybe they had been, and it was his fault for falling prey to addiction. They were all doing the same party drugs, but he was the only one who went off the rails. No one wanted to hang out with him after that. Then again, if they'd been friends, maybe they would've tried to help instead of pretending he no longer existed.

Jeremy jogged up the stairs that led to the lookout tower. "Hey, man," he said to Butch, who was on oversight duty.

"Hey. What, no fuckin' beer?" Butch grumbled.

"Sorry, man, but I have a half-eaten candy bar." Jeremy laughed at the disgusted look on the burly biker's face.

Butch was a good man. His old lady was part of the club, and unlike many other guys here, Butch never stepped out on her. If he did, Jeremy never saw it or heard about it. Tanya was missing an eye from an accident and wore a patch, so some of the new guys liked to make pirate jokes, which was never a good idea. The last new guy found himself sailing through the bar window, just like in an old western movie. They had two daughters who didn't live on the compound, and sometimes he wondered if they managed to keep what Butch did for a living away from them. That would be extremely difficult, but Butch couldn't be the only one who had made it work.

"How is cleanup going?"

"Fuck, I've never seen anything like this. They will be at it all day tomorrow, but this area will draw in the buzzards and coyotes by morning. Man, is it gonna stink for days," Butch said as one of the guys drove up to the gate with a trailer full of bikes. Butch hit the release, and the large metal gates rattled as the two sides separated. "You know, normally, we would make them yield and offer those left a chance to join. This was...I never want to see anything like this again, and I've seen some pretty terrible shit."

"You think killing them all was bad?"

Butch shrugged. "Who am I to say? Not my job to make those decisions, but what's done is done. Only fifty-two of them survived, and they've agreed to join after they do their initiation and punishment."

The two of them stood quietly and watched the lights move in the distance. The soft rumble of the backhoe could just be heard when the breeze picked up. A mass grave for hundreds of men and women. He could barely wrap his head around it or what it meant that he'd seen this and had been part of it. Being part of the motorcycle club, he had been forced to kill a few people in self-defense, but hundreds seemed unfathomable. What the three of those Hummers had done was unbelievable.

He turned and looked down from the tower at the small group around the bonfire. Jeremy couldn't even fathom what it must have been like to live and breathe experiences like that all the time. How did they even function? How could someone's brain compartmentalize what they'd seen? What they'd been ordered to do?

Movement caught his eye, and his gaze flicked to a person slinking around the shadows of the buildings. To see someone moving around wasn't unusual, but to see someone sneaking was.

"Hey, Butch, do you see someone over there?" He nodded in the direction he meant.

"Naw, sorry, man, that's too far, and it's too dark for these old eyes," Butch grumbled.

"You need me to stick around for a while?"

"Naw, the old lady is already asleep, and I'm too wired to rest. Just if you come again...."

"Beer. I got it." Jeremy smirked as he climbed back down the stairs. Flicking open the button on his knife, he started down the long wall of the sleeping quarters.

Morry suddenly shot to her feet.

Without thinking or wondering what was wrong, he sprinted toward her, then realized that she was on the phone.

"We'll be right there." Morry smiled as she hung up. "Wolf is waking up. Apparently, you boys brought the good mojo with you."

"I always bring the good mojo," Arek said, then gave Jeremy a wink as Morry rolled her eyes.

Morry was right, Arek grew on you, but he was pretty sure that the sticky fungus that came to mind wasn't what Arek would've chosen to resemble.

"Well, don't just sit there. Let's go," Morry ordered, getting everyone moving.

They headed to the medical building, but Jeremy kept looking for someone lurking in the darkness. Maybe he was seeing things because he never saw anyone. Everything looked calm and in place. The lights in the hallway of the medical wing seemed extra bright tonight, and he squinted at the white neon glare.

Morry unlocked the door with her card pass, and soon they met Doc Henry in the hall.

"So, how is he?" Morry asked.

"As bossy and ornery as that dog of his, but otherwise, it looks like he will be just fine physically. Mentally, we still need to see."

"What of the accident? Does he remember anything," Trev asked.

"I asked him if he remembered being in an accident, and he

said sort of, but then his head started to hurt. It may take him a day or two, perhaps longer, to remember. He suffered a very traumatic experience on top of hitting his head hard. Just take it easy with the questions. Right now, rest is the best thing for him."

"Will do," Morry said as Duke's bark echoed in the hallway.

"Yeah, yeah, we're coming," she said to Duke as the small party pushed into Wolf's room.

Duke immediately accosted everyone and even rubbed up against Jeremy's leg. Duke was so excited he didn't seem to know who to go to first, but it was Arek who got down and rolled around on the floor with him—oddly fitting.

"Well, aren't you a sight for sore eyes?" Morry said, smiling widely. "You have a nasty habit of ending up in a hospital bed."

The man Jeremy had yet to meet was partially propped up in bed, his eyes open and a scowl on his face. "I'm fine. The doctor is trying to tell me that I'm going to be stuck in this bed for weeks. I think you need to get someone with a better medical opinion," Wolf grumbled. "Good to see all of you. I'm sorry it was because I ended up in an accident." Wolf rubbed his head, squinting like he was trying to see something. "There is something I need to tell you...It's important."

Morry's smile faded as she leaned over and hugged Wolf. If he was sore, he didn't wince once. When Morry told Jeremy stories of their time overseas, she'd mentioned that Wolf was made of nails and could be missing both legs and would still find a way to walk. That was just who he was.

One at a time, the others touched fists or shook Wolf's hand, but it seemed as friendly and warm as a hug. It was in that moment he truly understood why they called themselves broth-ers. It wasn't just a nickname or a term because they'd served together. There was more to it with these five. The way they looked at one another and touched, you would've sworn they were related and had grown up together. Jeremy bet that if Dean were in the room, he would receive the same warm welcome.

The group looked at one another but didn't say anything.

"Tell me what's wrong. Why do you all have that look on your face," Wolf asked, his eyes landing on each of them and then lingering on Jeremy.

Breaking the silence, Jeremy stepped forward and held out his hand. "Good to meet you, Wolf. I work with Morry and...."

"They're shagging," Arek finished as Wolf gave his hand a firm shake.

"Seriously, man. Do you ever shut up," Kes asked the question Jeremy was dying to ask.

Jeremy stepped back, and the room fell silent once more. They stared at one another as if their silence was speaking for them, and he desperately wanted to know what was happening. What else was Morry keeping from him? Every time he turned around, there seemed to be something else to learn or something Morry wasn't saying or keeping secret. It made him wonder if he would ever know the whole Morry or always be left in the dark. The thought didn't sit well with him at all.

"No, this isn't the right time. Just let your body and mind heal," Trev said, but that only made Wolf push himself up higher in the bed.

"Trev, with all due respect, no, Sir. Tell me what happened, and...." Wolf stopped and looked around the room like it was missing someone. "Someone...Shit, why can't I remember? I need to get up. There's something I need to do."

Morry gripped Wolf's shoulder hard and forced him to remain in bed. "Don't you dare make me strap your ass to this bed. I have enough manpower to make it happen. Now, what do you need to do?"

Jeremy couldn't help but feel for Wolf as he stared up at Morry. His eyes seemed confused, like he had been swimming for the shore, then lost sight of the land and didn't know which way to go.

"I...I...Morry, it's important." Wolf gripped Morry's arm. "I know it's important." He laid his head back against the pillows. "Do you know something I need to know?"

Trev stepped forward. "It is not important tonight. We just arrived, and you just woke up. Once we've all had a good night's sleep tonight, we will talk about it tomorrow. There are many pieces we don't know, but I am hoping you can help us with the missing details." Trev stepped a little closer to the bed. "Tell me, what is the last thing you remember?"

Wolf's eyes filled with tears, his fists gripping the sheets. "Sitting in Jimmy's living room and telling his parents about how he died. About how brave he was to sacrifice himself to save the rest of us."

"Okay, that's good. Very good, Wolf," Trev said calmly. "We will start there tomorrow."

Trev smiled at Wolf, and Jeremy understood why he was in

charge. Trev seemed unflappable, and he had a way about him that made you want to agree.

"Time to rest, soldier. We have a lot to do tomorrow, so you better rest up."

"Yeah, maybe I just need to rest," Wolf said as Duke jumped up on the bed and laid down with his head on Wolf's chest. "Thanks for coming, all."

Morry leaned over and hugged him again. "Don't worry. We're not going anywhere, and we'll figure this all out."

"Can I just interject here and say you look like a pile of crap, and it's wonderful to finally have you not looking like a fucking god for a little while. Now I can take back the top spot on the hot tier," Arek boasted and puffed out his chest.

"I didn't miss you, and you never had the top tier," Wolf said, but the corner of his mouth curled up.

"What? Don't say such mean things. They sound truthful coming from you," Arek said, and Jeremy chuckled. Okay, Arek did know how to lighten a mood.

"Get out, all of you. I need to think," Wolf said and settled back, his eyes fixed on the ceiling.

"And rest," they all chimed together like a choir.

"Yes, and rest," Wolf agreed, but Jeremy had a feeling that Wolf wouldn't stay down long.

They stepped out into the hall, and Trev closed the door before he turned to the rest of them. "I didn't expect him to be missing that much time."

"Do you think he'll get it back," Morry asked, crossing her arms over her chest as her eyes filled with worry.

"I don't know, but if anyone were going to, it would be Wolf. I don't think we should press him for answers, though. It could make the amnesia worse. For now, let's just hope it all comes back to him."

Morry narrowed her eyes at Trev. "What do you know that I don't?"

"Tomorrow. It's too late to be getting into any of this right now. Trust me. It is nothing that can be solved right now."

Morry chewed on her lower lip, but Trev's steely, cool stare won out. "Fine. I'll show you to where you'll be sleeping."

"Very well," Trev said.

The three rooms were side by side, and just like Morry, they pulled the Hummers up so the vehicles were as close as they could get to the rooms without parking them inside.

As they walked slowly to Morry's room, he couldn't help but think about everything that had happened in such a short time. Jeremy slipped his hand into Morry's. Her fingers tightened around his, and his heart swelled to twice the size. He glanced down at her from the corner of his eye, taking in her profile, which was bathed in moonlight. There were just some moments that, for no reason at all, took your breath away, and this was one of those moments for him. She took his breath away.

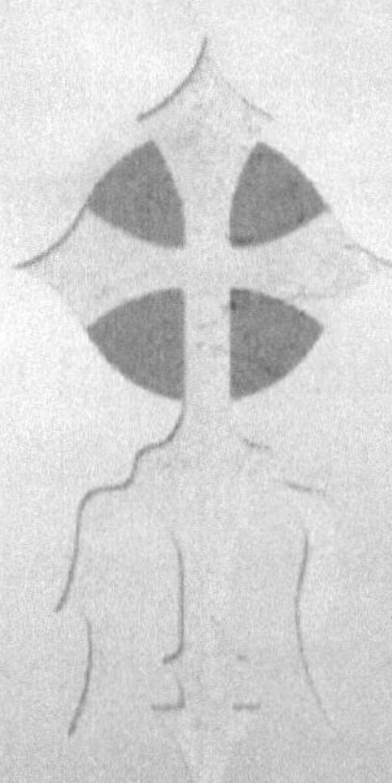

orry was drained by the time she walked into the bedroom. She'd run the gauntlet of emotions today. Starting out nervous and terrified to face her father. Then relieved it had gone so well. Which was quickly followed by shocked of the attack and thankful when her boys showed up. And finally, excited Wolf was awake, and most of her family was together. The images of what happened out there in the desert were weighing on her. She'd put on her warrior's face to do what was needed, even though she didn't want to. Some of those guys would be new recruits or had no idea why they were attacking the Legions. At the end of the day they were all a threat, but it didn't make taking their lives any easier.

That was the fucking crap thing about life. It forced you to do shit you didn't want to do when you were at your lowest point. It was almost as if God was showing you that no matter how much crap was flung in your face, you could and would find a way to put one foot in front of the other. If you didn't, you were left behind because the big blue ball kept on turning.

As soon as the door closed, she turned and pushed Jeremy up against it. The shocked expression only lasted a moment before his lips found hers. He said he loved her. He told her, and the thought froze in her brain like it was hit with liquid nitrogen. She barely accepted that she had feelings for him—was sleeping with him. The leap to love was a terrifying cliff that had never ended well. The guys she dated in high school never worked out. Then there was Andrew, who was still making her life hell, and TK, who'd fucking proposed and died in her arms a few hours later. Her life's track record of love was filled with potholes and land mines.

Yet, as his lips moved against hers and his hands gripped her waist, she felt like this was exactly where she was meant to be. To say that out loud, though? That was too much and too soon for her to handle right now.

She pressed her body against his, and he groaned into her mouth. She pushed down all the worry and tension from the day. The shit out in the desert, Wolf's accident, her son, and Maeve. It was all still there, but he made her feel like it wouldn't eat her alive from the inside out.

Breaking the kiss, she couldn't help staring into his eyes. He ran his thumb over her lips, and she sighed at the gentle contact.

"I wish I could make you feel better, make you laugh and relax like your friends do," he said. "I just want to be able to do for you what you've always done for me."

"Please tell me you're joking," she said, smiling at his confused expression.

"No, why would I joke about that? I saw how relaxed you were and how happy you are to have your friends around, and—"

Morry placed her finger on his lips, stopping him from saying another word.

"Jeremy, you do more than anyone else could. Yes, it's great to reminisce with the guys. They are my friends and family, and we went through something that only we can ever truly understand. Each of us lost someone we loved and watched countless others die in horrific ways. When we get together, it lets the buildup off our chest, like a kettle needing to let out steam. And yes, we try to remember the good times so that the bad doesn't constantly cloud everything we do." Reaching up, she slipped her fingers behind Jeremy's neck, loving that he pulled her closer.

"What are you trying to tell me, then?"

"I'm trying to tell you that I may not always laugh with you like that, nor am I able to reminisce in the same way, but you make me feel like I'm human and cared for and...." She paused and searched his face. "You make me feel safe in my skin, and that is— I have no words for what that means to me."

"So you believe I'm not about to run off with the next sweet- butt who walks through the gates?" He challenged.

"I'm working on that particular piece of baggage. You can't expect me to be perfect overnight."

"You are perfection. You just don't like to accept that someone sees you that way," he said, and her face and ears went hot as she blushed. Grabbing her hand, he kissed her palm and pulled her toward the bathroom. "I'm going to show you what I mean."

He always made her feel like she was young and foolish again. The girl that flirted, partied with friends and giggled over the cute boy. The girl who drank expensive coffee and walked arm in arm with Lindsay. The girl she thought was long dead.

They entered the bathroom, and Jeremy directed them to the one luxury she'd installed in her room, the whirlpool-style tub. It might have been foolish to fall for him—hell, it just might be the stupidest thing she'd done yet. The thing was, Morry didn't care anymore. If she fell and it didn't work, then at least she'd allowed herself to try. And if for some reason, he really did see them together long-term, and they got the chance to grow old together, then it would be another miracle in her life.

The sound of running water filled the room, along with the sweet scent of the bath salts. Jeremy turned to face her, and she bit her lip as he stripped off his cut and hung it up carefully on the back of the door. She loved the respect he showed for traditions, it was just another thing she could add to her ever-growing list of things. His T-shirt was next to follow. She couldn't take her eyes off his every little movement. Next were his boots, and as he bent over, the muscles along his back and shoulders flexed, making her mouth water. She felt like she needed to pinch herself to make sure that this was all real. This freaking hot ass guy who could have any girl on the property— including all at once— said he wanted only her.

As his jeans pooled to the floor, he was left standing before her in all his God-given glory. The tattoos on his arms announced how long he'd been here. With each new piece adding to the canvas of his life story since arriving. Her eyes tracing the artwork to his pec and the design with the words *Last Chance*.

They were words she would say to him daily. *This place... this moment in your life... this is your last chance.* Those two words held a double meaning tonight. This place had been Jeremy's last chance, and it felt like he was hers.

"Fuck, you're so beautiful, Morry. Like run-into-a-post-while-driving-because-you-were-too-busy-staring kind of sexy." She felt the blush creep across her skin and rolled her eyes. "Don't do that. Don't roll your eyes at me."

Jeremy stepped toward her, and she stared up into eyes so intense they took her breath away. Grabbing her shoulders, he turned her, so she faced the mirror while he stood behind her. Her heart galloped in her chest, and the tank top and jeans felt tight and uncomfortable against her skin.

"Tell me what you see," Jeremy said.

She locked eyes with him in the reflection. "This is ridiculous."

"Is that the answer you'd let anyone who walked through that gate get away with?"

Morry squirmed as her pulse rose a little higher. "No, probably not," she admitted.

"Then tell me what you see. Tell me who the woman in the mirror is."

Swallowing hard, Morry searched her face and bit her lip as she tried to see herself not as the scars but as the woman.

"I see someone who has been through a lot of crap and has

deep scars, but someone that still fights."

She couldn't stand looking at herself and turned her gaze to the floor, but Jeremy wrapped his hand around her throat and forced her to look up, tilting her head back until it was pressed against his chest. She was once more staring into his eyes. The heat of his body and the feel of his cock pressing into her back were enough to detour anyone's thoughts.

"Keep going," he ordered his lips against her ear. His tone was surprisingly authoritative, and she trembled in his hold.

"I don't want to do this," she said, her voice no more than a whisper.

"Fine, I'll tell you what I see. You're a woman who loves so deeply that it terrifies you. It rips you apart when someone you finally let into your life breaks your trust and hurts you. You would sacrifice your life to save others, even if you've never met them."

Morry closed her eyes, trying to hold back the sting of tears as Jeremy picked at the pieces of herself she tried so hard to hide.

"I see a woman who is passionate and strong, a good friend, but a fucking great mother. You're also sexy as hell, and no scar on your face could ever detract from that. You call yourself old at thirty-five, and maybe with everything you've lived through, that is how you feel, but all I see is someone who has ridden storms and survived."

A tear trickled down her cheek, and she watched it drip off her chin and land on his arm. He was ripping a hole in her heart and repairing it at the same time.

"You're a woman who lost her mother at a young age and lived with a man who insisted you call him General growing up. You have a son who adores you and fought battles I can't even imagine. You've loved hard, lost even more, and experienced all this world has to offer, good and bad, and you're still standing. That is who I want to be with. I don't give a fuck about wild parties and notches on my belt for the women I managed to fuck that week. None of it interests me."

Jeremy slowly turned her around, and she had to cover her mouth as she fought hard to hold back the last barrier before the floodgates opened. How did he always manage to do this to her?

"Look at me, Morry," Jeremy said, and she slowly lifted her eyes to his. "You saved me when no one else could. You made me respect myself and love who I am, and it's time you did the same for yourself. You are worthy of anyone and anything you want, and I'm shocked that somewhere along the line, I've managed to trick you into thinking I'm good enough to even stand beside you, let alone call you mine."

"Who are you? No one talks like this. You're like a unicorn," she cried, and his lips curved up.

"I like unicorns," he said and she couldn't have stopped the short laugh if she wanted to.

Dropping his lips to hers, he kissed her hard, and she could taste the salt of her tears on her tongue.

"I love you," he said, breaking the kiss and pulling off her tank top. "And I'm not going anywhere unless you kick my ass out that door." He kissed her again, and she groaned as he picked her up and sat her on the counter. "I want you to know that I don't want or expect any special treatment when it comes to the club. If I need my ass kicked then kick it, that hasn't changed."

He kissed her again and everything became lighter. The pain in her chest seemed less, the worry in her mind a fraction better.

"I'm going to pamper the crap out of you...When we're in private, of course."

"Of course," she said, smiling as he pulled off her boots.

She stood so he could get her jeans off, and as she stepped free, she placed her hands on his muscled chest, tracing the words *Last Chance* with her fingertip.

"You're amazing. I..." She licked her lips as she searched her heart for what she wanted to say. "You terrify me," she finally said. "You scare the living crap out of me because you make me believe anything is possible." She met his intense stare and pressed herself into his body, loving the feel of his warm skin against hers. "I love you, Jeremy."

His face transformed, and he beamed at her like she told him he won the lottery. She squealed as he bent over and picked her up.

"Woman, you better be prepared to be sick of me 'cause I'm going to steal every second I can. Starting with this bath."

Jeremy stepped into the tub and sat down with her between his legs. She sighed and stretched out in the warm water. She couldn't even remember the last time she'd received a massage, but her eyes closed, and she relaxed under his touch as he worked at the tight muscles in her neck and shoulders.

"I'm sorry you had to see that today. That kind of crap is not something I would wish on anyone."

"Can I ask you something?"

"Yes, you can have the left side of the bed tonight," she said, and he chuckled, making the warm water slosh gently.

"Good to know, but that wasn't my question. I wondered why you sell guns when you obviously don't like killing. I mean, it seems like a strange thing to get into."

Reaching forward, she grabbed the soap and lathered her hands. She poked Jeremy in the knee and understanding, he lifted his leg out of the water and wrapped it around her body. Fuck, he was so unbelievably hot. Even his fucking legs were sexy. She rubbed her hands along his toned calves as he moved on to her upper back.

"When I took over the Legion, they ran drugs and women. I killed everyone loyal to the old leader by lining them up execution style. Then, one at a time, I shot them for the rest of the members to see."

"Damn, that's fierce," Jeremy said, and she shrugged.

"I guess. I needed to prove I could be badass and worthy of the leadership position. Once I was done, I held up the gun and said from now on, this is what we'll be selling. Anyone who wanted to continue to do drugs or sell drugs and women could fucking leave." She paused as she recalled that day like it was yesterday.

"You're fucking crazy," Razor yelled, pointing at the five dead men on the ground. "You gonna go around and execute anyone who doesn't agree with you?"

Morry sauntered toward the large biker, puffing out his chest as he tried to make himself seem larger like a bear would.

"*Call me whatever you want. I'm not your old president, and we are doing shit my way. If you don't like it, there is the way out.*" *Morry held the gun out toward the open desert.* "*In fact, anyone who thinks that I'm too much of a girl or still wants to deal what the old club did can leave.*"

All the members stared around at one another. There were fifty or so still breathing, but she knew that before they bowed down, more would die. As she predicted, Razor and nine others broke away from the group and made their way toward their motorcycles.

"*Tell me something,*" *she said to those standing in the half circle.* "*Do you think it is wise or stupid to let them live?*"

The man that she knew as Butch looked her up and down. "*Is this a trick question? You planning on killing me for my opinion?*"

"*No. I want a real answer, I want to know what you think,*" *Morry said.*

"*Well then, it's stupid, as far as I'm concerned. Razor is not the type to take being kicked out quietly. He'll be back and with backup.*"

The rest mumbled their agreement as they nodded their heads.

"*Very well.*"

As the first motorcycle roared to life, she pulled out her second gun and aimed. With an accuracy that only came from too much practice, she fired at the first and last motorcycle, piercing the gas tanks. The explosions were instantaneous, and those around her ducked and covered their heads, but she didn't flinch. Some instantly died other screamed as they ran around on fire, but it was all background noise in her mind. It was mild and child's play in comparison to the crap she'd already lived through. She was sure some therapist would say that she wasn't tough, that she just experienced enough trauma that her brain no longer registered what the difference was between right and wrong, and maybe they were right. But, whatever the reason, she felt nothing.

She aimed at the next two, then the next two. She swung the gun at Razor. The lone bike had veered off from the fires as it peeled away. She fired and hit him center body mass. Razor flew off, and the bike went in the other direction. Smoke rose into the night sky, blanketing the small compound with the scent of burning oil and flesh.

Marching toward Razor, she took the chance that the men behind her wouldn't shoot her in the back. If this was the start of her group, she needed to trust them at least that much. The sand and small pebbles crunched under her feet as she neared the driveway where Razor had gone down. He was still breathing, his blood seeping into the dirt. His eyes found hers. He didn't ask to spare his life, but his eyes couldn't hide his fear.

"Maybe in your next life, you'll think twice before you think it's a fun idea to sell young girls to be sex slaves. And I have to tell you, it fucking warms my cold dead heart that my face is the last you will see."

She moaned as Jeremy's fingers dug into the knots in the middle of her back. "After that, I decided that I needed to find someone to sell to that I could live with, and I thought I had. Those I sell to are organizations in countries where the people are oppressed and terrified. Sponsors and corporations that all have the same beliefs, but need to hide all the transactions, so no one is the wiser use us and help fund the cause."

"What do you mean, you thought so?" Jeremy slid his hands under her arms to cup her breasts.

She leaned back, letting him soothe her and ignite a fire throughout her body that could wipe away any form of stress.

"Trev told me that, for some time now, the guns haven't been going where they should've been, and instead, a gang in California was getting them. Definitely not what I wanted."

Jeremy rolled her nipples between his fingers, and she gasped as the sensation shot straight between her legs. She wiggled against him and loved feeling his hard cock pressing into her.

"How's your tension level now?" he mumbled teasingly into the side of her neck before sucking on the sensitive skin.

"I think I'm still a little bit tense." She felt him smile before he ran his tongue up her neck to her ear.

When he growled in her ear, he sounded like he'd sucked back a pack of smokes. "We can't have that. I better try harder."

Oh, he was hard, alright. He was like a piece of fucking steel sticking into her back, making Morry hot as he shifted back and forth just enough to rub his cock into her. His hands slid down her body until he could deliciously tease the inside of her thighs.

"Mmm, I want you closer," he said.

She had no idea how he planned to make that happen until he gripped her hips and pulled her up until her head was on his shoulder. Looking down, she could now see his cock standing between her legs. Morry was tempted to reach forward and stroke that thick shaft, but Jeremy was quicker, and all thoughts of moving from her current position flew out the door as his fingers slid up and down her pussy lips.

"Fuck, you're so wet."

He swirled his finger around her clit, unrelenting as he groaned in her ear. Morry arched her back, lost to the intense sensations taking over her body.

"Oh, fuck yeah. That's it," Jeremy coaxed.

His finger dipped inside her, and she gripped the sides of the tub, digging into the hard surface.

"Yeah, wiggle against my cock. I fucking love that. You get me so hard. I want to come all over you right now."

Jeremy didn't just say something. He growled it with such intensity that it was like his voice touched her in places his hands couldn't reach. She rocked her hips up to meet his finger when he slipped a second one inside. The water sloshed back and forth with the rhythm of her body as she climbed closer to her orgasm.

"Yes, Morry. Fuck my fingers. Ride them hard."

He nipped the side of her neck, his teeth pressing in enough that the need for release rose to a whole other level. Jeremy wrapped his other arm around her waist and held her tight against him.

"Jeremy, fuck yes. I'm going to come."

His fingers quickened as his thumb danced lightly over her clit, driving her wild. Each touch was another shock to her system. There were no words to describe the euphoric feeling that swept over her as she bucked harder against his fingers. Morry yelled his name as she crested the peak and came hard on his fingers. Like every time they were together, her mind went blank, and Jeremy and the pleasure that consumed her was all there was.

She slumped and panted hard as she tried to catch her breath, loving that he held her and let her get her bearings. Rolling over in his arms, she slid up his body to look down into those piercing blue eyes.

"You make me crumble apart, yet you always put me back together again."

She smiled and kissed him before he could say anything. Never breaking the kiss, she straddled his body, reveling in how he groaned and gripped her ass hard as she rubbed herself along his cock. The water swooshed around her as she rocked herself up and down his body.

"Fuck, Morry," he said and laid his head back on the tub as she gripped his cock in her hand.

Rising, she rubbed the head of his cock along her wet lips, savoring the look of pleasure on his face. Jeremy sucked in a deep breath as she slowly lowered herself down on him. Just like the first time they were together, she gasped at the sheer size as he stretched her to her limits. She couldn't seem to get enough.

As the final inch slipped inside her, she realized this was what she'd been searching for all along. That Jeremy was who she needed. He'd come from the most unlikely source and somehow fit her perfectly.

"I want to make love to you," she said so softly against his lips that she wasn't sure he heard her until he smiled. Her heart seized and stopped pounding in her chest as she stared into eyes that mirrored her feelings.

Her movements were slow at first, and her lips never stopped touching his. She bit his lip and groaned as Jeremy's hand slid down her ass. He applied enough pressure to her rosebud that every time she slid down his cock, the tip of his finger pressed into her ass.

"Do you like that?"

"Fuck yes. I'm just worried your cock will rip my ass in two," Morry said, and he chuckled.

"Trust me. You're going to love every searing second of it. Then you're going to scream my name louder than you ever have as I make you come again," he said, cupping her face as he took over kissing her.

Their tongues battled as his movements became erratic beneath her. The water rocked as hard as they were and flowed steadily over the side of the tub as he pounded up into her.

He was hitting all the right places, and Morry was panting, close to coming for the second time.

"Come with me. I want you to come with me." She groaned as she tried to hold off the building pressure.

"Oh, baby, I can come any time you want," Jeremy said, and he wasn't exaggerating.

As she released the hold on her climax, so did he. His orgasm had her wave of pleasure stretching out longer, and she loved when he growled her name. Jeremy gripped her ass so hard she would have his fingerprints tomorrow, and she couldn't think of anything as satisfying as seeing those marks and knowing why she had them.

They collapsed together, her cuddling against his chest and his arms tight around her. She listened to the beat of his heart. The rhythmic sound soothed her, and for the first time in a very long time, she felt truly safe, wrapped up in his arms.

"I love you," Jeremy said, kissing the top of her head. "God, it feels so good to finally say that out loud."

She lazily smiled and gripped him tighter. "I love you too."

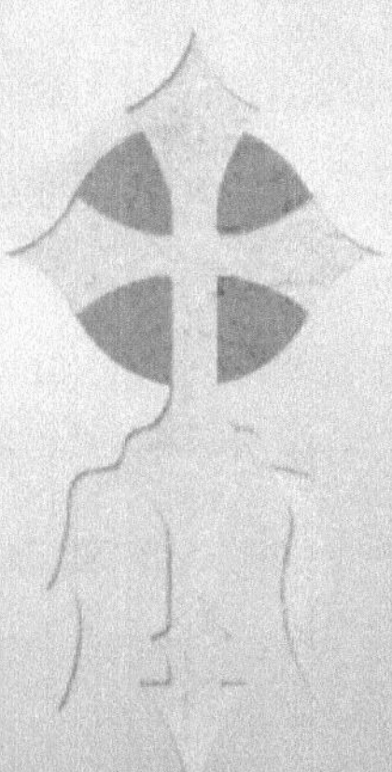

CHAPTER 25

Morry stood in the doorway and watched as Wolf went through all the memory questions the doctor asked. He seemed annoyed with the entire process but was doing what Wolf did best, excelling.

"Blue, green, grass, Ryan Reynolds. Can I stop now?" Wolf said as the doctor set the last image down.

"For now. I'm going to ask you harder questions in a couple of hours," Henry said as he jotted down notes.

"How is this supposed to help me remember anything?" Wolf said, crossing his arms over his chest.

Henry stood and gave Duke, who was lying quietly on the bed, a scratch behind his ear. "These are simply memory exercises. I know it's frustrating, but you already remembered this morning that when you got back, you started working as a U.S. Marshal. That is information you couldn't remember yesterday. It's coming, and I feel confident making the questions more difficult which will help stimulate your brain further."

Wolf sighed and turned to look out the window. "I'm telling you. I need to remember faster. Can't you do something to shock my system into remembering?"

"I don't advise doing anything drastic that will be traumatic to your brain or your memories. It could push them further away." Henry fixed his glasses, which never seemed to want to stay in place, and Morry stepped out of the room to let them continue speaking.

Morry sipped her coffee as she walked down the hall and out of the medical building. She could hear Kes and Arek arguing before she turned the corner toward their rooms.

"I'm telling you, man. I don't fucking snore," Arek said.

"Oh, so you're telling me that the snorting hog in heat sounds is just your normal breathing?" Kes drawled, and she almost spit her coffee back into her cup.

"I do not sound like a hog in heat," Arek said, his voice rising in pitch like he was horrified by the thought.

A series of loud snorting noises filled the air, and she burst out laughing as the two men came into view. Arek stood with his hands on his hips and glared at Kes, who was making the incredibly annoying noises. As usual, Trev ignored them both like they were pesky flies as he sat in a chair and sipped his coffee.

She'd designed the visitors' wing to have sitting areas outside their doors. Not that staring at a motorcycle compound was the view most would want. Trev looked up and waved her around the other two men, who looked like they would come to blows over snoring.

"You would think that after all this time, they would learn to get along, but they still sound like an old married couple," Morry said as she sat down beside Trev.

"They would first have to concede to be grownups. I fear that may never happen." He gave her a small smile. "How is Wolf this morning?"

"He's annoyed and still insistent that he needs to remember something. I get the sense he's panicked about it, and I wish I knew how to help him."

She watched as more of the equipment used to burn and bury the bodies came through the gates and was taken to the back of the property. A backhoe had seemed like a frivolous and over-the-top expenditure when she bought it, but now the large piece of machinery had been a godsend. Though, this was not exactly what she had in mind when she purchased it.

"I want to tell you about what I found out from the investigation of Wolf's Hummer," Trev said.

It was Murphy's law that her phone picked that moment to ring. She stared at the name of the specialist she'd contacted for Kyle. "Sorry, give me a second. I need to take this." Standing, she moved farther away from the two bickering men. "Hello?"

"Is this Morianna Waters?"

"Yes, it is."

"This is Doctor Zittle returning your call. I will get right to it. I spoke to Kyle's doctor and received all the latest blood work, scans, and liver levels."

"Okay, and what do you think?"

"I'm sorry, Ms. Waters, but your son's condition is well beyond what I can help with unless you have a donor."

Morry pinched the bridge of her nose.

"So how long does he have," she asked, not wanting to know. There was no worse feeling than seeing your child ill and being unable to help them. From the beginning of his illness, they always had multiple options, but now they were only down to one.

"It's hard to say for certain at the rate his liver is diminishing, but...I would say six weeks."

Morry slumped against the support beam of the building and had to hang on as her knees went weak. She closed her eyes as her mind tried to tell her that what she'd heard must be wrong. The doctor had to be wrong.

"I'm very sorry to have to call you with this news, but if a donor is found, I will clear my schedule to make the transplant happen. I really am sorry."

She nodded, even though he couldn't see it. "Thank you," she said, her voice straining as she tried not to cry. Hanging up from her call, she turned to face Trev, but all three now stared at her.

"What's wrong," Trev asked as he stood. His eyes were as firm and fierce as she'd always known them to be. Even when they were all at their worst and wanted to give up, Trev was the one who kept them from turning on each other and kept them going.

Even now, he looked ready to take on whatever the challenge may be.

"That was the specialist I called to look over Kyle's case. He thinks that, at best, he has…," Morry paused. Her mouth wouldn't spit out the words. If she said it out loud, it would make it more real. This couldn't be real.

Trev walked over and placed his hands on her shoulders.

"Tell us what you need, and I will find a way to make it happen," he said, his voice full of concern as the tears trickled from the corners of her eyes.

"He needs a liver transplant, but for a long time, he was low on the list, and now that he's at the top, they can't find a match," she said and closed her eyes. "I can't lose my son, Trev. It will kill me. I just can't."

"So you need a donor? That's easy enough," he said, and she looked at him like he'd lost his mind. "You need someone with O neg blood. They are a universal donor. I will check with all the retired vets and see if anyone is willing. I have a database we can go through. Also, have all the bikers who are willing checked. You may have a donor right here and not know it."

Without even thinking about it, she grabbed Trev and hugged him. "Why are you always able to see the easy answers?"

Trev wasn't what she would call a hugger, but he wrapped his arms around her and rubbed her back. "It's always easier to see the tree that's needed when you're not lost within the forest."

"If this is a group hug, can we get in on the action?" Morry stepped back and glared at Arek. "What? I was only asking because Kes wanted to know."

Kes rolled his eyes and shook his head no, and she couldn't help but laugh.

"I need to speak to Henry," she said as Trev picked up the tablet he'd put down.

An hour later, the announcement saying they needed help and for those willing to get a blood type check had gone out over the P.A. system. Morry was shocked to see how long the lineup was. Of course, right at the front of the line was Jeremy. He was the first to walk out of the shop area when she said she needed someone with O neg blood. Greasy hands and all, Jeremy stood patiently waiting for Henry to take the sample.

Trev made a few calls and found two potential donors who were getting tested to see if they were healthy enough to donate. It shouldn't have surprised her that Trev would find the solution that had been staring her in the face the entire time. Not that she would admit this to the guys, but sometimes, always striving to be better made her blind to when she needed to ask for help.

The minutes ticked into hours, and she couldn't stop pacing outside the clinic room, where everyone was getting their results one at a time. Henry said he couldn't just announce it. To do that went against doctor-patient confidentiality and ethics. Sure, now he wants to be a rule stickler. He said it put unfair pressure on those who could donate to have everyone know they could. Of course, she knew it had to be their choice. It wasn't like it was a walk-in-the-park procedure. Whoever it was would be laid up for weeks, but the thought of someone living here being a potential donor and choosing not to help her son sat like a weight on her chest.

Every conversation and relationship she'd made since taking over was running through her mind. Had she burned bridges with anyone? Did they love or respect her enough now to help? Were their livers even healthy enough since they all drank alcohol like it was water?

She turned to march back in the other direction when the door opened from the large waiting area, and Butch came out. He gave her a sad face and shook his head no. With each person who wasn't a match, the panic she'd managed to bury began to poke its head out of the sand.

"You really should eat something," Trev said as she walked past where he was leaning against the wall.

"I can't. I'll just throw it back up," Morry said. Stopping, she did jumping jacks and then dropped to do burpees. Fuck, she hated these things.

"Would you like me to count you down?" Trev drawled, and she couldn't help but smile.

"You're an ass, but I love you." Jumping to her feet, she stared at Trev. He went through as much or more than she had and stood as strong and unwavering as any oak tree.

"You know that, don't you? That we all love you?"

If *she* wasn't good with emotions, then Trev avoided them altogether. He shifted uncomfortably and looked away from her eyes.

"The gratitude you all want to place at my feet is unneeded. You all got yourselves out of that desert. I did nothing special."

She scoffed and let out a sarcastic laugh. "Trev, if you truly believe that, then you're not as smart as you think you are."

Whatever smart comment he was about to say was put on hold as the door opened again, and Jeremy came out. She stared into his eyes, and he nodded his head.

"Are you kidding me right now," she asked, taking a tentative step toward him. "Please don't nod yes if you just want to mess with me or don't plan on helping, even if you are a match. I can't handle that." The pounding of her heart was second only to the sound of blood whooshing in her ears.

"I wouldn't mess with you like that, and I've already told Henry I'll do it. He's in there calling the specialist right now," he said, walking to meet her in the middle of the hallway. Relief washed over her in a tsunami of emotion she couldn't bottle. The tears she'd been holding back broke free.

Jeremy pulled her into a hug, and she gripped him like he was a ghost who might disappear. Her body shook with relief, and she wondered at how the world worked. Dean had almost killed Jeremy and instead chose to help him by bringing him to her. What would've happened if Jeremy hadn't gotten caught up with Dean that day? What if she hadn't been able to get him straight and off drugs? What if he'd walked out the door the day he was given his get-out-jail-free card and never looked back?

"I love you, Morry. Of course, I'll help Kyle," he whispered in her ear. "For once, I can be the hero in our story."

"Thank you," was all she could get out around the lump in her throat.

Pulling back from the hug, she wiped at her eyes and realized that Trev had disappeared, giving them this moment alone.

"I need to call my father and see if he was able to help my cause," she said, then started to laugh.

Jeremy's eyebrows shot up as he stared at her, but she couldn't seem to make herself stop and only laughed harder until she was gripping her stomach and unable to get a breath in.

"Um…," Jeremy said, and his confusion only made the hysterical laughter worse.

She managed to get control of herself enough to shake off the spontaneous insanity. "I can't wait until Andrew finds out you're the donor. Oh, the look on his face. He's going to be pissed." Her eyes flicked up to Jeremy. "And I fucking love it."

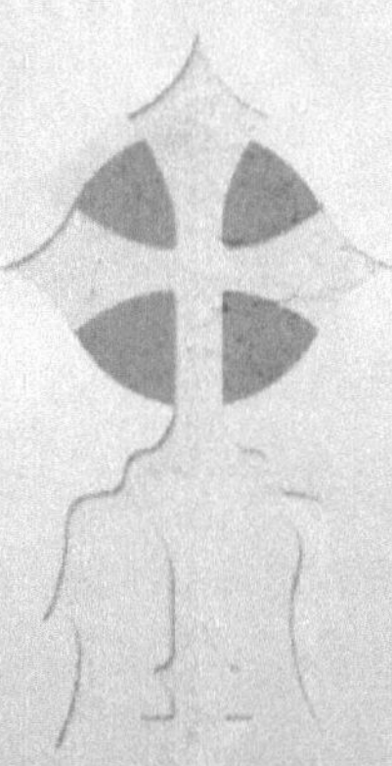

CHAPTER 26

Morry was enjoying this moment more than she should. There was no telling what her father had said or done, and she would owe him big at some point because a favor from her father never came without a price. She might have to make his favorite cookies, or it could be something else, but there was always a tradeoff.

Morry leaned back in the office chair, watching Andrew pace the perimeter as he screamed and ranted like he'd lost his mind. She asked Trev to be here for this conversation, and he dressed up for the occasion. He looked suave in his suit and tie, and his eyes laser-focused on Andrew. There was nothing he would miss, and that was why she needed him here. Her emotions always ran hot when it came to Andrew, and not in a good way.

"I can't fucking believe this." Andrew faced her and shook his finger, which only added to the crazed tomato look he had going on. His normally neat hair was flopping around on his head, and she was sure he would give himself a stroke with how worked up he was.

"How did you do it? Who did you fucking buy off? Because you and I both know that judge was going to rule in my favor," Andrew yelled and placed his hands on his chest.

"Why are you always so dramatic, Andrew?"

"Dramatic? I'm entitled to be pissed off."

She stood and slammed her fists down on the desk. The rage Andrew brought out in her was like a living, breathing creature. More than anything, she wanted to leap over the desk and strangle him to death.

"Entitled. You're fucking right you're entitled. You're an entitled prick. Kyle is also my son, not just yours. I've done nothing wrong as a parent, and twice now, you have attacked me and tried to take him away."

Andrew took a step back as she yelled. She didn't lose her temper like this often, but when she did, you'd better watch out. All the anger pent up during the past few months was boiling over. Her face was hot, and her body was shaking. Trev gripped her arm, and she took a deep breath.

"Let's get one thing very clear. I will never let you take my son from me, and if I have to do things I'm not proud of to make that happen, that is exactly what I will do."

"Are you admitting you did something shady?" He huffed like he was a paragon of sainthood and put his hands on his hips. "Of course you are. The great Morianna Waters can do no wrong, anyway, so what does it matter, right?"

Trev squeezed her arm, and as she met his cool gaze, she knew she needed to calm down. Whatever her father had done wouldn't hold if she gave Andrew more ammunition.

"You can draw your own conclusions, Andrew, but ending up in a screaming match with you is not why I called you here."

"Yeah, what is so damn important that you called me away from Kyle? Why didn't you just come to the hospital if you wanted to see him so badly?"

Morry bit her lip, her nostrils flaring at the condescending tone. Did he talk to Lindsay like this? I bet he didn't. For whatever reason, Andrew had turned into a grade-A piece of shit ever since she filed for divorce. He was the one caught cheating and decided to broadcast his bare ass to the world, but it was her he treated like shit.

"I called you here because I knew that this was how you would react to the news, and our son doesn't need to hear us going at it like rabid dogs," she said.

Trev removed his hand as the tension in the room diffused.

"You have a point there. No point in everyone being kicked out of the hospital," Andrew said. Somehow, he managed to say it so that all she heard was that it would've been unfair if he got kicked out, but not her.

"The second reason I called you here was to tell you that I've found Kyle, a donor, and he's agreed to donate part of his liver."

All the color drained from Andrew's face, the condescending and angry glare washing away. "What?"

"You heard me. I've spoken to the best specialist in the country, and he's agreed to do Kyle's surgery next week."

Andrew stumbled to the seat on the other side of the desk and sat down. "Oh my god, I can't believe this. How? Who?"

She swallowed down the smirk and the temptation to say something sarcastic. "He wishes to remain anonymous for now, but I will tell you that he is one of the bikers from the Legion."

Trev had talked her and Jeremy into keeping the information of who the donor was quiet. He said there were many reasons. One of them was that it would only give Andrew more cause to be pissed off that he'd been deceived the day she went to the hospital. They'd also broken the law by impersonating a doctor.

Trev was right, of course, but she couldn't deny that she looked forward to seeing his face when he found out.

Andrew shot to his feet like he'd been fired from a cannon. "No. No fucking way is my son getting a piece of liver from one of those—those—heathens," he yelled, pointing out the window toward the clubhouse. Morry licked her lips and tried for calm, but every second with this man in the room only made her more murderous. "I'm not going to let this happen. I'll call the judge, and...."

Morry slammed her fist on the desk so hard that the little lamp bounced and fell off with a crash. "I'm so sick of you and your attitude," she seethed.

Andrew winced like he thought she was planning to shoot him as she reached for her phone. Pulling it out, she opened a text from Kyle and held out the phone for Andrew.

"Look at him, Andrew. Look at our son."

"I know what he looks like."

"Look at him," she screamed, and Andrew stepped back. "Now."

His Adam's apple bobbed as he swallowed hard and stepped close to the phone. She waited until his eyes were focused on the image before she spoke again.

"Look at him," she said softly. "He's dying. He's dying, Andrew. The doctors give him six weeks to live at best. Six weeks and our boy will no longer be here."

Tears welled in Andrew's eyes as he stared at their son's smiling but jaundiced face.

"Can you stand there and honestly tell me that you would prefer he die than get the surgery he needs because you hate me and what I do that much? You hate those men more than you love your son and want him to live?"

"I don't hate you," he said so softly that Morry barely heard the words.

She looked over at Trev, and he took the cue. He stood and left the room, closing the door behind him. Walking around the desk, she sat on the edge staring at the man she once thought she would be with for the rest of her life.

Morry crossed her arms over her chest. "Andrew, I don't understand any of this," she said and watched the large bay door open and then close again as four of the motorcycles emerged and made their way to the gate. "You've hated and resented me from the moment I filed for divorce. Were you pissed off that I was the one who filed before you? Please help me understand how we got to this point."

Andrew ran his hand through his messy hair. Before Kyle got sick, she'd never seen Andrew look out of sorts or disheveled. But there were rings around his eyes now, making him look like a raccoon, and his shirt was untucked from his jeans.

"I don't hate you. I wish you would stop saying that," Andrew said, much calmer, like she'd poked a hole in his balloon and all the hot air had seeped out. "I hate that this is what you decided to do when you got back, but I don't hate you. I...I still love you."

Her mouth fell open and would've hit the floor if it could have. "Say what now?"

"Morry, what I did was wrong. I was lonely and angry, and Lindsay was there, but I never stopped loving you and wanted to work things out. I was so upset when I was served, and you hadn't even spoken to me about filing for divorce."

Morry held up her hands to try to stop him, but he just kept on talking. "I still love you, Morry, and I want us to get back together. I'm hoping you'll give us another try."

"Have you lost your-ever-lovin' mind?" She shot to her feet and moved back around the desk to put it between her and her obviously delusional ex.

His brows pulled low as he scowled at her. "I'm trying to tell you how I feel, how I've always felt, and here you are being sarcastic."

"No, I'm not being sarcastic. I'm being serious. Andrew, do you have any idea what it was like to be sitting there, have my computer ring, and see you and Lindsay together? Do you even understand that image is forever burned into my brain? Her naked ass pressed up against my laptop screen as you fucked her?"

He looked down at the ground and opened his mouth, but she didn't give him a chance.

"No, I'm not done. I lived over there with one female officer to approximately a hundred men. At the drop of a hat, I could've fucked any of them, and you would never have been the wiser, but I didn't. I never even thought about it. My family was here. You were here, Kyle was here, and the point is that I...I was lonely too, but I didn't fall into anyone's arms. That is all on you."

She leaned forward and gripped the edge of the desk. "I filed for divorce because I didn't want to make things work. Do you understand that after my heart was ripped out, I had to stare my unit in the face and hold my head up high like I hadn't just been humiliated in front of them in the most graphic way possible? I respected myself too much to return to the same river, Andrew."

"I'm sorry. It's all I have. I can't go back and change what happened. All I can do is hope that you would want to give us a chance to put our family back together," Andrew said and shrugged.

Now that the shock had worn off, the anger was quickly rising to the surface. "Let me make sure I understand this correctly. You cheated on me with Lindsay for whatever your reasons were, but you never really liked or loved her, and even though you proposed and married her, you wanted me back? Do you even see what a douche move that is? Lindsay adores you, always has, and you would toss her aside now to get back together with me." She couldn't believe that she was defending Lindsay's honor. Hell had frozen over. That was the only explanation.

"To put our family back together, yes, but when you say it like that, it makes me sound like an asshole." He crossed his arms, and she shook her head, unable to wrap her mind around his logic.

"Andrew, that's because it is an asshole move. It doesn't just sound like it." She blew out a long puff of air. "This is not why we are here. I wanted you to know that Kyle's surgery will be next week. I'll send you all the details to sign off on." Reaching down, she grabbed the fallen lamp and set it back on her desk. She needed to buy a lottery ticket because the bulb hadn't even broken. Sitting down, she grabbed the paperwork on her desk, then slowly looked up when she realized that Andrew hadn't moved.

"What are you still doing standing there?"

"You won't even give it any consideration?"

She gave Andrew a pointed look. "No."

"Why not? I mean..." he started, sounding like a whining child who wasn't getting his way.

"For fuck's sake, Andrew, I'm with someone else, and unlike you, I'm happy. I have no interest in getting back together ever. You burned that bridge...No, actually, you blew it the fuck up and then set the remaining pieces on fire when you challenged me the first time for sole custody. Never mind the damage you've done this time around. Now get out of my office. I have work to do."

Andrew's face had begun to redden again, but whatever he was going to say was interrupted as the door opened. Trev stood in the doorway like a looming sentinel, his eyes boring holes into Andrew.

Stomping across the floor, he made a spectacle of leaving, but she called his name when he reached the door. "Oh, and Andrew?"

He turned to face her.

"I'll be visiting Kyle later today."

Turning on his heel, he stomped out the door and brushed past Trev. If only Andrew knew that any of her Righteous brothers would kill him if he pushed too hard. She wasn't prepared to go there. At least not yet.

"He's so charming," Trev said, his dry sarcasm pulling up the corner of her mouth.

Of all the things Andrew could've said today, wanting to get back together had not been on her list of possibilities. They had their moment, but it was over, and she'd moved on a long ass time ago.

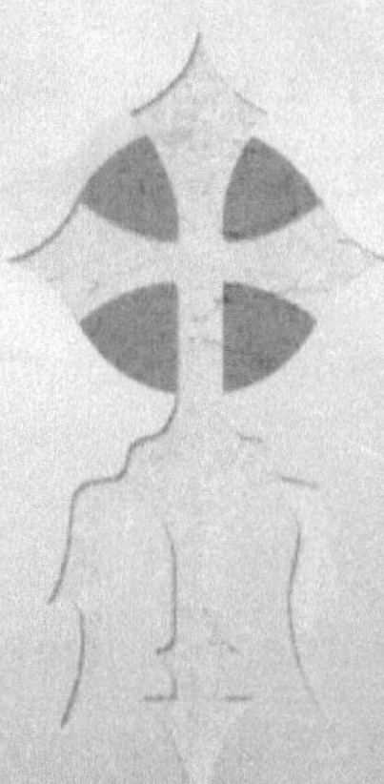

Chapter 27

"You're mine. From now on, you're only mine," he whispered in her ear. "I'll love you with my last breath and protect you until my heart stops beating," Wolf said and smoothed back Maeve's dark hair. Smiling, he kissed her lips, but then the image dissolved before his eyes.

"No, Maeve, don't go," he yelled, but it was too late. She was gone.

The image took on new life, and as it cleared, he was behind the wheel of his Hummer.

He looked over at Maeve, and as their eyes met, the Hummer jerked hard, the back end swinging wildly. Sparks flew into the air as the last of the tires' rubber ripped off the rims. He tried to hold the vehicle steady on the road, but there was no controlling it now, and as the rims hit the soft shoulder, the Hummer flew off the road, heading for the steep *embankment. Reaching out, he held his arm over Maeve in a last-ditch effort to protect her one last time.*

Wolf sat up straight with a gasp. "Maeve," he said and then grabbed his pounding head. It felt like someone was trying to stab him in the eye. "Shit."

Duke whined as his golden eyes stared back at him in the darkened room.

"I need Morry."

He looked at the side table, but they never gave him a phone. Grabbing the little string to call the nurse, he went to pull it but froze. They probably had orders to force him to rest and would try to put him back to sleep, but rest was not what he needed. He needed to find Maeve.

He couldn't stop the frantic pounding of his heart or the panic that wanted to take over. The last time he'd felt like this was when his sister died. He took a deep breath and tried to stop the shaking in his hands. How long had he been unconscious? Did they know where the guys working for the Righteous had taken her? Was she alive? Is that what Trev was trying hard not to say?

Trev's eyes had been filled with worry. Fuck, no. He wasn't losing her.

He silently screamed as he moved his legs off the side of the bed, then had to hold his head in his hands. All the images of their time together flooded his mind like a dam broke.

Balling his fist, he fought through the pain lancing his side and piercing his mind. He needed to get to Morry, and then he needed to get his hands on one of the Hummers and a gun. Glancing across the room, Wolf spotted cupboards that were all labeled.

Slowly slipping his feet to the floor, he swore under his breath as his knee screamed at him. "Fuck, okay. You can do this."

Wolf slid down to the floor so he was on his ass, and using his good leg and arm, he pushed himself backward until he reached the supply area. Duke followed him and kept poking at his face as if telling him he needed to go back to bed or hurry up. Reaching up, Wolf grabbed the edge of the long counter and slowly pulled himself to his feet. Sweat was beading on his brow by the time he was fully upright, and he had to lean against the counter as every part of his body screamed that he was being a fucking idiot.

"No, you need to get answers," he mumbled as encouragement. He'd been through worse pain and harder situations than a car crash.

Looking at the little white labels neatly stuck to the wood, he spotted one that said bandages and wraps. Shuffling along until he could get the cupboard open, he found what he needed. Pulling out two tensor bandages, Wolf pulled the hospital gown out of the way and quickly wrapped his knee with one roll and then the other. Placing his toes down, he tested it. His knee still had a lot of pain, but it was less.

"Now I need a cane or...perfect," he said and slowly walked to the far corner to grab the shiny metal thing that held bags of blood or whatever was supposed to be dripped into the body. His hand gripped the cool metal, and with the metal walking thing on one side and Duke on the other, he made his grand escape.

All was going too well, and he should have known better. To get out, you needed a card pass.

"Son of a bitch," he muttered as he rattled the locked door. He was trapped, and the fear he'd beaten back slowly started to take over. "Stop it. You're going to pass out," he said, then stumbled sideways as little black dots floated in front of his eyes.

"No, you can't. You can't pass out," Wolf growled at himself but had to lean against the door as all his muscles went heavy.

The black dots were spreading, and he licked his lips as he lowered himself to the ground. If whoever wanted Maeve hurt her, he was going to kill every last one of them. None of them would be safe until he wiped them from the planet. The fear was quickly swirling into anger that was burning white hot. Duke laid down beside him, and as their eyes met, Duke whined.

"I'm sorry, buddy. I just need a few moments to rest."

Morry sat up straight, sweat trickling down her back. Her eyes darted around the room as she tried to determine what had woken her up. Memories, so many memories, were racing through her mind, and then the smile on her son's face when she walked into his room last night. So why was she so anxious? Morry glanced down at Jeremy, sleeping soundly, his arm over his eyes. She took a moment to appreciate the view and still couldn't believe everything that had happened to lead to this moment.

Just as she decided to crawl under the blankets and wake him up, her phone vibrated on her nightstand. Reaching over, she grabbed the glowing device and hit talk.

"Henry, what is it? What's wrong?" Jeremy immediately sat up beside her. She rubbed her face. Of course, Wolf would try to leave. She should've put fucking guards on his door. The crazy ass. "I'll be right there."

"Wolf," Jeremy asked, and she nodded.

Swinging her legs out of bed, she grabbed her camo fatigues. "Yeah, the crazy ass decided to leave his room and collapsed at the locked door."

"Wow, you weren't kidding," Jeremy said and got up. She glimpsed his hard ass before he covered it with jeans. Okay, he was turning her into a sex addict. She couldn't get enough of him.

Pulling on a hoodie, the dog tags around her neck rattled as she pulled them from inside the material. "You don't have to come," she said as Jeremy pulled on his own sweatshirt.

"Honestly, I wouldn't be able to sleep without you," he said casually, but the words stopped her in her tracks. "What? Why are you staring at me like that?"

Jeremy walked over, and she rose on her toes to kiss him. There was no hesitation, and his hands gripped her ass, pulling her tight against his body.

"It scares me how much I love you," she said softly against his lips.

Jeremy nipped her bottom lip playfully. "I'm not going anywhere. Every inch of you is mine, and I'm not letting go."

"I guess we should go make sure Wolf hasn't done himself any permanent damage or killed Henry yet," she said.

"When we get back here, I'm taking you all over again," he said as if reading her mind.

"Such hardships."

Jeremy laughed as he opened the door.

Her room was near the guest area and the medical building, so it didn't take long to reach the outer doors.

"Hey, the door to the storage building is open slightly," Jeremy said, pointing to the building across the way. "I'll go close it. One of the guys must not have shut it tight."

"Okay, I'll see you inside."

Morry could hear Trev arguing before she reached the next set of doors, and he didn't have his happy tone. That was the voice he used when he was livid. It didn't happen often, but when it did, watch out.

The door beeped and unlocked as she swiped her card and walked in to find Trev nose-to-nose with Wolf. Even though Wolf was injured, he looked ready to fight, and Duke was barking and running around them.

"Hey, this is a fucking hospital and my place. None of you get to fight one another in my home, and certainly not in a medical building." She pointed to the red and white sign on the wall that said no fighting. This was not her first time dealing with men who thought they were superheroes.

Neither of them looked her way, but their body language relaxed.

"He won't get out of my way or tell me what I want to know," Wolf growled.

"You're supposed to be resting. You collapsed because you're not ready to get up," Trev said.

"Don't give me that bullshit. You're the one who will get in our face and order us to keep going," Wolf argued, and he had a point.

"We were in the middle of nowhere and being hunted down. I'm pretty sure that is what you call extenuating circumstances," Trev countered, which was also a good point.

"Okay, enough. It's fucking three in the morning. No one is going to be saving the world right now. Wolf, get back into bed and tell us what you need to tell us. Trev, you will answer all his questions if he promises to remain there until at least eight o'clock."

The two men eyed each other and then looked over. "Deal," they said in unison.

"Great, let's go then. Back to your room."

"Could one of you tell me why men never grow up?" All those in the corridor, including Doc Henry, looked at her.

"Speak for yourself. I'm grown up," Trev said.

"You may indeed be the only man I've ever met who decided to grow up," she said, earning a snort of disgust from Wolf. "The key word is may."

They helped Wolf to bed, and as he relaxed, she could see how much effort his little excursion had taken out of him.

Wolf's eyes found her. "I remember. We were trying to get to you," he said, and her brows drew together.

"We? There was no one else in the Hummer," she said, as fear sent her pulse racing. Had they missed someone? Were they lying out there all this time?

"We were staying at Jimmy's cottage hiding out because we didn't know who to trust, and I didn't know she knew about the Righteous. She hadn't mentioned that she knew you. Fuck."

"Whoa. Who," Morry asked again as the nervous tension made the hair on the back of her neck prickle.

"Maeve. Maeve was with me, and...." Wolf rubbed his face. "They took her. They chased us down everywhere we stopped, and I shouldn't have stayed so long. I was being selfish with our time."

Shock rendered Morry speechless. Reaching out, she gripped Wolf's arm, and his terrified expression amped up her own fear. "Who? Who took her?"

"I don't know for sure, but they hired guys from the Righteous, and those fuckers tried to kill me three times to get to her."

"Oh my god," she said, jumping to her feet to pace the room.

All this time, she wondered where the hell Maeve was and couldn't understand why she couldn't find any sign of her. None of this was making sense, though.

"Who would want Maeve? I don't understand this."

"I think I may have the answer to that," Trev said as he leaned against the wall. She and Wolf looked over at him, and he sighed. "There have been issues within the group for months. I started to get a bad feeling just before Miller suddenly rose from the dead and claimed the group would be destroyed. One thing after another has kept happening. When Maeve was arrested, I got an anonymous phone call from a masked and untraceable voice saying that I needed to go to the precinct because someone there needed representation."

"That's how you took on Maeve's case? Why didn't you tell me? I thought all this time she called you like I trained her to do." Maeve crossed her arms over her chest.

"I was keeping it all very close to the vest. Honestly, I wasn't sure what was going on and didn't know who to trust. Don't get me wrong. I trust the two of you as much as I do Arek, but not the phone lines, emails, or anything else. I felt we'd been compromised and wasn't sure where the threat was coming from."

"But you do now?" Morry put her hands on her hips. Right about now, she wished she had something strong to drink. Fuck, things were just going too well.

"What I know is that we broke Maeve out of the transport vehicle and dropped her off in Vegas," Trev said.

"That was when I got the call to hunt her down," Wolf interjected. "I was sent two orders, one from the Righteous and the other from the Marshal's office. My boss called me personally. He never calls anyone. That should've told me there was something wrong."

"No point in beating yourself up. The point is, all the information that Kes, Arek, and I have been gathering is all leading straight back to Dean, or more accurately, his family." Trev said.

"Dean? That doesn't even make sense. Dean hates his father and wouldn't have anything to do with his family."

"I'm not saying he does. It just seems to be where all the issues are coming from, and that's the facts. Who is behind it? Well, that's another issue."

Morry rubbed her jaw as she thought. "Do you have any idea where they would've taken her?"

Trev lifted a shoulder and let it drop. "I have a couple of theories I'm working on, but I'm not fucking sharing them with this one...." He pointed his thumb in Wolf's direction. "Until I have a few more things figured out. Don't need him running off half-cocked to save the woman he loves and fucking shit up."

"Your confidence in me is staggering," Wolf mocked, crossing his arms.

"Tell me I'm wrong. Where exactly were you running off to like a lame dog in a hospital gown? Hmm? You going to drive through hours of desert to bust down the doors of a cartel home and demand the love of your life back? Let's just think about how well that would go over?"

"You're an asshole," Wolf said.

"But I'm also right. This needs a fucking plan and a good one."

"Um...I'm sorry. Did he just say that she is the love of your life?" Morry's hackles went up at the thought of Wolf taking advantage of Maeve.

Maeve wasn't a child, but she worked hard to get herself dug out of some very dark crap, and if Wolf had done anything to undo all the work she put in, Morry would pull her gun and shoot his other leg.

"Yeah, we are...she's my *Walela*, my everything." He placed his hand over his heart. "I know that sounds crazy, especially with the age difference, but she makes my heart beat like it's the first time. We were trying to get to you, Morry. When it came out that she knew you and who I was, we tried. This is where we were heading when they found us." He held open his hands and stared at his palms. "I tried to save her. I tried to protect her. And I failed. I failed my sister and Jimmy and now Maeve."

When his eyes found hers, she felt her own filling with tears. There was so much pain shining from his eyes, and she understood.

"No point in blaming yourself, Wolf," Trev spoke up. "Neither of you. The soldiers are just like us and trained just like us. You were outnumbered with limited resources and unsure who you could trust. That's exactly what whoever this is wanted. To keep us looking over our shoulders."

Morry walked to the front of the bed and grabbed one of Wolf's hands. "Trev is right. Whether this is the Cartel or someone else, they have access to those we thought were friends. This is going to need a fucking top notch plan. We can't just storm every castle we think they might be hiding in."

"I know." Wolf closed his eyes as he squeezed her hand.

"Rest up, my friend, and I will show you everything I have after a few more hours of sleep. I'm fucking tired," Trev said and stepped out of the room.

Morry made her way to the door and stopped to look back at Wolf. "I know you're worried, but Maeve has more tenacity than anyone I've ever met. They're going to be sorry they messed with her. Trust me. If anyone can walk out of burning flames alive, it's Maeve."

Wolf smiled as she closed the door.

"Make sure he doesn't try that shit again, and call me immediately if he does," she ordered the two guards.

Shaking her head, she fell into step with Trev and then glared at the side of his face. "Don't ever cut me out of the loop again," she said, and his eyebrow rose as he looked at her. "I fucking mean it. Nothing is classified between us after all the shit we went through. Understood?"

The corner of his mouth curled up. "Understood."

CHAPTER 28

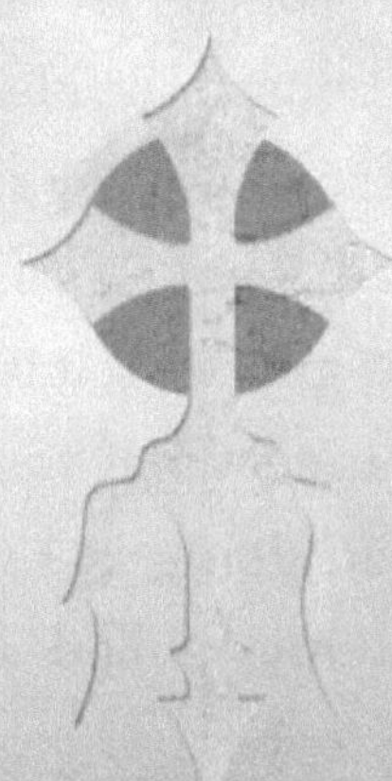

Jeremy stared at the narrow crack of the door. He reached for his gun and realized he'd forgotten it.

Shit

He stood perfectly still and listened for any noise, but all seemed quiet. Using a finger, he gave the door a gentle shove and cocked his fist, ready for a fight. Nothing seemed out of the ordinary when he first stepped inside, but he narrowed his eyes at the far wall. There was a soft glow in the corner.

Slowly easing his way over to the worktable where some tools were laid out, he grabbed a crowbar. With each step, he knew that someone was up to no good. There was no reason to be in here this late, especially with a flashlight, which was what the glow was.

It was either that or it was a fucking alien, and if it were some little green Martians, he would scream like a little kid as he high-tailed it out of there. Slipping his hand into his pocket, he pulled out his cell phone and got it open just as whoever it was stepped away from the corner that housed the electrical box.

The person stopped as soon as they saw him, and in the flashlight's beam, he recognized Stephen's face. Jeremy knew something wasn't right with this guy. He felt it the first day he'd arrived and was bold enough to wander away from his assigned duties.

"Stephen? What are you doing in here, man? You gave me a fucking heart attack." Jeremy smiled and sighed like he was relieved to see it was only Stephen.

"I think you can drop the act," Stephen said, and Jeremy let his smile fall.

"The question still stands. What the fuck are you doing in here?" Jeremy saw something on the floor, and it took a moment for his brain to register that it was a booted foot.

"Don't worry, he's already dead," Stephen said and kicked the leg of the downed man.

Jeremy's fist clenched around his phone, and as it did, he swiped to get to the emergency alarm. Stephen suddenly yelled like he was possessed by a demon and turned the flashlight, so it was shining in Jeremy's eyes. Jeremy stumbled back, slamming into the large stack of wooden crates.

He saw the boot coming and got his knee up and arms down just in time to block most of the blow, but the boot still slipped through and caught him in the stomach. All the air was forced from his lungs. His fists went up as the guy landed a hard blow to his jaw, and something hard hit his hand, sending the phone flying and skidding across the concrete floor.

"Son of a bitch," Jeremy swore, jumping to the side. The next blow hit the crate harmlessly.

"Fuck," Stephen swore.

Jeremy swung the crowbar hidden behind his leg, and Stephen ducked, but his flashlight crashed to the floor, flickered, and went out. They were plunged into darkness except for the glow of his cell phone, lying on the floor like a little beacon.

He swung again and once more narrowly missed Stephen's face. He'd been training here with the guys and Morry since he arrived, but this guy moved extremely fast. There was no way in hell he'd only had six months of training. The way Stephen moved was professional. He moved like Morry.

Stephen charged low at his waist, and Jeremy couldn't get out of the way in time. He managed to get his knee up into his gut before arms wrapped around his waist and drove him backward.

"Fuck," Jeremy yelled as he lost his footing and fell.

They slammed into the ground hard, and he tried to protect his head as much as possible from cracking on the hard floor, but he still hit hard enough to feel dazed. The crowbar shot out of his hand and slid under the skids. Of course, it would.

He couldn't worry about that, though, 'cause it was clear that this was a fight to the death.

He'd already recognized Big Joe on the floor with a dark puddle around him that could only be blood.

Pushing up hard, Jeremy shoved Stephen off him as if he were nothing more than his daily weights and managed to get him with his knee. He didn't know where he hit Stephen, but it was hard enough for the guy to groan in pain. He punched at the side of Stephen's face —despite the shit angle—and managed to lay a hard hit to his side.

An elbow cracked Jeremy across the jaw, and as his hands loosened, Stephen rolled out of his grip.

"You should've just turned around and left. I didn't want to kill you. You seem like a decent guy," Stephen said.

Jeremy noticed Stephen leaning into an open crate. Spinning on his back, he caught Stephen in the side of the knee. The fucker yelled when it made a popping sound and staggered. But Jeremy could see the shadow of a gun already in his hand.

Scrambling to his feet, he ran for his phone, picked it up, and hit the emergency button. The red lights in the building began to spin, and the siren could be heard blaring outside.

"Don't fucking move," Stephen snarled as the cool metal of a gun pressed into the back of his head.

"Good luck getting out of here alive," Jeremy said.

Jeremy had known fear many times. He was kicked out of his home and lived on the streets. He'd been beaten and raped until he wished he was dead. He'd feared disease, hunger, and how to score his next fix. Worst of all was fearing to succeed while equally terrified to fail. Coming here had been the scariest and most wonderful thing that ever happened to him, and in the blink of an eye, a single man threatened to take away this slice of happiness he'd finally carved for himself.

"Well, I guess you're not as stupid as I thought you were. Move it. You're coming with me." Stephen shoved the gun into the back of his head. Jeremy raised his hands and walked toward the door like a man walking the plank.

He had no idea if he would live or not, and all he could think about was Morry and Kyle. If Jeremy died, so did her chance to save her son. His heart hammered hard as they neared the main door. He could barely hear the blaring siren over the pounding of his pulse.

Jeremy wasn't sure if God existed—his path had made him question faith and what that meant so many times—but if there was a God, he prayed to him now.

Morry stepped outside and looked around, an eerie feeling creeping over her skin.

"What is it," Trev asked, his voice quick and his eyes sharp.

"It's quiet, like too quiet. People are usually outside the bar smoking until at least four in the morning, and someone is always heading out or in on a bike. But there's nothing."

Trev stepped back and lightly tapped on the door where Kes was staying. The sound was minuscule, yet Kes opened the door, gun in hand. "Get Arek. Tell him to find high ground and go with him to keep an eye on his six."

"What do you think is happening," Morry asked. Her eyes scanned every inch of the place but saw nothing moving. Even the air was still tonight like it was holding its breath to see what would happen.

"I'm not sure, but there is tension in the air," Trev said, voice her own inner feelings.

She knew what he meant. How many times had they walked into a small village or the remnants of one where only rubble remained and knew something or someone was out there? They'd been honed to feel it like a sixth fucking sense.

Arek emerged from his room with his sniper case in hand, and the two men took off into the shadows. Arek was a pain in the ass ninety percent of the time, but when you needed him to be on point, he never let you down. Just them being here with her made her feel better. It wasn't like she couldn't take care of herself, and she didn't need a man to make her happy. But to have her brothers around her was like a blanket on a cold winter's night, and Jeremy had become the fire she wanted to sit by.

"Do you think an attack is coming, you see anything on the ridge?"

They both looked out toward the skyline for any movement, any sign of someone trying to sneak onto the property by repelling down the massive rock face. She instinctively cocked her head and listened for a helicopter, wishing Wolf was outside. He could hear things no one else ever could.

"No, I think that whoever this is, they're already on property," Trev said.

"Okay, now you're freaking me the fuck out. I hate it when you say shit that sounds creepy. You used to love telling horror stories overseas until no one could rest." Trev smirked, but it didn't reach his eyes as they searched the darkness.

"No better way to keep guards awake," he said. "Do you have your gun?"

Morry reached for it in her jeans and swore. "No, I ran out of the room and forgot to grab it." Trev's gaze shifted to hers, and she felt him telling her off. At that moment, she felt like a cadet all over again. Fucking Trev had a strange ass power to him.

Trev opened the door to his room and slipped inside, returning a moment later with two guns handing her one. Trev tapped the face of his watch and spoke low into it. "Sweet Delilah, Baby Girl, and Lady Luck, this is Three, Four, Three, Zulu, Foxtrot, Bravo, Whisky, code word, Father Time. Come online."

Morry watched in fascination as the dashboards in the Hummers lit up. "Oh, sure, you get all the cool toys, and here I thought I was the only one with the advanced gadgets," Morry teased.

Trev smirked and relayed his next command. "All Hummers, guns ready." The click and soft whir made her shiver as the guns slowly rose from the tops of the deadly vehicles. "Sweet Delilah, how many friendlies and bogies are on the property?"

"Only one potential hostile detected."

"Show me where all humans within a mile radius are located. Hostiles in red and friendlies in blue," Trev said casually.

She could see him as the next James Bond character. If they hadn't been kicked out when they got back, she had no doubt he would be an Admiral by now. There wasn't a boardroom, courtroom, or room full of dumb, wet-behind-the-ears cadets who didn't sit up straight when he spoke.

Morry leaned over Trev's arm to look at the small screen, and as soon as she saw where the hostile dot was, her heart dropped. "Oh, God. Jeremy."

She stepped forward, but Trev grabbed her arm to keep her under the overhang and out of the open. "No, not until we can see the threat. Be smart. Don't let the fear rule you now."

"But we know they are in there," she whispered, her voice harsh with the fear that she was going to lose Jeremy or had already lost him. No, she couldn't let herself think like that.

"There is also one deceased. Would you like to see where?" Baby Doll said.

Trev lifted a brow at the Hummer. Unless given a command, they weren't supposed to guess what you wanted, but it *would* be Kes's Hummer that acted freaky. It suited him.

"Well, that did nothing to ease my fear," she mumbled.

Morry covered her mouth as the little green dot appeared in the same building she knew Jeremy had gone. The fact that he hadn't made it to Wolf's room and wasn't standing beside her right now had chills spreading throughout her body.

"No, this is not happening," she breathed out.

Suddenly, the sirens and lights flashed. Someone had hit the emergency button.

She stared at the line of closed doors. She expected everyone sleeping to come running out of their rooms, but no one did. It was still a ghost town like everyone had been abducted.

"Something is wrong, and I don't mean the siren," she said, looking up at Trev.

"Agreed." He tapped his watch. "They are in their rooms but not moving."

He twisted his wrist for her to see. "How is that possible?"

"All the reasonable possibilities are not good. Are you able to access the main sleeping quarters from this end of the building," Trev asked, and she had to force herself to concentrate on him instead of what was happening inside that storage building.

"Um, yeah. There's a door at this end, just around the corner." She glanced at the front doors that were still quiet. Her mind raced as she tried to piece together what could be happening with her men, while her heart was scared to death for Jeremy.

"Good..." Whatever Trev was going to say died in his throat as the storage building door was kicked open with a bang.

Jeremy stepped outside, his movements slow, his hands in the air. She couldn't stop a sigh of relief to see he was still alive. If he hadn't been...She couldn't even think about it.

As soon as she saw the gun pressed against Jeremy's head, she knew that whoever held it would die. Trev didn't try to stop her this time as she stepped out from under the overhang. Morry marched out until she was stopped.

"That's far enough."

She recognized Stephen's voice right away, even with the loud siren. She wanted to kick herself in the ass for not just shooting the guy in the head when she had doubts the other day. The look he'd given her out on the run told her that he wasn't as shy and useless as he wanted everyone to believe. But she wanted to help TK's brother, so she'd pushed the nagging feeling aside. Hadn't she already learned her lesson when it came to her instincts? Never again. She was never second-guessing that intuition if they made it out of this.

"Put the gun down, Morry," Stephen ordered.

She looked at the weapon in her hand and then back up at Jeremy. She wished she had a clear shot, but the guy was ducking so low that she could only make out his hair over Jeremy's shoulder.

"Are you hard of hearing? Put the weapon down now," he said louder this time, pushing his gun into the back of Jeremy's neck hard enough that he winced.

Fuck, she hated to disarm herself but slowly laid the gun down on the ground.

"Good, now kick it away," he said.

She grumbled every swear word she could think of under her breath as she kicked the gun with her toe, so it slid farther away.

"There, see? That wasn't so hard, was it?"

She hated the arrogant and condescending tone. It made her want to punch Stephen in the face and cut off his balls.

She ignored the snide remark. "Let him go," she yelled back. "I know it's not him you want."

"Do you think I'm stupid?"

"Well, you came here, to begin with, then you lied to me, and now you have a gun to one of my men's heads. I would say that ranks up there with unintelligent moves," she said, trying to sound blasé about the fact that he had Jeremy, of all people.

She looked into Jeremy's eyes. He was trying to tell her something, maybe convey what he was feeling. As she stared into those blue eyes, her adrenaline spiked a little higher, threatening to make her panic. She wasn't the panicking type, but she couldn't lose Jeremy now that she'd finally let herself feel again. He'd ripped off the scars and slowly mended what was broken.

"He's not just anyone, now, is he?" Stephen said, but she ignored the question. "He's the boy toy, your fuck buddy."

"What do you want, Stephen?" she drawled and stepped a little to the one side to see his eyes behind Jeremy's taller shoulder. "You came here, which means you must want something from me. What is it that you want? Money, drugs, guns?"

"None of it. I came here to destroy you." Those words sat heavy. That meant he planned on hurting her, and he had in his grasp the one person here who could bring her to her knees.

Peering out of the side of her eye, she couldn't see Trev anymore and knew he'd slipped into some shadow.

"Where are they," Stephen asked as if reading her mind.

"Who, my Legion members? I don't know. How about you tell me since none of them are coming out of their rooms? What the fuck did you do to them?" she growled, letting her anger show.

"They're sleeping, but they will be dead soon enough. Now, where are they?"

"Who?"

"Your friends. The ones with the Hummers. The other Righteous members."

The fact he knew who the Righteous were, startled her. "I don't have a clue. I'm not their keeper," she said honestly. She actually had no idea where they were now, so technically, she wasn't lying. "My best guess is the same thing as the rest of the Legion members."

She could see enough of Stephen that he took a moment to look around and saw only closed doors and no movement.

"I'll ask you again, Stephen, why are you here? You just want to run your mouth off, or are you planning to kill me?" She shrugged. "I'm not sure what beef I have with you when I'd never even met you until you came here, but I'm listening. You fucking have my full attention."

"That I do."

She ground her teeth. "Does this have to do with your brother?"

Morry didn't dare take her eyes off Stephen, but she could see movement just behind him, on the top of the warehouse. The flicker of a shadow was brief, but she knew who it was, and she didn't want this to happen.

Not that helping Stephen would ever fix the fact that TK was dead, but she felt it would've gone a long way toward her receiving forgiveness.

The laugh that echoed toward her was maniacal, and the hair rose on her neck. It was the laugh of someone who'd accepted death.

"You're so fucking clueless. I thought you would be smarter than that, Morry, with all your fancy resources. The way the others talk about you is like you're some sort of wonder woman. Really, you're just a broken and pathetic with a fucking boy toy."

Ouch. Morry didn't give two fucks what he thought about her, but it was how he spoke that bothered her. Who had he been talking to? What he said made her think it wasn't anyone from here.

Jeremy growled as Stephen grabbed him by the hair and kicked him hard enough that he went down on his knees in front of her. Stephen looked around. "I guess no one is coming to help you."

A creepy smile turned up the corners of his mouth as his eyes danced with an evil she'd seen too many times before. There was no stopping this man. He believed whatever he believed to the point of radical behavior.

"So where do you want me to shoot him? In the head and make it quick? Or how about in the back to paralyze him? Better yet, why don't I shoot him in the liver, and then your kid will die too? That way, not even his corpse will be viable for donation."

Only anger and rage were alive in her. "So you plan to kill a fourteen-year-old boy, too? Wow, such a fucking man you are. I bet your family is proud of you," she said. His eyes hardened. She'd hit a sore spot. "I didn't realize that kids with only six weeks to live were a target for...who exactly?"

"You have a pretty smart mouth for someone who is no longer in control."

She shrugged. "If control is what you're after, you'll be hunting until the day you die. Control is only an illusion."

"I really should start by cutting out your tongue. Women like you need to learn their place—"

Whatever he was going to say next died with a muffled pop. The sound echoed in her ears.

Stephen's eyes went wide as if his body registered that something serious had happened, but wasn't sure what. As the final remnants of his life dissipated from his eyes, he crumpled to the ground. Jeremy looked at Stephen, then grabbed the gun from his hand.

Morry ran the rest of the way to Jeremy and wrapped her arms around him as he stood. He held her tight.

"I knew I didn't like that guy," he said. "I didn't think I was getting out of that alive," he whispered into her hair. "I've never been so scared."

"Thinking you're not going to live is terrifying," she said, and Jeremy laughed.

"I don't mean I was scared to die. I meant I was scared that I wouldn't get to save Kyle," Jeremy said.

She pulled back and stared into his eyes. It was like the damaged teen had grown into a man and then found the wings of an angel somewhere along the way.

She didn't know if she deserved to have someone like this in her life, but fuck, she didn't plan on letting it go.

"I love you, Morry, and as soon as the fucking stores open today, I'm buying you a big ass ring, and I'm not taking no for an answer. You're marrying me. I just saw my fucking life flash before my eyes, and the only thing that mattered in it was you."

"Hey, I need your help over here," Trev called out.

"This conversation is on hold until later," she said, her voice choked up, but she smiled.

Pausing for a moment longer, she stared down at Stephen and wished she understood what had happened to make him like this. Was he that distraught over his brother's death? Did he hate her that much for what happened? She didn't even know that his family knew. Had he ended up with a group of military haters? And how did he know about the Righteous?

Too many questions, and she didn't know if they would ever get answers now that he was dead. And yet, she'd take the mystery over losing Jeremy a million times over.

CHAPTER 29

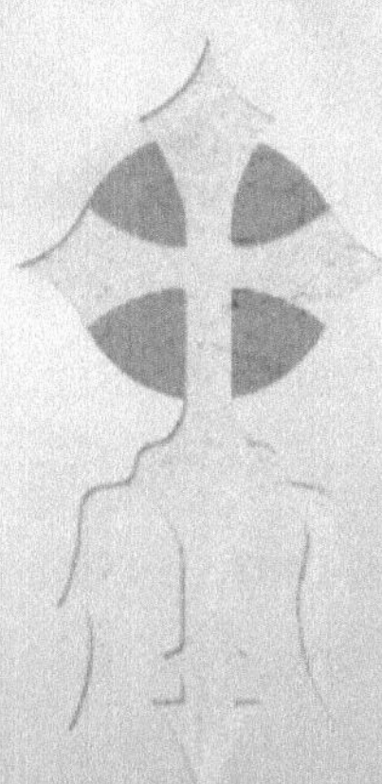

Jeremy ran beside Morry. She may have been terrified, but her face never gave it away. He was certain that if roles were reversed, he wouldn't have been as calm and would've been yelling for someone to shoot Stephen. Lesson learned he was never fucking going into a dark building with the door open without either backup or turning on every fucking light with guns strapped to every part of his body.

"Go check the bar for anyone," Trev called out.

"Why? What's wrong," Morry asked even as they veered their course to the front of the bar.

"Some type of gas." Trev held up a mask. Jeremy had no idea where he got it. Was the guy a fucking wizard? Had he pulled it out of his ass?

"Lady Luck, come here," Morry called out to the Hummer like it was a dog.

Sure enough, the vehicle backed out of its spot and raced over. She pulled open the back door, reached inside, and turned around, holding two gas masks.

He should've known. If he went looking, he might find a long-lost or dead, famous person in those fucking Hummers.

"What does that thing not do?" he said, accepting the offering.

"I haven't figured out how to get her to do my laundry yet, and I'm not too interested in having sex with it," Morry said as she pulled on her mask, but he couldn't help but laugh.

"You better not," he mumbled.

They ran for the bar but bounced off the door when they got there. Morry held her shoulder. "What the fuck?"

"Let me," Jeremy said and lifted his boot to kick the door. It moved a little and then closed again. "I think someone is lying against it. I'm going to push it." Jeremy grunted as he pushed with all his might. Whoever was on the other side was heavy as fuck.

"I see an arm," Morry said, pointing inside. "Hold up there." She slipped under his arm. "It's Judd," she called, the sound muffled with the mask on.

Grabbing his arm, she pulled him out of the way, then turned him to get him out the door. "Fuck, he's heavy," Morry complained as she got him outside.

As soon as Judd was out of the way, he pushed open the door and locked it in place so it wouldn't close again.

"Come on, Judd. You better not be dead, you asswipe," Morry growled, her fingers going to his neck. "He has a pulse. Go get one of the others." Standing, she unlocked the second door and pushed it open to lock it into place.

Jeremy stepped into the dim bar area and looked around.

"Butch is alive, so is Ginny, and I've got the new prospect in here. He isn't looking so good." Jeremy picked the guy up and tossed him over his shoulder before marching to the open door. He laid the guy down beside Judd and went back inside.

"I'm going to open some windows," he said after he pulled Butch and Ginny across the floor so they were closer to the open door.

Morry was giving the new guy mouth-to-mouth. Shit, he could've had her kiss him a long ass time ago if he'd thought about passing out.

"Is he going to live?"

The new guy gasped, his eyes opening wide before he rolled onto his side and began to cough.

"Looks like it," Morry said.

Walking away, he jumped up on the closest bench, fiddled with the locks, then pushed the window open wide. It was rare that they were ever open with all the dust in the desert, and the fourth one seemed determined to stay closed.

"Any more inside?" Morry called out.

"Doesn't look like it," he answered, looking around. "But I haven't checked the back." He jogged into the kitchen and looked around, but all was quiet. He looked up at the ventilation vent. The little strings tied to it showed that air was moving. That had to be the source. How? No idea.

"No one in the back, but the air is on high. That has to be the source of entry for whatever knocked them out."

Morry called out to the Hummer. "Hey, Lady Luck, scan for gas agents," she said as he met her outside.

"Dangerously high quantities of CO_2 found in the south building."

"What's the source?"

"Unknown."

"Well, that doesn't exactly make me feel warm and fuzzy," Jeremy said as Judd started to come around and began coughing. Butch and Jen were next. They looked a little green as they sucked in deep breaths.

"I didn't think I'd ever say this, but I'm happy to see you're alive," Jeremy said to Judd, who smirked as one of the other Hummers revved. Jeremy stared at it as it flew past the bar. Of course, there was no driver, which only added to the cool and disturbing feeling the vehicles always gave him.

"What is it doing," he asked as Morry slowly stood.

"I don't know."

It turned and lined up, facing the double doors of the living quarters. The tires spun as it raced for the building, and with a loud crash, the Hummer smashed right through, sending dust and debris flying.

"Oh shit," Jeremy mumbled.

Morry was off, running for the doors and the Hummer that was slowly backing out. He was hot on her heels.

Trev stood just inside the door with someone draped over his shoulders. "The door had been sealed. I managed to open most of the windows, but we need to get the gas out of here faster. Some are in bad shape," Trev said as Kes and Arek came down the hall, each helping someone.

"I'll go see if I can find the source," Jeremy said, taking off for the back of the building.

He'd worked on all the units for this place with the maintenance guys more than once. With a leap, he grabbed the ladder and hauled it down before scrambling up to the roof. Jeremy sprinted to the heating and cooling units, pulled open the doors, and froze.

"Oh, shit." Were the only words he could come up with as he stared at the bomb that was quickly counting down. Jeremy ran to the edge of the building, yelling for Morry or any of the others.

Kes was the one to poke his head out. "What's up?"

"Ah, we have a big mother fucking problem up here. A bomb is attached to the heating and cooling, which is attached to all the tanks and the gas in the building.

"Fuck, how much time?"

"Like ten minutes, if that."

Kes waved at him. "Get your ass off the roof, then. We need your help to get everyone out."

"You can't disarm it?"

"I was a fucking pilot, not part of those crazy fuckers in the boom boom brigade." Kes shook his head and darted back inside.

"Well, that's fucking great," Jeremy mumbled as he ran back toward the ladder. He skidded to a halt at the sight of the hose coming from one of the massive storage tanks, pumping into the ventilation system.

He glanced at the bomb showing seven minutes. "Shit. This is probably a stupid decision."

Jeremy ran to where the hose was attached and pulled with all his might. It came apart easier than expected, but now he had a hose pumping gas everywhere. He tossed the end over the side of the building. Hopefully, that would be enough.

Racking his brain, Jeremy looked around for a way to stop the bomb when an idea came to him. "Okay, this is definitely stupid," he said as he ran back to the bomb and looked at it. He lifted it carefully to see if it was attached with wires, but it only seemed to be sitting in the unit.

Yay for lack of sophistication. Picking up the bomb, he prayed that someone loved him enough not to let him explode. Carrying it as gingerly as a new born baby, he made his way to the ladder and held it in one hand as he climbed down.

Nothing had ever felt as slow as he watched the numbers tick. As fast as he could, he raced around to the front side. "Less than five minutes," he yelled over and over again. Those who were feeling better were covering their faces and trying to help get the rest of the people out.

"What the hell are you doing?" Morry yelled as he raced by with the bomb held out in his hands.

"Damn, that fucker is crazier than we are," Arek said.

That was the most accurate thing Jeremy had heard the guy say since he arrived. Putting it in one hand, he ripped off the gas mask—it wouldn't help him anyway if the bomb went off in his hands.

"Open the gates," he screamed over his shoulder.

The large gates pulled apart as he kept running. Not far off the path from the main entrance were some dunes that, if you stepped on them, you would easily sink up to your knees. Many of the new members had gotten themselves into trouble more than once.

He looked at the device showing a minute and a half left as he pulled up and turned to face the dunes. It had been a long time since he'd thrown a baseball, but he had a gun for an arm. It was why he'd played center field. Turning the device in his hand, he didn't picture what would happen if it exploded. He closed his eyes for a second, and when he opened them, he saw a cheering crowd. It was the bottom of the ninth tied game in the world series, and the ball was just hit to him.

He raced back and grabbed the ball out of the air, then took aim and fired toward home plate and the runner trying to steal the game. He watched the ball sail through the air as it left his hand.

"Jeremy. Run." Snapping out of the vision, he turned and ran back through the gates, diving behind the Hummer that had raced over. The explosion was loud. Sand erupted into the air to rain down on him. He covered his head and sighed as the Hummer rumbled, taking the force of the aftershock.

He slumped on the dirt, his ears only ringing slightly, but other than that, he seemed to be alive and in one piece. Okay, he was taking Morry on vacation as soon as he was cleared from his surgery because this week had been fucking nuts. Whoever said that everyone needed excitement in their life hadn't had a gun to their head and a bomb go off in less then an hour.

Feet skidded to his side. "Are you okay," Morry asked, her hand gripping his shoulder.

He rolled over and smiled. "Yeah, I'm good," he said. He started to smile and then grabbed her rolling her body underneath him as the storage buildings exploded in succession. The stored ammunition fired, hitting the buildings and everything else.

"Get under the Hummer," he said.

She slid under, and he followed. It sounded like a fun day with fireworks. He held Morry's hand and could clearly remember when he was a child and would happily shoot off little rockets or sit with his parents to watch the Fourth of July celebrations. But this one was far deadlier.

As the explosions and the sounds of ammunition going off died down, they scooted out from under the Hummer. At least ten people were lying on the ground, bleeding. The storage building, bar, and clubhouse were gone as black smoke billowed in the air.

Morry stared at the mass chaos and damage, her eyes blinking until he wrapped his arm around her shoulders.

"It's all gone," she said, looking up at him.

"It's just buildings. Are you okay?"

"Yeah, but...Oh no, Butch," Morry said, and they ran toward the man who had become a close friend since Jeremy arrived. Trev was already kneeling by his side, trying to stop the bleeding, but even he could tell it was bad.

Butch gripped Morry's hand as she knelt by his side. Blood trickled from his mouth, but he managed to smile. "It's. Been. An. Honor," he said and then coughed hard, blood pooling in his mouth. Butch's eyes turned up to the dark sky as silent tears poured down Morry's cheeks.

Jeremy pulled Morry to her feet and wrapped her up in his arms. It would take a lot to rebuild, but more than that, the loss of their people would hit Morry hard. She would blame herself. He already knew it and was prepared to make sure she knew every second of every day that it wasn't true.

Trev stood and looked around before his eyes found him. "What you did saved a lot of lives. I would be honored to have you on my team any day," Trev said before nodding and walking away.

"I love you, you crazy ass," Morry said, pulling back to look up at him. "But don't ever fucking run with a bomb again, or I'll kill you with my bare hands."

He could only smile as she kissed him, then stomped away to take care of others. Fuck, he loved that woman.

EPILOGUE

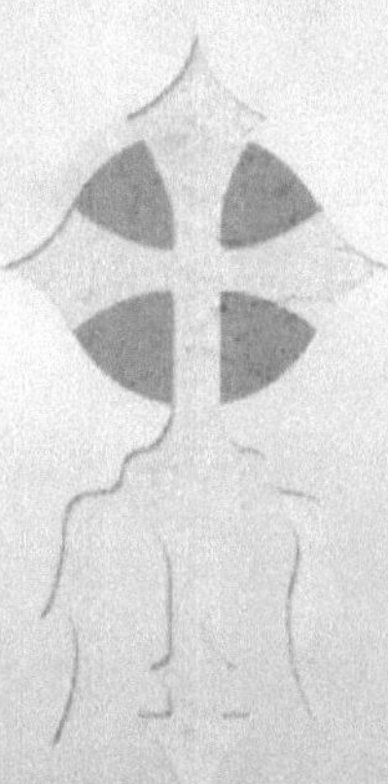

Morry stood at the graveside, watching as they lowered Butch's body into the ground. He had so much more life to live. It shouldn't have ended like this. Almost everyone had left, including his family, but she'd chosen to stay behind for a little while longer.

"So what is the next step," Morry asked as she looked up at Trev, who was standing quietly on the other side of the hole. Wolf was next to him, sitting in a chair, petting Duke's head. Any other time she would've loved to have the group together for a reunion, but not for this.

Jeremy gripped her hand tighter, and she looked into the eyes of all those she trusted the most in the world.

"The only thing you need to worry about is Kyle's surgery," Trev said. "Kes and I have spoken and decided to rebuild what you lost." He held up his hand before she could argue. "We want to do this. The attack was at your place but make no mistake. It was aimed at all of us."

She nodded. "Thank you." She shook her head. "I still can't believe that he wasn't Stephen. I never met him, but you would think I would've known."

"He looks similar, and if I hadn't spoken to Tyler's family in person when we got back, I wouldn't have known either." Trev rubbed at his chin. "The bigger issue is that whoever sent him knew how much TK meant to you. They took advantage of that connection to place a mole inside. Whoever this is, knows us well."

"I need to get to Maeve," Wolf said. "And I need to know what Dean has to do with all this because at the moment it's not looking good. He is the only one of us not here and the only one of us that knew how close you and TK had become or who Maeve really is. Hell, he's the only one that knew Miller's connection to Mel and Trev." Wolf crossed his arms over his chest.

"I know it looks bad, and I still don't think it is him, but we'll find out the answers," Trev reassured them.

"What about Dean?" Jeremy said.

"We can't seem to reach him," Morry explained.

"Well, that's probably because he hasn't been around for months, almost a year," Jeremy said, and all eyes turned in his direction.

"What?" Morry was shocked.

"Yeah, I mean, I thought he was just on vacation, but I started to worry when he still hadn't come home. I saw them leave, so I didn't think anything bad was going on," Jeremy said.

Trev rubbed his chin. "Start at the beginning," he said.

Jeremy relayed the story of heading back for his normal visit when he saw the black limo and Dean and Yasmine getting inside. When he was done, he looked at all the shocked faces. "I'm starting to feel like I should've said something a long time ago."

"That may have been helpful, but it doesn't explain who he went with," Trev said.

"Would it help if I gave you the plate number?"

Morry couldn't believe what she was hearing. She knew Dean. He wouldn't just take off without telling any of them. Jeremy handed over his phone with a picture showing a limo passing and the license plate.

"What if it comes back to his father? Do you think he turned on us?" Kes said, and Morry wheeled in his direction.

"Not a chance, and if any of you even slightly believe that, then you can leave right now," Morry growled at Kes and then looked at Wolf.

"I'm just saying we should be looking at all the possibilities," Kes argued.

She took a heated step in his direction, but Jeremy pulled her back, and she took a deep breath. "Your father was an ass to you and your family. Would you go back? What if your father forced you to rape women and kill people to toughen you up? How about then? What if he beat you until you couldn't walk? Would you willingly let your wife and children be around a monster like that?"

"Okay. I'm sorry. You're right," Kes said, looking away from her angry stare.

"It is his father's car," Trev said, his voice calm as he handed Jeremy his phone. "But it doesn't explain why. Why wouldn't he put up a fight? We all know that Dean is as capable as any of us, if not more."

"Tate," Jeremy said.

They all looked at him. His face turned a sickly shade of white as all the color drained from it.

Jeremy's eyes found hers. "Dean was walking with Aiden, and Yasmine was carrying Isabella, but I didn't see Tate."

"His father had his son. Son of a bitch," Morry growled. "That is where they will be. Him and Maeve."

"What makes you say that," Wolf asked as he slowly rose to his feet.

Morry sighed. "Because Dean sent me to find Maeve and protect her. He didn't tell me why then, but after what you've told me, I do know now. The son of a famous cartel hands me the daughter of another."

She looked at all the guys, but it was Trev that swore under his breath.

"They were supposed to wed," Trev said.

"Then we need to get them back," Morry replied, and everyone nodded. Morry placed her fist to her heart. "Brothers, we stand together."

The guys mirrored her position. "Apart we fall."

"Let's go get this son of a bitch," Trev growled.

Coming 2023 - Book 7 - Dark Reunion - The Final Chapter in The Righteous Series

THANK YOU

Thank you to all those that decided to pick up this book and read it. It is only with readers continued support that Indie Authors, such as myself, are able to keep writing which is why your reviews mean so much to us. If you enjoyed this book, please consider leaving me a review.

BROOKLYN

If you like it dark and edgy then look no further. Brooklyn Cross has always had a deep passion for writing that stemmed from a wild imagination. When she is not busy typing away about the next character you will fall in love with, you can find her walking with her dogs on the farm and sipping a hot cup of coffee.

In addition to getting her degree in business she was highly competitive in the equestrian sport of dressage, with aspirations of an Olympic dream. She is an entrepreneur at heart and has coached and trained many of a riding enthusiast or their wonderful mounts, but always found herself drawn to writing full-time.

"Writing is what I love. I just want to be authentic with my characters. To tell a story that others can immerse themselves in and enjoy, but also relate too. If I can make you smile, laugh, cry, or your heart pound then I have done my job. To drop people into my worlds and for a short time have you live alongside my characters, is what I have always wanted."

CROSS

Below are the links that you can use to find me if you'd like to follow me on my social media platforms.

Book Bub: Brooklyn Cross Books - BookBub

Goodreads: Brooklyn Cross (Author of Dark Side of the Cloth) | Goodreads

TikTok: Author Brooklyn Cross (@authorbrooklyncross) TikTok | Watch Author Brooklyn Cross's Newest TikTok Videos

IG: Brooklyn Cross (@author_brooklyncross) • Instagram photos and videos

FB Group: Crossfire - A Brooklyn Cross Reader Group | Facebook